The Risk of Happiness:
The Punk Rocker

by

Cathrine Goldstein

The New York Artists Series

The Risk of Happiness: The Punk Rocker

Cover Art by *RJ Morris*

The Wild Rose Press, Inc.
PO Box 708
Adams Basin, NY 14410-0708
Visit us at www.thewildrosepress.com

Publishing History
First Champagne Rose Edition, 2019
Print ISBN 978-1-5092-2434-0
Digital ISBN 978-1-5092-2435-7

The New York Artists Series, Book 3
Published in the United States of America

Reale whistled and winked at her. Damn, he was too happy.

Johnny never looked up, completely locked into his tablet. Huh. She had a strict, no-tablet-at-the-table rule, but right now, she'd make an exception just to find out if she had broken her own strict, do-not-sleep-with-your-rock-and-roll-ex-boyfriend-no-matter-how-sexy-he-is rule.

"And um, where did we—or more specifically, did you—sleep last night?" Her heart pounded in her chest.

"Don't you remember?" He waltzed past her and placed his scrambled egg pan onto the stove before stuffing two slices of whole grain bread into the toaster.

She turned to him, mortified. "No. Uh, I'm sorry. But uh…"

He smiled, grabbing his pan again and crossing to the table, expertly sliding eggs onto Johnny's plate. "Seconds." He nodded toward Johnny proudly.

"But, you slept where exactly?"

"Babe. You were drunk. I carried you in the house, changed you into your PJs, and slid you into bed. I slept on the couch. Scout's honor." He held up his peace fingers, making a V.

"That's the wrong sign, dumbo." She smirked. "So nothing happened?"

He came closer, whispering so Johnny couldn't hear. "As tempting as it was, what with your ruddy glow and contagious laugh, I figured after you had sung every song on my last CD to me, twice, you were perhaps a bit too intoxicated to partake in any additional activities that evening. Or morning."

Praise for Cathrine Goldstein
and The New York Artists Series

"The perfect blend of sexy and entertaining—I could not turn the pages fast enough!"

~Riddles Reviews (5 Stars)

"It will make your heart flutter in all different colors."

~Poetry T.

"This book would make a perfect romance movie! ...I was laughing, crying, cheering, then smiling at the end when they found their HEA. One of my favorite books this year."

~Chanda N., NetGalley Review

"What a fun read! The characters were so good in this book, they were complicated and yet fun. ...The ending was so GOOD!!!"

~April B., NetGalley Review

"Recommended as a 'Must Read!'—Standing ovation to the author!"

~Love Maddie

"I absolutely Loved this Rock Star Romance!! ...This book was so well written ...It was sweet, steamy, funny...and tissue worthy."

~Gia C. (5 Stars)

Dedication

As always, for Jay, Penelope, and Pickle (Sarah)

Prologue

Six Years Ago

From her vantage point high on a stool, Amanda Simmons glanced around the crowded bar. She kept an eye out for the music exec here to scout her boyfriend, punk rocker Reale Lynxx, and his edgy start-up band, Lynxx. Her gaze flashed to the small, dimly lit stage and landed on all six muscled feet of Reale, dressed in his customary opened black shirt and ripped jeans. Damn, he was sexy. She took a deep breath of the musty air that reeked of stale beer and fresh body odor, placing a cool hand to her forehead to make the throbbing stop. A headache. Served her right. After lying to Reale and feigning a migraine today, she deserved it. But she had to lie about the migraine. How else could she explain the morning vomiting?

"Need a refresher?" Some preppy guy in khakis and loafers nodded to her drink. He was standing next to her, too close, leaning back against the bar.

Amanda glanced up at him, appraising his image, crew-cut hair and a stand-up collar polo. He looked like a model from a nineteen-eighties catalog or any one of the young men at her mother's country club. The kind of man her mother wanted her to marry so Amanda could escape the clutches of her "rock and roll wannabe" boyfriend. She looked past the guy and toward the stage. Reale furrowed his brow but kept playing. He glared at Preppy.

"No, thanks." She pointed to Reale whose eyes were locked on what was transpiring, although they shouldn't have been. He should have been so focused on his performance he never even noticed her. But it didn't work that way for them. He was so tuned in to her she'd get a text from him even if she was at school and having a bad day. It's as if he could sense her needs. Well, it was high time she sensed his. "That's my boyfriend," she mumbled.

Preppy skulked off, and Amanda sat up taller as heartburn scorched her esophagus. She rubbed away the pain and fiddled with the silver band she wore on her swollen ring finger. It was the exact match to the one Reale wore on his. He looked up from a guitar riff, and as the crowd went wild, he winked at her. A wave of nausea passed over her.

How could she do this to him?

A flash of an expensive gold watch on someone's wrist caught her attention, and she turned to spot the music executive who had made his way to a lone empty barstool near hers. He was inputting some info into his phone before bringing it to his ear to speak.

"Good. Really freaking good," the man shouted into his phone, and she craned to hear more. She only caught snippets of the conversation but got the gist. Reale was getting signed tonight.

Amanda took a long swallow of her water with no ice, chewing the short red bar straw. Tonight could be everything for Reale and his band, or it could be nothing. But the churning in her stomach and the adrenaline coursing up and down her arms told her it wasn't nothing. It was something. Something huge. And somehow, it had all fallen onto her lap. She could make this or break this for Reale.

Well, one thing was certain, she wouldn't stand in his way.

Loosening the grommets in her thick black belt, she yanked at the waistband of her faded jeans and rubbed away another bout of nausea shooting across her gut. With one quick glance around, she spotted Preppy plopping down at a worn, wood table located close to the stage. As Preppy signaled for the waitress, Amanda hopped off her barstool and slung her one bag—an old, canvas army duffel holding all her worldly possessions, including the coffee mug Reale had made for her—over her shoulder. She moved toward Preppy like she was trudging through mud. Her hands were shaking and her legs dragging. Reale watched her. He cocked his head, shooting her a confused look.

She turned her back to him and wiped a tear forming in the corner of her eye. It couldn't matter. She had come here tonight knowing what she had to do. She loved him so much she had to let him go.

Amanda marched up to Preppy and crooked her finger, beckoning him, and he rose to his feet. With her stomach in knots, she placed a trembling hand to her aching gut. Her gaze locked on Reale. From stage, he stared back at her, his guitar wilting in his grasp, his face crestfallen. It was now or never.

With one final glance at Reale, she turned and grabbed Preppy's polo shirt collar. Pulling him to her, she landed a kiss on his wet, slobbery mouth.

And chaos ensued.

Chapter One

Today

"Johnny!" Amanda stood next to her beach chair, shouting to her five-year-old son who was too close to the water's edge. He had never learned to swim, but raising a child on her own, on Long Island, was too expensive for the luxuries she would have loved to offer Johnny, like Mommy and Me classes or swim lessons. She clamped her hands on her hips, watching him closely. Her thin, white, gauzy swim cover clung to the perspiration on her back and hips. She hated the water, and as long as Johnny was a safe distance away, she didn't venture any closer.

So why were they on vacation at the beach? She shook her head. Because her best friend, Jessica VanDyke, had offered her the tiny vacation home on Fire Island for the week. Seeing as Johnny had never before been on a vacation, and all she had to pay for was the ferry ride from Bay Shore over, well, she'd jumped at the chance.

But why wasn't he listening to her? "Johnny." She repeated his name in her stern voice, the one that normally made him take action.

Still nothing. Damn. The roar of the ocean was too loud, and he couldn't hear her.

She began her trudge closer to her son, walking

over the hot sand, doing her best to dodge sharp seashells. He wasn't far away; she would never allow that. Just a few long yards, but the ocean noise made it feel as if he were all the way in a different state. Despite the warm sun, she shuddered. She could never imagine being away from Johnny. Not for a minute. Even the thought of all-day kindergarten terrified her. And the school they were zoned for... Oh. She strongly disliked that school. Every time she thought of that place an excruciating ache formed deep in her belly. The reason he was going to that school was her. He didn't necessarily have to.

Tossing her head, she unstuck her hair from her greasy, sunblocked face as the wind whipped sand into her eyes. Why was it people loved to go to the beach, exactly? "Johnny?"

Nothing. He was too engrossed in the waves breaking around his ankles. He was farther in than they'd agreed. He wasn't supposed to *touch* the water, that was their agreement and—

She stopped and smiled as she gazed at her son splashing in the mere inches of ocean water by his feet. He ran in and out of the wash of the surf. He was fine. She should let him be. He was a boy, and boys needed to run and push boundaries. All kids did. Lord knew she had been no different—right through her college years she pushed every boundary she came up against.

The sun reflected off his blond, wavy hair, and his full lips were parted into a full-blown grin. He looked like an angel. He was having the time of his life, on the first vacation of his life, and she should back off. Jess told her time and again she was a helicopter mom, and she needed to let Johnny grow up. And she would, as soon as she knew he was ready and okay. In the meantime, she hovered over every playdate, every nitrate-free hotdog that needed cutting, every pile of laundry and sheets, making sure she used the gentle, fragrance-free detergent that didn't bother his skin, and every show he watched to make sure it was educational. Of course she was overcompensating for him not having a father and no extended family, but it was more than that. She loved him, and she would do anything and everything for him.

She sighed as Johnny ran in a circle up onto shore and back into the water's edge. He was fine, within grabbing distance if she needed to, and she had warned him never to turn his back to the ocean. She had read *The World According to Garp*. She knew they had to be wary of the undertow; they were at an ocean after all. The ocean. She shook her head. Why the heck had she chosen the ocean side of Fire Island for Johnny's first experience with water? Why not ease them both in with the Great South Bay? And this was their first day of vacation, which meant he would want to dare the ocean every day for the next six days. Was she insane? What was she thinking?

She stepped closer again, tensing. His circles were growing larger. Was he going too far in? Coming out of the water meant turning his back to the surf. She exhaled as he rushed back onto the beach, his skin tanning with every second he stayed out in the direct sun. She pushed her sunglasses up higher on her nose, furrowing her brow. Was it too hot? Was he sunblocked enough? She glanced at her watch. The last application of his organic sunblock was forty-five minutes ago. It would be time to reapply in—

"*Johnny!*" He was gone.

No, no, no. She sprinted full speed into the water, waist deep. It didn't matter that she hated the water. It didn't matter that she didn't swim. "*Help!*" she screamed as loud as she could, hoping and praying the lifeguard would hear her. "*Johnny!*" She screamed his name over and over as the waves crashed mercilessly around her, and she steadied herself against the punishing surf. She peered into the dark water, begging and pleading with God to help her find her son. "*No!*" She screamed louder. "*Johnny*! Oh, God, please." She couldn't cry—only act.

Without thinking, she plunged in head first, forcing her eyes open underwater to find her son. The salt burned her eyes, but she held them open. "*Johnny!*" She wailed his name as she thrashed about, swallowing a gulp of sea water. She forced herself to her feet, grabbing a breath of air, and dove in again—desperate to find him. She wouldn't come up without him. He was here, she could feel it.

She turned as the ocean broke over her back, and she saw a flash of blond hair. She trudged to him with all her might and then grabbed the limp body of her son. She forced herself upright against the ocean, her strength coming from adrenaline and sheer will. She had heard stories of women who had moved cars off their crushed children—yes, she understood, completely. Right now, she could fight back the ocean if she had to.

"*Huh!*" Gasping for air, she stood as best she could as a man came at her, plowing through the water. "Take him!" she screamed, handing Johnny's body to the man. He scooped Johnny in his arms and ran to the shore.

Oh, thank God. Thank God. Thank—

Smack! With a gaze at the beach and the people huddled around Johnny, she was once again forced underwater. A wave crashed hard against her legs, pulling her under. She bounced off the ocean floor; it was hard and something scratched her arm. She fought to right herself, but the punishing water clapped above her and dragged her back. The undertow. She flailed her arms, desperate to surface, not because of her will to live, but because of Johnny. Without her he had no one. She couldn't let that happen.

Smack! The ocean broke above her as she struggled for air. Suddenly something pulled at her arms. Something was wedged in her armpits, dragging her. She could only pray it was dragging her toward the shore and not farther out to sea. Johnny could not wake up alone.

"Got her!" a man's voice yelled as the scrape of the hot sand abused her battered and bruised body.

Forced to her side, she coughed up seawater and vomited on the beach. She gasped her next breath, her throat and lungs burning. She wedged her heavy arms beneath her as she tried to push herself up.

"Stay down." A man's voice spoke to her as she fought to make sense of it all. She must be close to dead because the voice was deep and melodic. It sounded like Reale's voice. If she was supposed to relive her life before she died, it would make sense she would relive her happiest times.

"Johnny?" Her voice was raspy, and it ached to speak. Her wet hair was heavy on her face, and she wanted to push it away, but her arms wouldn't obey.

"Your boy?" He didn't wait for a response. "He's

okay. He coughed up ocean water, like you, but he's fine. He's sitting over there." The man pointed in the direction higher up the beach.

"Can I...?" She motioned to sit up.

"Your head needs to be checked. The medics are with your son now. Stay down until they can—"

"Please?" She stayed on her side, her word weak.

The man's hands slid under her shoulders, and he eased her up to a seated position.

It ached to move, but she craned her neck toward Johnny. "They're working on him. Is he okay?"

"A few cuts and bruises. He's fine."

"Thank you." She pulled her gaze away from her son and toward the man who had saved her life. "Thank you so much for saving him and for—" Although her eyes burned, she forced them upward.

All her pain fell away as she sat up fast, placing her hands behind her, bracing herself. Her breath rushed in and out of her aching lungs. "Reale?"

He didn't make eye contact. "I'm, uh, on vacation. I didn't think anyone would recognize me without my band."

For the second time that day, her heart nearly stopped. "I'm not anyone," she whispered, pushing the hair from her face, settling her eyes on his.

Recognition flashed through his gorgeous blue eyes. "Mandy?"

She nodded, tears bursting from her eyes as he leaned forward and held her in his embrace. She let herself be moved as he pushed back, holding her at arm's length. He stared as if she were an apparition who would suddenly disappear.

Reale Lynxx. Here. With her. After all this time.

How and why she couldn't discern. All she knew for a fact was that Reale Lynxx had just risked everything to save the life of her child, and in doing so, had unknowingly saved the life of his own son.

Chapter Two

This wasn't possible. Reale let go of Mandy and stood, backing away. Here she was before him: Amanda Simmons, the woman who'd ripped his heart from his chest and drove a Mack truck over it. Damn. He ran a hand through his cropped hair, pacing back and forth before her. The sand burned his feet, but he didn't give a damn. How was this possible? He had chosen this beach because he had to get away, and it was the one place he could go that would give him a reprieve from thinking of her. *The one place*. She hated the water, and obviously, she still couldn't swim, so what? He tensed as he straightened to his full six-foot height. She must be with her husband—the man who made them vacation at the beach. But where was the jerk now that she needed him most?

"Where's your husband?" His words were gruffer than he expected, and she recoiled from his question, like he had slapped her across the face.

"I don't..." She shook her head, looking small and defeated.

His shoulders relaxed, and they shouldn't have. He shouldn't give a damn about whether or not her husband was with her. Or whether or not she was married. Or whether or not she thought of him every single day...like he thought of her. His demeanor softened, and he lifted the corner of his drenched T-shirt, wiping his brow. The salt burned his skin, but he didn't care. He'd been burned before.

As he wiped his cheeks and clean-shaven chin, he caught her staring at his waistband. He glanced down to see the corner of his most recent tattoo peeking out of his swim trunks. Unless she could read Kanji lettering, she wouldn't be able to make out what it said, but she could see something there—something he'd decided to have burned into his flesh four years ago when Lynxx went on tour to Japan. How the hell was he going to explain this tattoo to the woman who had annihilated his heart and obliterated his soul? He yanked the shirt down forcefully, and she turned away.

Putting a fist to his mouth, he cleared his throat. "Well, I should…"

"Reale."

She turned to him again, and in her voice he heard all the pain and anguish he had felt for all these years. Damn it. He wanted to be mad. He really wanted to be.

She struggled to her feet, and he fought the instinct to help her. She dropped to her knees, swaying.

"Oh, damn it." He rushed to her side and wrapped his arm around her waist, and her body relaxed with his touch. He stood several inches over her, and without thinking about it, he turned his head toward her, burying his nose in her hair as he had done so many times before. He inhaled deeply. She smelled like salt water and beach, but underneath it all was the same clean, pure scent of Mandy. His nervous stomach relaxed.

She fought to turn her head toward him, a move she had made so many times when they were walking down any village street, when she would crane her neck, waiting for his kiss. He leaned down as she turned, looking up.

"Mandy…"

"Can you help me walk? I have to get to Johnny."

To Johnny. Of course. Here he was thinking she was feeling what he was feeling, but all she needed was for him to help her. Once again he wasn't good enough. Once again he was going to be tossed aside for something she felt was more important—

"Mommy?"

"Johnny!" She broke free of Reale's grasp and rushed to her son. She threw her arms around the boy, and together they crumpled to the burning sand.

The image of them together, crying, was so powerful a lump formed in Reale's throat. What a jerk he was. He was feeling rejected again, but something so much bigger was happening. This had nothing to do with him. This was about a child who needed his mother, and a mother who forced herself to survive to be there for him. And he was witnessing it all. He was seeing, firsthand, the power of love, and it was freaking incredible. He fought back the tear forming in the corner of his eye.

Mandy stood on shaky legs, wrapping her arm around Johnny. Slowly they walked toward Reale. Off to the side, Reale's manager, Daniel, and his security detail, held back a forming crowd. Thankfully this was a private beach, and Daniel was doing a good job forcing the few beachcombers to put away their cell phones. Reale took a deep breath as Mandy and Johnny came closer, his feet unable to move.

"Reale." She nodded to him. "I want you to meet someone. This is Johnny. My son, Johnny Simmons."

Johnny *Simmons*. Reale took in the boy—longish, blond, wavy hair beginning to dry and curl up in the sun, bright blue eyes, lean and scrappy. Well, one thing was for sure, Mandy had a definite type. Johnny could have been his. He pushed away the ridiculous thought. Yes, she had betrayed him once, but no one, especially not the woman he had once known and loved, could ever do something as heartless as to knowingly keep a father from his son. He extended his hand. "Hi, Johnny."

"Hi." Johnny shook his hand, making eye contact. "Hey. Aren't you that singer?"

Reale nodded. "I am."

"Cool. You know, Mommy has—"

"Johnny, that's okay," Mandy cut him off. She leaned down toward her son. "Let's let Reale—"

"Mommy has every CD you've ever made," he finished his sentence, undaunted.

Reale chuckled, glancing at Mandy whose cheeks were reddening. He smirked, feeling happier than he had in a long time.

"And I've got your poster on my wall."

"Really?" Reale raised his eyebrows and then turned to her.

She bit her lip and looked away, as the boy nodded enthusiastically.

Reale smiled, feeling in control for the first time in years. "Tell you what, little man, how about I come by one day and sign that poster for you?"

"Reale." She snapped her head around, shaking it.

"What?" His stomach clenched. He was more than a little annoyed she was shutting this down.

"You can't promise a child something and not see

14

it through."

Not see it through. Reale saw red. His heart pounded so loudly it echoed through his head as the roar of the ocean dulled behind him. The people on the beach grew blurry, and his palms became sweaty. He balled his hands into fists, releasing them immediately. "I don't think, Mandy, you're in any position to lecture me about not seeing things through."

Her eyes glazed over, and she nodded. Her gaze was locked on his. "You're right. I'm sorry."

Damn. He had fantasized about hearing those two little words over and over again for the past six years. Mandy was sorry. Sorry she didn't believe in him. Sorry she'd listened to her meddling mother. Sorry she had walked out on him. On *them*. Yet he didn't feel any better. Watching her fight back her tears, he felt even worse.

Johnny looked up to his mother and then to Reale, and suddenly Reale felt compelled to say the one thing he thought he never would. "I'm sorry too."

Her big, beautiful green eyes widened and turned upward toward him. "You have nothing to apologize for, Reale." She stepped forward and placed her warm hand on his arm. "Nothing."

And just like that, a million pounds fell off his shoulders. All this time, for all these years, he had wondered what he had done. All those times he had tried to find her that first year so he could apologize for whatever he had unknowingly done—but he hadn't done anything. She was clearly standing here, six years later, telling him none of this was his fault. He glanced at her hand on his arm—it felt soft and right. She dropped her hand, standing straighter, and a burning sensation coursed up and down his body as his initial euphoria waned. Once again, his body felt limp and heavy. Somehow, being right didn't make it hurt any less.

The hot sun burned his fair scalp, and Mandy shielded her eyes with her hand. "I have to get Johnny inside and out of the sun."

Reale tensed. "Don't you need to go to the hospital? CAT scans or something?"

She shook her head, worry clouding her expression. "The medics cleared us. He didn't hit his head, but they told me to watch him. If he shows any symptoms of concussion, I'm to rush him right in."

"And who's watching you?" He started, surprised he still cared so much.

She smiled. "I'll be fine."

He nodded. "Well, I guess as a nurse you'd know."

She shook her head, glancing out over the ocean. "I, uh, I'm not a nurse."

"What?" He stepped forward, taking her hand, fighting the impulse to place his free hand on her cheek and then to gently tilt her chin upward.

She made unsteady eye contact, raising one shoulder and dropping it. "Plans change sometimes." She broke free from his grasp and placed her arm around Johnny, drawing him nearer to her.

Reale turned to his manager who had fought back the people on the beach until it was down to the occasional passerby who glanced their way out of curiosity. Daniel was talking to a few members of the press; no doubt he had called them with the scoop: "Bad Boy Punk Rock Star Saves Drowning Boy." As much as Reale hated it, he couldn't blame Daniel. It wasn't easy to be his manager, and right now Reale needed all the good press he could get. Especially after that accident. Ugh. He had come here to forget the accident, but how did he forget endangering the lives of dozens of children?

"Reale?" Mandy's soft, melodic voice pulled him from his thoughts. "I was wondering. Would you like to come by later? For dinner? Johnny and I are making our famous—"

"Yes."

Her eyes widened at the urgency of his answer. Who could blame her? How could he say yes that easily, after all this time? After all that pain?

"I, uh. I would like that, Mandy."

"Well, maybe you want to know what's on the menu?"

She smiled in a way that warmed his frozen heart.

"I don't care if it's spaghetti from a can." And he didn't. He just wanted to be with her. He looked at Johnny. With both of them.

Her face lit up. "Well, I promise it's better than that." Then her beautiful, soft face scrunched up into a scowl. "Of course, bring anyone you'd like. I mean, if you're vacationing with someone. Savannah something I think I read about?"

"I'm not."

Her eyes met his, and they flashed with relief.

"What time?"

"Well it's vacation for us, so we're staying up late. How 'bout dinner at five thirty?"

He laughed freely, and it felt good. Five thirty was about the time he normally dragged himself from bed.

"We usually eat at five," Johnny leaned forward

and whispered, like he was letting Reale in on a big secret.

"Sounds rebellious and cool," he leaned down and whispered back.

Mandy grinned, her smile reaching her eyes. "It's a date, then." She stepped back, placing her hand to her mouth as her face blanched. "I mean, not a date, but…"

"It's a date, then." Reale nodded to her, assuring her. Why, after everything, did he still have the desire to comfort her?

Her face relaxed, and she smiled again. She turned, pointing over her shoulder to a small, white cottage set back far from the water's edge. With its picket fence, long walkways, and manicured bushes, it looked like something off a postcard from Cape Cod. "That's where we're staying."

"That little house?" How was that safe? With a young woman and a little boy alone, anyone could get in. He glanced at the neighboring houses. Okay, at least she had people around, but still.

"Isn't it cute?" She turned back to him expectantly. "It's my friend Jessica's. She's letting us stay for the week."

"The week?"

She nodded, her eyes on his. So he had one week to sort this all out.

"What can I bring? To dinner." He looked into her eyes.

"Nothing. Oh, I guess, something to drink if you'd like it." Her tone was soft and troubled, like she knew all the gory details of his latest drunken debacle. "I make the exception with wine, but I don't keep any other alcohol around."

He nodded in understanding.

"We, uh." She tossed her head toward Johnny. "I have to get him out of the sun for a bit. We'll see you at five thirty?" Her eyes were so hopeful and kind; they were the eyes of *his* Mandy—not that strange woman who'd kissed another man and then left him at the bar all those years ago.

"Five thirty." He nodded.

"Great. And Reale…" She stepped forward, closer to him, and he inhaled deeply. "Thank you, so much. There are no words to thank you for what you did."

He nodded, becoming paralyzed. How desperately he wanted to reach out and touch one long, wet piece of hair, but he didn't dare. Instead, he watched as she walked away, glancing back over her shoulder to smile at him. That radiant smile warmed him to his core. Sure, he could get even right now. He could no-show tonight, letting her feel even an ounce of the pain he had felt—and still felt—daily. But as the two of them walked away, hand in hand, he felt such a connection to them, such a misplaced *responsibility*, he knew, no matter what, he could never be the direct cause of their pain.

Besides, it was only dinner. One simple dinner. And yet… Forget platinum records and millions of dollars. The prospect of dinner with Mandy and Johnny was making him happier than he had been in six years.

Chapter Three

Amanda stared at her reflection in the oblong, free-standing, full-length mirror stuffed into the corner of the bedroom in the little house she was borrowing from Jess. Not terrible. Yes, her nails were a mess—she never had the money or time for the luxury of a manicure or pedicure—and her yellow summer dress hung loosely from her tall frame since she had lost about ten pounds since the last time Reale had seen her, but all in all, she was okay. The old beach house was dimly lit, and the mirror was old and cloudy, so it didn't give her an accurate representation of what she looked like, but that was okay too. For once she couldn't focus on the worry lines on her forehead or the crinkles at the corners of her eyes, and that was fitting for tonight. Tonight—seeing Reale after all this time—was a fantasy, so why should she see clearly?

She leaned closer to appraise the scratch on her cheek. It was red but superficial. A few days of ointment would clear it up. Makeup would infect the scratch, so she kept her face clean, wearing just some mascara and lip gloss. Besides, tonight wasn't a date; it was a thank-you dinner. She plopped her hands on her hips and noticed the cuts on her forearms. Those cuts, from where she'd hit the bottom of the ocean, were a different story. Those had the potential to infect if she wasn't careful. But she would be careful. She sighed, watching her reflection as her shoulders rose up and fell down. Careful was her only option, because here she was, about to enter into a dangerous situation for the second time today.

She fiddled with her fingers, running her right hand over her ring finger, feeling for her silver band—a habit she'd forced herself to break years ago when she removed the ring, sealing it in a plastic baggy and sliding it into the back of the top drawer of her dresser. She took a deep breath, glancing at the simple, white leather watch on her wrist: five twenty. A shiver ran up her spine as she considered the real possibility that he may not show. Then what? Well, she would explain to Johnny that Reale was sorry, but he had music business that pulled him away. Then when they got home, she'd sneak into Johnny's room late one night and sign the damned poster herself. She would make sure Johnny never, ever felt the type of hurt she had.

Maybe it would be better that way. After all, what would tonight do for them anyway? Give them a chance to bond over old times? To rehash what had happened? To talk about what was going on with Reale and why the media was in a frenzy as the "bad boy of punk rock" seemed to be coming apart?

She exhaled and smoothed her hand over her hair. Yes, as much as it would be a disappointment, it would be better if he didn't show up tonight. So she'd made extra Spaghetti Carbonara; she and Johnny could eat it for lunch tomorrow. No, nothing could come from tonight except hurt. If things were comfortable and nostalgic, she would be devastated when Reale left. If they were awkward, it would taint all the wonderful memories they had. And if they flat-out had fun,

Johnny would be sad when they went home to their normal life after a night of hanging out with a rock star. She pulled a lip gloss from her tiny straw purse on the bed. Damn. She should have thought this all through. Maybe she'd bumped her head harder than she realized? She unscrewed the cover of her gloss and with a shaking hand put the wand to her pale lips. With one pass of the light pink color—

Knock, knock!

She jumped, startled. She struggled to slide the wand back into the gloss.

"Mom?" Johnny called from the other room. "It's Reale! He's at the door, and he's carrying a giant gift bag!"

"Would you please answer it and tell him I'll be right there?" Damn. She shook her head and took one final glance in the mirror. She was playing with fire, and someone was going to get burned.

****

Reale stood at the door to the tiny cottage, doubting everything he had done over the past six hours. Second-guessing himself was second nature to him now, but why had he agreed to dinner tonight? With Mandy? After all this time?

Balancing the oversized gift bag in one arm, he lifted his other hand that was holding a bottle of wine and rapped on the door. He glanced at that freaking bottle—how long had he spent debating it at the liquor store? He didn't want to show up with "rock star billion-dollar budget" wine. That was crass. And he didn't want to bring the swill he and Mandy used to drink either. That would have been either rude or pushy. What he settled on was a good, thirty-five-dollar bottle of wine. Something normal adults brought to each other's houses when they were a dinner guest. Of course, he hadn't asked what they were eating…that would have dictated the wine. He decided on a Bordeaux, hoping she'd like it. Once upon a time, she would only drink red, and of course, organic and sulfite-free because of her migraines. Maybe that was the only thing about her that hadn't changed?

Before he could contemplate dropping the gifts and running, the door swung open to reveal Johnny's smiling face. "We have Monopoly!"

Reale chuckled. Everything this kid said seemed to end in an exclamation. Was he really that happy? Thinking about it, Reale remembered living with Mandy—and yeah, he'd worn that same silly grin on his face every day too. Johnny moved into the living area, and Reale stepped inside the warm, small cottage, taking a whiff of dinner. *Mmm.* It smelled fabulous, like good pasta, and he relaxed over his wine choice.

"Mommy will be out in a minute. She's changing."

He nodded, never taking his gaze off Johnny. Damn, something about him seemed familiar. Johnny smiled back, and he seized his chance.

"So, uh, Johnny, does your mom get changed to go out a lot?" Oh, man, this was low. Had he really stooped to these depths?

"Uh-huh. Every day."

His stomach clenched, and he clutched the bag tighter. Every day. *Every single day* the woman went out? No one dated that much. Unless…wait. Johnny was five years old. Every year of Johnny's life represented a year Reale and Mandy were apart, and although that felt like an eternity to him, it still didn't make Johnny worldly or able to interpret subtext. He spoke more directly. "When Mommy goes out, does she go out with someone? A man?" There, he had asked it.

Johnny laughed. "Mommy? No!" He slapped his leg like he was a ninety-year-old man laughing at an old George Burns skit. "Mommy goes to work and then home to me. She's a mommy!"

He laughed along with Johnny, relaxing way more than he should have.

"Wait here. I want to show you something!"

Johnny turned and took off into a bedroom adjoined to the opposite end of the living area. Reale took a moment to look around the cottage, taking in the simple, old décor: dull, brown couches, wood paneled walls, glass-top coffee table with sailing books perched on top, and one lone ship's wheel on the wall. Off to the corner was an out-of-date kitchen with an old white stove covered in pots and pans. He walked to the kitchen to place the wine on the counter and noticed a round kitchen table flanked by four round-backed chairs. The table setting caught his eye because it stood out from the rest of the gloomy décor—it was beautiful, with blue placemats and white plates. In the middle of the table was a small, square vase with a bunch of white beach heather. He placed the wine bottle down on the tan laminate counter and touched a piece of the delicate heather. *Huh.* This setting was the only bright thing in the entire cabin.

Until she walked in.

He spun around to face Mandy who was standing in the living room.

She tossed her head toward the wine. "Is that for us?" She walked to the bottle and tilted it to read the label. She glanced up at him, her giant eyes glassy. "It's, uh, perfect. Thank you. I can only drink the organic, sulfite-free. That was very considerate."

He nodded, his tongue thick and unusable. Unlike his mouth, his eyes were still working, and his gaze ran up and down Mandy in that gorgeous yellow dress that sat off her shoulders gathering just below her amazing breasts before falling gracefully to mid-thigh. How easy it would be to gather the gauzy material in his fists and tug it up, over her head... No. He inhaled, fighting to gain control. Thankfully, the black shirt he wore over his faded jeans was loose and untucked, offering him some camouflage. How was it his body still responded like this after all this time? Forgetting the bag still in his hand, he placed his free hand to his heart, smiling. "You look gorgeous."

Her face reddened, and she smiled, looking away and back to him. "Really?"

"Yeah, really. Even more beautiful than I remembered."

She recoiled. Damn it. He said too much too soon.

"I mean—"

She stepped forward and placed a hand on his forearm, smiling up at him. "I know what you meant, Reale. Please don't worry about every little thing you say to me. There's no way tonight won't be clumsy and awkward. I probably shouldn't have invited you, and I'm shocked you came...but..." Her gaze dashed down to the floor between them.

"But?" He stooped down, trying to force her eyes up to look into his.

She held his gaze steady with hers. "But I'm glad you did."

"Me too."

She kept her hand on his, and his entire body warmed. He inched closer to her, and the gift bag crumpled between them.

"Reale?" Johnny came running into the kitchen and slid to a stop by their feet. "Look!" He held up a book, sliding back and forth in his socks on the linoleum floor.

She smiled, backing away. She walked to the stove and busied herself with dinner preparations while Reale took a seat in one of the kitchen chairs, dropping the gift bag onto the floor. Johnny stuffed the book into Reale's hands. Standing next to Reale, Johnny opened the book.

"Look!" Johnny pointed a short, stubby finger at a picture of a rollercoaster.

"Nice rollercoaster. Do you like riding them?"

"I want to." Johnny nodded. "But she won't let me." He pointed his thumb at Mandy, and Reale chuckled.

"*She's* right here, young man." She turned to Reale and Johnny, holding a sprig of basil in her hands. She tore it into tiny bits as she spoke. "And you know the rules, no amusement parks until you're old enough to go to big-kid school." She used a stern voice, but her eyes were alive with happiness.

"What?" Reale mockingly furrowed his brow. "What kind of rule is that?"

"A safe one." She turned back, tossing basil into a pot.

"Maybe…" He winked at Johnny. "Or maybe one trip to a smaller amusement park is the perfect way to spend a summer day before school starts."

He and Johnny giggled, but she turned back to them as a look of defeat clouded her gorgeous face.

"Johnny? Can you please go wash your hands for dinner?"

Johnny dropped the book onto Reale's lap and disappeared to the bathroom near his bedroom. As soon as he was gone, Reale turned to Mandy.

"I'm sorry. I got caught up. A rule's a rule. No matter how dumb." He waggled his eyebrows, hoping for a smile from her.

"Dumb? Really?" She nodded, walking closer to him. She was standing so close he could feel the energy coursing off her and smell her freshly washed hair. "I don't expect you to understand, but when you live on a budget, like we do, you can't afford to run off to amusement parks. Even a small one will cost us a hundred bucks for the day, easily. I can't do it." She shrugged.

He tossed the book onto the table and stood before her. Damn, he wanted to make her hurting stop. How easy it would have been for him to pay for anything they needed, but it wasn't his place. Sure, for a flash he considered this whole evening was a ruse to try to get him to give them money, but thinking about it, it didn't make sense. She hadn't planned on nearly drowning today. She hadn't known he was vacationing on Fire Island—hell, *he* hadn't known he was vacationing on Fire Island until Daniel told him just a few days before he left. It wasn't like it was in the papers. As far as he knew, people assumed he was holed up in his house in the Hamptons with its own private beach. Reale Lynxx, front man for Lynxx, the hottest punk rock band of today, didn't need to hide away on Fire Island in June like some Wall Street tycoon sneaking off with his mistress.

"What do you do, Mandy?"

"I'm a waitress in a diner." She pursed her lips together. "Not so glamorous, but I make good tips, and I have my weekends off with Johnny. My friend Jessica—the one whose family owns this place—she or her mom keep Johnny while I'm at work. I don't know what I would have done without them all these years."

"What about your mom?"

"She passed away three years ago."

"I'm sorry."

"Are you?" She raised her eyebrows as she spoke. "Because as awful as it sounds, I'm not even sure I'm sorry. She never met Johnny. He doesn't know he had a grandmother."

He bit his tongue, forcing himself not to ask the next logical question. Does Johnny know his dad? And why isn't that jackass taking Johnny to ride a rollercoaster? Asking those questions, dredging up those feelings, would dampen the night for both of them. Judging from Johnny's age, his conception happened soon after Reale and Mandy had split or—he shook his head—Johnny's conception happened while they were still together. And that would have meant while they were still together, she was with another man... He ran a hand across his clean-shaven chin.

"I thought for sure she'd want you to raise your child in Greenwich."

"She did." Mandy swallowed hard. "But not Johnny. She wanted me to raise the 'right' child at the right time. She turned her back on us and died of breast cancer a couple of years later."

"She must have left you an inheritance."

"No. She spent a fortune on medical bills. Anything she had left went to her new, young boyfriend."

"I am sorry. For all of it."

Her eyes glassed over. "Thank you." She forced a smile. "That was an uplifting way to start the night."

She tossed her beautiful hair that looked the same as he remembered it—long, thick, honey blonde, and soft. How many nights had he pulled her to him, spooning her, while his short scruff tangled in her hair?

She smiled and glanced at the table. "I know this table is set, but what do you say we eat outside? There's a beautiful porch on the ocean side. It's where we eat all our meals. Well…" She flashed a real smile then and bounced her head back and forth. "Where we've eaten those few meals we've had since we got here last night."

"Sounds great. How can I help?"

"I'll grab some plates. How 'bout you grab the wine and follow me?"

He smiled. Heck yeah. He'd be happy to follow her. Anywhere.

Chapter Four

Amanda took in the gorgeous evening. The night air was warm, and it was wonderful to have a break from the relentless sun. Nighttime was always her favorite time of the day—from twilight on. Back in her days with Reale, they would spend countless evenings drinking cheap wine on their fire escape while he wrote music and she studied. Sometimes they would stay out on that fire escape until three or four in the morning. She loved those wee hours in Manhattan—yes, maybe it was the city that never slept, but it mellowed after midnight. After midnight the city changed its personality from a hungry dog to a languid cat. And she loved it.

She adjusted herself in the simple plastic lawn chair and pushed back from the table. Dinner was much more relaxed and pleasant than she ever expected it to be. For one thing, the seating arrangement was handled by Johnny, who plopped himself smack in the middle of Reale and Amanda, making it less awkward than if they had been huddled next to each other at the small, square picnic table. For another thing, Reale's drinking didn't appear to be the problem the media said it was. Not that she'd trust the media, anyway. And not that she was keeping tabs—she was the last person who had any right to judge anyone—but she was thrilled he kept to one glass of wine, no matter how delicious. And lastly, they had had dinner conversation like normal people, talking about everything from Reale's music to Johnny losing his first tooth. And to top it all off, Johnny was happy. It was wonderful to see him so excited to talk to a man since he never had the chance. Sure, her boss Nick was a nice guy, a grandfather type, but Johnny only saw him at the diner while Nick was working.

As she leaned back in her chair, holding her small mason jar half-filled with wine, she felt something she never did anymore: relaxed and at peace. How odd after the day she'd had, with Johnny nearly drowning… She closed her eyes, reliving the water smashing against her aching body as she glimpsed a flash of Johnny's blond hair, and she shuddered. She'd never be able to sleep tonight, but at least she was content. For the moment.

"You cold?" Reale nodded to her, his gaze falling on a stone fire pit a few yards away, closer to the beach. Then his eyes found the outdoor Jacuzzi shaped like a two-person basin, with high metal walls surrounding it on three sides. A low shelf sat on one side, holding three candles. It looked so…inviting.

She shook her head, trying to clear her confusing thoughts, and he joined her in sitting back from the table, lounging in his chair with his emptied plate in front of him. One lone piece of basil remained on the pink-stained plate, and it made her happy he'd taken thirds of her cooking.

"Un-unh." She shook her head. No way was she allowing any of them closer to that treacherous water. "Thanks. Just had a flash of what happened today. I can't believe it was this morning."

"I know." He took a sip of his wine as they watched Johnny run across the lawn to retrieve the cushion-tipped arrows he had shot from the new child's size bow Reale had brought him, complete with all the bells and whistles a semi-pro archer would need. It was way more than a five-year-old needed, but Amanda was touched and grateful. Besides, she had been something of a competitive archer back in high school, and she'd always hoped Johnny would follow in her footsteps—about that anyway. This was the perfect way to start.

She nodded to Johnny. "How'd you know to get him that? I never know the right gift. Even for him."

"It's a guy thing."

He shrugged it off, but her body warmed with his words. It had been so long, six years, since she had thought about being with a man. And now, with Reale sitting here, his every move reinforcing his uber masculinity… His hair, much shorter than before, spiky on top, speckled with white highlights; his chin, clean shaven; his chest wide, hiding inside his black shirt. He was so handsome, but he had changed from the young man she had fallen in love with to this hardened thirty-five-year-old sitting before her. Her gaze fell over the contours of his thin face—had the rest of him changed as much as his appearance had? She sighed, placing her wine on the table. Maybe she had had enough. She lifted her gaze and found he was staring at her. Intently.

"What?" Her word was a whisper.

"I'm thinking how you haven't changed a bit in all these years."

She scoffed. "Oh, I don't know."

"I do." He nodded, and she felt a definite pull toward him. She laid her hands on the table before her, and he sat forward, reaching out to take both of her hands in his. He cupped them in his strong grasp, and she sighed.

"I miss you, Reale." She said the words before she could think it through.

"I miss you too, baby."

She gasped, her body alive with a current of desire and longing. She squeezed his hands as he stroked hers, their hands touching, caressing, melding together as she desperately wanted their bodies to do. What was happening here? After all this time? Could they—?

Bam! Before she could complete her thought, one of Johnny's arrows came at them and landed on the table, almost knocking over her centerpiece of white lavenders. Their hands broke apart as she jumped to her feet.

She reached out and grabbed the vase of flowers, trying to steady it and regain control. "Johnny, I asked you to shoot away from us." Her voice was too snippy. She took a deep breath and calmed her tone. "Please."

"Aw." Reale sat forward, his eyes still sparkling. "It's hard to shoot when you're starting out. He just needs a few pointers."

Before she could comment, Reale was out of his seat and by Johnny's side. As she watched them together, Reale's arms around his son, helping him hold a bow and shoot an arrow, she became overwhelmed. He had saved Johnny's life today—both of their lives—and now he was here, acting like a father to her son. Their son. *His* son. Sure, it would be wonderful to have help raising Johnny, but this wasn't about her. It was about the two people she loved most in the world, and how they were connected without knowing it. Her eyes grew prickly, and her neck itched. Her body swayed toward them. She couldn't stand still anymore. She couldn't keep this secret any longer. Guilt rose from her toes to the crown of her head, her body hot and tingly. What right did she have to keep them apart for all these years? What was she thinking?

Like a person on death row, she felt a crushing need to confess it all. Before she could make sense of what she was doing, she sprinted out onto the lawn just in time to get hit, square in the heart, by one of Reale's arrows.

"Ow!" She rubbed away the sensation that hurt even less than a bee sting.

"Mandy." For the second time that day, Reale rushed to her side. "Are you okay?"

She turned to him. "I'm fine." Embarrassment warmed her cheeks. Shot in the heart by one of his arrows? Really? Could fate be any more obvious? She turned to Johnny. "But it could have been an eye. You have to be more careful." The crushing look of defeat on Johnny's face stopped her cold. "And…I have to be more careful." She smiled at her son. "That's why you have to be sure you never aim at anyone."

"I didn't—"

She put up her hand to quiet him. "And you have to be sure never to do what Mommy did—walk in front of someone who was shooting an arrow."

Thankfully the damned blow, no matter how minor, stopped her from confessing. It wasn't the time or place for that. Thing was, would there ever be a time or place for that? Would she ever tell? She had her reasons for running from Reale when she was pregnant. He needed his freedom to build the career he had now—the career he deserved. *Should* she ever tell? And what's more, how much of the man she once knew was still there? How much had been lost to drinking binges and wild parties, and if what she had read was true, endangering the lives of children?

She rubbed away the red spot on her chest. It went perfectly with the rest of her cuts and bruises. Damn. Which fate should she believe? The one that had him save her life and then set him up like Cupid, delivering an arrow to her heart? Or the one that showed her both times she met him today caused her bodily harm?

It didn't matter right now. What mattered first was making sure Johnny was okay, by proving this was her mistake, not his.

"So." She stepped forward and smiled at Johnny. "Since I was the one who got hit, I think it's fair I get the next turn." She raised her eyebrows, and Johnny came running to her, throwing his arms around her waist, hugging her. She laughed.

"Here!" He was giddy as he handed his mother the bow. "Reale said we can only hit at the target, so aim at that." He pointed to the large bulls-eye target Reale had brought with the bow and arrow.

"Got it." She lifted the bow and loaded an arrow. Then she pulled back.

"Wait, wait, wait." Reale came up behind her. He wrapped his arms around her as he had done to Johnny minutes before. He felt so good. She inhaled his scent—dark, musky, virile. She never wanted this to end.

"You seem to have forgotten." As he kept his strong arms around her, she whispered, "I was on the archery club in high school."

"Didn't forget," he whispered back. "That's why I brought it. I wanted an excuse to hold you."

She grinned as he pulled back tighter, increasing the tension.

****

"He's out."

Mandy walked to Reale, carrying a tiny stuffed elephant. She looked gorgeous but worn out. Was he an ass for staying this late? But they were having such a great time, a nice, normal time—something he hadn't had in six years, and he didn't want the feeling to end. Aside from the inappropriate thoughts swirling through his brain about removing that loose, flowing dress and kissing her all night long, he would have been content tonight to curl up on the couch with her and watch a movie together—something they used to love to do in their tiny apartment in the West Village. Back in the day when he used to tap into the neighbor's cable, because he couldn't afford service of their own. And now—now he could buy the cable company, but he had no Mandy. Clearly, his life had taken a turn for the worst.

"He wants you to have this." She tossed the elephant at Reale and plopped down on the couch next to him, just as she always had. "You made some impact, mister." She punched his shoulder playfully and nodded to the elephant on his lap. "He never parts with Peanut."

"Peanut?"

"He's five." She shrugged and sat back, her body moving closer to his.

How many nights had they sat like this huddled over a takeout container of greasy lo mein? He took the elephant in his hand. "You think I made an impact?"

"Absolutely."

She nodded enthusiastically, and a warm feeling churned in his gut. He liked making a positive impact on a child. Once upon a time, before all the craziness of fame hit, he used to imagine when he made it big he would be one of those celebrities who would join Big Brothers and mentor kids in need. He would prove just because a boy may be growing up without a dad, it didn't mean he couldn't become the man he was supposed to be. A good man. A man who held doors for women. A man who's there for his children and supported his family. A man who helped people in need. A man like the man he wished he had become. Damn. Daring a glimpse into her soft green eyes, he allowed himself the one frivolous thought he never allowed. Maybe it wasn't too late to become the man he wished he was?

He cleared his throat and looked over the little blue elephant wearing a fancy saddle. "Is this a circus elephant?"

Her face scrunched into a scowl. "Good grief I hope not. I would never have gotten it for him if I thought…" She appraised the toy thoughtfully. "Nah." She relaxed back against the couch, and his arm ached to wrap around her. "Just a decoration. We're clear."

"You've always been worried about animal rights."

"Not enough to become a vegetarian though." She tilted her head. "Not by choice, anyway."

Damn it. There it was again. The only woman in the world he had ever loved, and she was clearly telling him she was broke.

"Mandy. If you need something to tide you over…"

"What?" She sat up, turning toward him, her

gorgeous eyes widening for a second before they narrowed, glowering. "Why would you even ask me that? We're doing fine, thank you. No, maybe we don't have the millions of dollars you have, but Johnny and I have each other. He eats three healthy meals a day plus snacks, I'm not on any type of assistance, he has toys and play dates and a yard to play in and—"

"Hey." He placed a finger to her lips. Obviously he had touched a sore spot. "I'm sorry. I didn't mean to infer you needed my help. I was just offering."

She bristled. "Thank you. But no, we're fine."

"Mandy, I'm sorry. Really."

Her tense body relaxed. "No, I'm sorry, Reale. Johnny's a sore spot for me. I want to make sure I'm doing right by him."

"Looks to me like you are."

"Yeah?" She turned her gaze to him, expectantly.

"Oh, yeah. He's a great kid. The best. And it's clear he adores you."

She tilted her head. "He may be a little too attached to me. I have to get him ready to be away from me full day come fall." She shook her head. "I don't know why kindergarten isn't half day like it used to be. Full day, in a school with *second graders*."

She nearly spit her words, using as much dramatic emphasis as if she had said, "Devil worshippers." He suppressed a chuckle.

"They share a cafeteria, you know. I mean, the second graders don't eat until after the kindergartens are finished, but still, don't you think a big cafeteria filled with pizza and choices of drink can be intimidating when you're not even four feet tall?"

"No." He smiled. "I think it'd be awesome." If he

hadn't known it just by watching them, it was clear Mandy had dedicated her life to Johnny.

"You know what else?" She tucked her legs beneath her and smoothed her dress over her knees. He caught a glimpse of her toned calves. "He needs a full-sized backpack. I mean, what can he be carting around that won't fit into his toddler-sized backpack?"

"Well, he's not a toddler anymore."

She looked over her shoulder toward the closed door of Johnny's bedroom. "No, he's not, is he?" She wasn't asking for an answer.

"He will be fine, Mandy." She spun around to face him again, and he sat up quickly, remembering how much she hated the word fine. Something was either great or awful for Mandy—fine implied ambivalence, and she wasn't ambivalent about anything. At least, that's what he used to think, back when he thought he knew her. "Not fine, great. He'll do great."

She smiled, and then her face clouded over.

"Mandy. Is it too weird to have me here?"

She sighed. "It's a little weird. But it's also wonderful to see you, Reale. Really."

"It's wonderful to see you too, Mandy." And it was. For all these years, for all the temper tantrums he'd thrown in her name, for all the giving up on himself and the rest of humankind because she had left him for no reason—despite it all, here he was, and it felt good. Really freaking good.

"Can I get you a drink?" She nodded to the kitchen.

"Just water, thanks."

She smiled and bounced off the couch, retrieving two bottles of water from the fridge. "Here." She walked back and handed him one. "Bottled water.

Another vacation splurge." She lifted her eyebrows and cracked open her bottle, sipping the cold water.

There it was again. She clearly had no idea she was doing it, but every time she referenced saving money—something they shared as a habit from their past—his heart ached. Damn, how he wanted to fix that problem for her.

"Johnny's asleep."

She spoke while screwing the cap back on her water bottle. How many bottles of designer water had he dumped over his head in the name of rock and roll? How many bottles of expensive booze had he smashed onstage? How many millions of dollars of *stuff* had he destroyed through the years? All that stuff, costing all that money—money that could have been used to help starving nations or given to further education or supported cancer research or passed on to help single mothers and children in need. He felt nauseated.

She continued. "I want to stay up and keep an eye on him. I know the medics cleared him, and there's no head trauma, but still. Can you stay a while longer? I understand if you can't. Or…don't want to." Her gaze dropped to the couch he was sitting on.

"I'd love to stay, Mandy." All night if she asked. And longer if she let him. Somehow, being this close to Mandy, he forgot how angry he was, and all he felt was peace.

She nodded to the couch. "These couches are nasty. What do you say we sit outside and enjoy the gorgeous night? Like old times." Again she started, seemingly surprised by what she said.

"Like old times. I like it." He stood and stepped forward. He took her hand in his.

Her hand was warm and welcoming, and her beautiful, soft cheeks reddened. "Reale—I don't mean to be pushy or take the lead like this. I'm sorry. It's the mommy in me. Aside from work and Jessica, I'm only ever with Johnny. I have to move everything forward or else nothing gets done. And I'm afraid I'm finding it hard to let go of that part of me."

"Why would you want to? I've always loved that about you. You're a natural caretaker."

She beamed at him, and he was suddenly weak. Had he really used the love word after six years? Who was this man he became around Amanda Simmons? And what was this power she wielded that could make him need her so desperately?

"Lead on, Mandy."

Hell yeah, she could lead him forward, out the front door, across the beach, and anywhere else she damned well wanted.

Chapter Five

Had he really said there was still something about her he loved? Amanda wrapped her arms around herself, fighting off the night chill. She stood on the lawn, the soft grass tickling her feet. She didn't want to feel sand beneath her tonight and probably wouldn't for a very long time. She was positioned close enough to the house to hear Johnny if he woke but far enough away to give her and Reale some privacy. She shivered again. She lived on the South Shore of Long Island, but she never spent any real time on the beach, so she had no idea how chilly nights could be. Even in mid-June.

"Cold?" He stepped up beside her, and she swayed toward him.

"A little."

He wrapped his arm around her and pulled her body to his. It felt so right to be there, cloaked in the dark of night, snuggled tightly to the hard, angular body of Reale Lynxx.

"You're so thin," he whispered.

"You too." She swallowed hard. She gazed out into the distance at the ocean crashing on the shore. It was beautiful, but she knew firsthand how terrifying it could be.

His gaze followed hers. "Think you'll ever go near it again?"

She shook her head. "No way. Once burned." She

turned to him, breaking his hold on her, and covered her mouth with her hand. "I mean…"

He nodded, looking back out over the ocean. "I get it. But let me tell you something from experience. You didn't die, even when you thought you would. And it's still as beautiful as it always was. And just as tempting—maybe even more so, because now you can begin to understand the depths of its powers. Maybe you weren't ready to handle it the first time you dove in. Maybe all you needed was a little space and perspective. Maybe you needed to mature before you could realize how much you have always loved it, no matter how it hurt you, and how you'll never stop loving it, ever."

"Oh, Reale."

She turned her body toward him, and he embraced her as she snaked her arms up over his shoulders and around his neck. In the shadows the moonlight reflected off his white highlights, and his bright blue eyes shone as he leaned down, his strong, full lips finding hers.

****

She broke away. The look of shock in her eyes made it evident she was as surprised as he was. What the hell was he doing? He had no idea, but it felt damned right. He kept his arms still, and she closed her eyes, leaning forward again. This time when he kissed her, he kissed her with every ounce of his soul. With everything he had once felt for her, and everything he felt again. She kissed him back with equal enthusiasm, and she pushed her body against his as he took her face in his hands, cupping her cheeks, careful of the scrapes and bruises.

He pulled back to breathe, whispering her name.

"Mandy, baby."

"Reale…"

She wrapped one long leg around his hip, and he was lost. He grunted into her mouth, pushing himself to her. Somehow, after everything, after every way he had messed up, she was here, offering him the chance to live again. And he was going to seize it, damn it.

He let go of his embrace to scoop her up, cradling her in his arms, never breaking their kiss. Her kiss was the most passionate, wonderful thing he had ever felt, and if she stopped him—if she said no—he would have left tonight, content. Just kissing Mandy felt better than anything he had ever done with any other woman, ever. Her mouth opened eagerly as she took in his tongue. Quickly he walked them into the house. He stepped inside quietly and carefully shut the front door with his foot. Still holding her tightly, he reached around to lock the front door, and she pointed to a hallway across the room.

"There."

He walked them down the hallway, kissing as they went. With his mouth still on hers he bent down and turned the knob of a closed door, opening into the bedroom. After he closed and locked the bedroom door, he stopped kissing her to place her down on the white comforter of the nicely made bed. She leaned back on her elbows, and he stood over her, smiling. "Are you sure?"

"More than I've ever been about anything."

He nodded. Not wasting time with the buttons of his black shirt, he yanked it over his head, and her gaze fell over his abdomen, settling on the tattoo at his waistband.

"I've never seen that." She pointed to the tattoo. "What is it?"

Her dress fell away, sliding up her lean thighs, and she pressed her legs together. She smiled, her lips puffy from their kiss. She was still the most beautiful woman he had ever seen.

He eased down the corner of his jeans and boxer briefs to reveal the full length of the tattoo. "I got it in Japan. It's Kanji writing."

"It's beautiful. What does it say?" She held his gaze with hers.

He walked toward her and crawled onto the bed. With his body positioned over hers, he eased her back gently. Her hair fell over the soft white pillowcases. She looked like an angel. His angel.

"It says, 'Mandy.' "

"Oh, ha, ha." She gazed at him out of the corner of her eye.

He shook his head, repeating his words. "It says, 'Mandy.' "

She gasped as tears formed in her eyes. He covered her mouth with his and laid his body carefully on top of hers.

She wedged her hands between them and pushed him slightly. He leaned up, looking into her eyes.

She bit the corner of her swollen lip. "I, uh, I have one too. Sort of."

"A tattoo?" He cocked his head.

"Not a tattoo, but… Could you…for a moment?"

Reluctantly, he rolled off her but stayed close to her side.

She pushed herself up onto her elbows again. "Johnny was a tough delivery. They weren't even sure I was going to make it. Touch and go."

He inhaled sharply. A world without Mandy was…unfathomable. He blinked away the horrid thought.

She cleared her throat. "When it was time for him to come out, I had cervical swelling—it was a form of edema—so much so, the doctor said no way. They wheeled me off for emergency surgery."

"A C-section?"

She nodded, reached down to the hem of her dress, and lifted it over her white lace panties.

"Mandy…" He growled at her panties, toned legs, and tight tummy.

She slid down the top of her panties, exposing a long, red, raised scar, just above her pubic bone. She shrugged. "I know it's not exactly sexy, so I thought you should know before."

He leaned forward and found her mouth with his. He kissed her deeply and then pulled back, looking into her eyes. "That's where you're wrong. It's incredibly sexy."

She let herself fall back as his mouth found its way down her tight abs and to her scar. He kissed it over and over again as she trembled and moaned in delight. Smiling, he climbed back over her, and laying his hands beside her head, stroking her cheeks, he kissed her with all the love in his healing heart.

He wasn't going to rush this. Not after all this time. Not after all the memories and dreams. No freaking way. He unlatched from her mouth and moved downward, kissing her neck. The thin straps of her summer dress slipped to the edges of her toned shoulders still speckled with a few red scratches from her accident. He kissed them gently.

"Reale, wait."

"Too much?"

"It's not that." She pointed to what looked like a small, white robot on her dresser. "The baby monitor. Let's me hear everything in Johnny's room. As long as it's on, I can relax." She dropped her eyes and raised them again. "Could you…?"

He jumped from bed faster than he thought possible and moved quickly in the dim yellow light of the small lamp perched on the distressed table next to the door. He flipped the side switch on the monitor. "This?"

She nodded. The quiet sound of Johnny's snoring came through the speaker.

Reale chuckled. "Mood music?"

She smirked and held out her arms to him.

He climbed back on top of her warm, soft body. *Oh, Mandy.*

"I hope the sound coming through the monitor's not a turnoff for you." Even in this dim light, her eyes were wet and soulful.

He shook his head. Amazingly it wasn't. It felt good to know the kid was okay, and now, she could relax completely—which was what he wanted, Mandy relaxed and free. "Nothing's a turnoff around you, Mandy. Nothing."

She smiled as he pressed his weight down on top of her. "Mmmm…" She closed her eyes.

She shimmied beneath him as his chest grazed hers, and her taut nipples poked through the lacy cups of that dress. Her nipples…damn. He closed his eyes, remembering the look and feel of her naked body beneath him. She always had the most beautiful nipples, dark red, large, and so responsive. He knew them and every inch of her body—large, soft, tear-shaped breasts, toned waist and hips, long legs with that perfect little mole on her right outer thigh—without ever needing to see it again. But that sure as hell didn't mean he didn't want to.

His gaze lingered on her pouty mouth as he inhaled deeply, his exhale a groan. She rolled her head backward, burying her gorgeous hair into the pillow. She closed her eyes and moaned in response. He pulled in his abdomen, trying anything to make room in his already too-tight jeans. Being with Mandy, feeling her soft body beneath him, damn. He was so freaking hard it was like he was a kid again. She raised one shoulder and lowered it demurely, driving a throbbing ache straight to his groin.

He rested his hands above her shoulders and lowered his bodyweight to his elbows. Reaching out with his long fingers, he eased the straps of her dress off her shoulders, and she wiggled her arms free, the cups of her dress just barely covering her breasts. All he needed to do was move the material the tiniest bit.

She gazed deeply into his eyes as she had done so many times before, and he gave a tug to the material gathering in his fingers, dropping the cups of her dress so her naked breasts burst free beneath him. Damn, how he needed to feel her. As he pressed down, his wide chest covered her completely. He lifted his weight again, and her hard nipples grazed against him.

"Mandy…" He moved downward, kissing her neck and collarbone. Finally, his mouth latched onto her nipple.

"Oh, God, Reale."

She arched her back, and he slipped one arm beneath her, holding her, drawing her closer, her belly snug to his shoulders. He needed more, now. Still leaning over her, he released the arm beneath her and rested his bodyweight toward his knees. He grasped both of her soft breasts in his hands, kneading them, while his tongue licked her nipple. He squeezed her breasts together as he passed from one nipple to the other, licking, nipping, his large hands encasing her breasts almost completely as she moaned in response.

"Mandy you feel so freaking good."

He released her breasts, needing her kiss. As he hovered above her, she leaned up from the pillow and embraced his face with her two warm hands that felt like magic. She met his kiss, devouring him as his tongue slid in and out of her warm mouth. Obviously she missed him as much as he had missed her.

"Reale..." She released her grip on him and reached for the sides of her dress, tugging at it.

In a flash he jumped off the bed, tearing her dress free from her body and tossing it to the floor. She sat up, resting on her knees, and reached for his button fly. Damn, Mandy, sitting there in nothing but a pair of white lace panties... Was he even going to make it back onto the bed? When she popped the last button of his fly, he burst forward, thankfully still contained by his too-tight boxer briefs. She slipped her thin fingers into the sides of his briefs and pulled downward. He stepped back from her and yanked off his jeans and briefs.

"Mmmm..." She half-closed her eyes.

Her response was throaty and guttural, and she smelled like pure, raw sex. She climbed toward the middle of the bed and rolled over, lying on her stomach. She gazed over her shoulder at him—Christ. Mandy. Lying there… How many times had they made love in this position? Sometimes she stayed long on the bed beneath him, raising her hips slightly, and other times they were rougher, with her belly to the bed and her hips high as he grasped her soft curves, driving himself as hard and deep as he could. But no, not tonight, as much as he wanted to be inside her, he wanted to connect with her even more.

He crawled over her and eased her panties down and off her legs, exposing her gorgeous ass. He looked away and breathed deeply. He looked back as she lifted her ass a tad higher, rocking the slightest bit. The tiny mole on her thigh made him smile. That was Mandy. His Mandy. Her white skin was translucent against her tanned legs, and a sudden feeling of possessiveness hit him like a high-voltage shock from his amp. No, he never wanted anyone but him to see her naked. Never. He lay down long on top of her, his hands covering each of hers, and splayed her arms, stretching them long to the sides, giving him access to her gorgeous neck. She giggled as he nipped her ear. Her breath raced as he made his way across her back, from shoulder blade to shoulder blade. He sat up onto his knees and dragged his hands down the length of her body, stopping at her firm ass, squeezing and cupping as he ached in response. God damn, how he wanted to dive in.

Using any last bit of restraint he had, he widened his legs and rolled her onto her back before straddling her. "Okay?" He leaned forward, nudging his nose against hers as he asked.

"Perfect."

"Do you want me to wear—?"

She shook her head. "I'm on the pill. It helps with the migraines."

He nodded. He wanted nothing more than to be inside her bareback, like he used to be, but after the life he'd led, would it be fair? Would he be putting her at risk?

"Hey." She reached up and stroked both his cheeks. "I know you. I know you're worried about me. But I also know you're incredibly smart. I'm sure you've been tested. Are you clear?"

"Yes." He was. Of everything he could think to be tested for. But this was Mandy, and he'd sworn years ago to protect her. And what's more, she now had a son to look out for. But the truth was most of the shit he'd done didn't have to do with sex or women. Yes, he'd been with his fair share since she left him, but at those times he always used protection. He shuddered at the thought of being with anyone but Mandy. Why couldn't he get rid of the past six years of his life?

"Then we're fine. As long as you can enjoy without worrying. I promise." She freed her legs from beneath him and stroked his clean-shaven chin again.

He closed his eyes, soaking in her magic touch.

He opened his eyes, and she was smiling at him. He leaned down, hovering above her, as he maneuvered himself toward her. He nudged at her, and she closed her eyes, shifting downward, closer to him. He pushed harder, careful not to hurt her, but she was damned tight.

"I haven't done this in so long." She blinked lazily. "I might be tight."

"Mandy…" He pushed harder, penetrating her. God how he wanted to know who else and when and how often, but at the same time, he didn't. It didn't matter. Nothing mattered except them. Sliding himself deeper into Mandy, he forgot everyone but her. "Oh, God, baby."

She wrapped her legs around his hips and her arms around his shoulders and pulled him closer to her soft, sensual body. She lifted her chin, and his mouth found hers, kissing her deeply. All he wanted was to stay deep inside her, moving slowly, kissing her over and over. He wanted to make love to her like he had never made love before. He wanted to prove how much he still loved her.

He pressed his weight down in just the right way as she tightened her legs around him. "Reale, I'm so close."

"Yeah, baby. I've got you." He held her tighter and pressed against her harder as he thrust over and over, deeper and deeper. Her body slid up and down on the bed as she moaned into his mouth.

She broke their kiss to gasp for breath, her arms grasping at him like she was lost at sea and he was her life preserver. Harder still he thrust as she moaned, her back lifting off the bed.

Her head dropped back. "Oh, God, Reale." Her tight muscles clenched and released around him, and she fell back against the bed, her eyes closed, her head turned to the side. She panted gently through parted lips. "I can't anymore."

"Baby." He thrust harder again as she gasped, and finally, burying himself as deeply as he could, touching those places he had dreamt of every night for the past six years, he let go. "Oh, God." He thrust one last time as he shuddered violently, moving her body beneath him. "Christ!" He shook his head as his muscles trembled and twitched and his normally strong arms collapsed beneath him. "Jesus, Mandy." He dropped his head beside her, a million pounds falling away—feeling a release like he had never before experienced. Ever.

He lay in a heap on top of her, forcing deep breaths through his nose. He wrapped his arms around her, pulling her as tightly as he dared. "Mandy," he whispered. His Mandy. Here. With him.

God knew what brought him here or how it happened, but he was here. With Mandy. *Huh*. Maybe God *did* know how it happened. It would have to be some magnificent being to bring Mandy back to Reale. *Whoa*. He'd better start going to church again like he did when he was a kid; every single Sunday wearing a brown, three-piece polyester suit with brown pleather shoes, at first a size too big, and soon two sizes too small—winter and summer—in a tiny sunbaked town outside New Orleans. Christ if it wasn't hot. How many days did he sit melting into that pew wondering if he had already been cast into Hell for what he'd done? But it seems he was wrong. Tying an empty can of corn to a cat's tail or skipping school twice a week wasn't enough to cast him into Hell. Damn, even what he'd done lately, any and all of the asshole spoiled stunts he pulled, didn't seem to toss him into endless fire. On the contrary, to be back with Mandy meant he had made it to Heaven. If God or the Universe or whatever benevolent All-Knowing Being brought them together again, then that being was sure as hell owed a big freaking thank you.

Yes, they were here again, and she was his…again. At least for tonight. No. It couldn't be just for tonight. No way.

Her body trembled beneath him, and he held her tighter. "Mandy."

Her body moved more forcefully, shaking him ever so slightly.

"Mand?" He lifted his torso to gaze down at her beauty. Her eyes were closed, and her cheeks and nose were red. She lifted her hands to her face, covering it.

"Mandy, baby, what's wrong?" He reached up and guided her hands away from her face. "Are you okay?"

She nodded.

"Why are you crying?" He lifted a hand and wiped away a single tear that rolled down her soft cheek.

She shrugged, tear after tear falling.

"Are you unhappy?"

"No, Reale. No. Of course not. I'm…" She looked away, sighing. "I haven't let go like that for six years. And being with you, after I thought I may never see you again…" She placed a hand to her mouth, releasing a sob.

"Oh, baby." He took her hand away and kissed her tears. "Hey."

He lifted his chin, nodding, and she turned to him.

"I'm here now. I promise."

"Promise?" She glanced up with so much vulnerability his heart ached.

He leaned down, nose to nose, planting a single kiss on her sweet lips. "Promise."

****

"Hey."

Amanda roused to the sound of Reale's deep, sexy

voice purring in her ear. "Mmmm…" She rolled over and stretched her arms overhead, smiling. She felt so good, so calm, and so happy. It must be a dream, one she had often—Reale nuzzling against her earlobe to rouse her, but she opened her eyes, and he was grinning at her, his bright blue eyes alive with happiness. Thankfully, it wasn't a dream. She reached out to stroke his stubbly cheek, and for a moment, everything but them fell away and she was twenty-one again, waking up in their tiny bed in their apartment in the West Village. Last night was perfect, like they had picked up exactly where they had left off the last time they were together. No, it was more than perfect—it was sublime.

"Crap!" She sat up fast, dragging the sheet upward and tucking it under her armpits.

"Not the reaction I was hoping for." He sat back, watching her.

"No, no, no…" She slid to the corner of the bed, yanking the sheet with her. She jumped to her feet and wrapped herself frantically in the sheet. "Johnny! I can't be sure he didn't hit his head yesterday. I was going to stay awake—I didn't mean to fall asleep."

Reale stood, joining her, and placed his arms around her. "He's fine."

"But you can't be sure. And I'm always the first one up." She broke free of his arms and scooted to the bedroom door. "I'm sorry, I have to make sure he's—"

"I got up with him about an hour ago. He's eating the all-natural cereal you had in the house. How does anyone eat that crap?" He raised his eyebrows, smiling.

She glanced at Reale. He was wearing his jeans.

"He's watching cartoons on my phone to help the cereal go down. Not those educational cartoons of

55

today, either, where they pretend to be fun but you're learning another language or fractions or something." He shook his head good-naturedly. "He's watching good ol' junk cartoons." He grinned. "The only thing he's learning this morning is how to hunt 'wabbit.' " He chuckled. "That health-nut junk goes down a lot better with a cartooned devil whizzing by."

"He…what?" She opened the bedroom door and snuck down the short hallway. Sure enough, Johnny was sitting at the kitchen table eating his nutritious cereal. She turned back to Reale, mesmerized. She kept her voice low. "He never eats that. It's a fight every morning."

"Can you blame him? I tried it. Tastes like tree bark and cardboard."

She crossed her arms playfully and tucked the sheet around her. "Surely it's not that bad."

"Really?" He grinned. "Have you tried it?"

"Uh, no." She dropped her gaze to the ground and then back to him. "I save that for him. I eat something else."

His eyes flickered with understanding. "Because it's too expensive."

She shrugged, not wanting to ruin this perfect moment.

He walked to her and stroked her hair. "Come on. Go throw on a robe so we can have breakfast with John. I made coffee."

Coffee. She sighed happily. "I just need a few minutes to clean up from dinner last night."

"Already done." He clapped his hands together. "I'm taking you guys somewhere today."

"Wait, what?" She craned her neck to see farther.

Sure enough. The kitchen was tidy. She shook her head, fighting to make sense of it all. "Uh, thank you for cleaning it all up. But wait, what do you mean taking us somewhere?"

"You're welcome. Thank you again for dinner. And dessert." He raised his eyebrows up and down, grinning. "And as far as going somewhere, it's a surprise."

"This whole vacation is shaping up to be quite the surprise." Her cheeks heated as she mumbled.

"For me too." He leaned over and kissed her on top of her head.

She bristled. She was getting swept away, and she needed to gain back some control. "I don't know if it's such a good idea."

"It's a great idea. Promise."

"I mean, I don't want Johnny getting used to—"

"Mandy. You're on vacation. Nothing about vacation is supposed to be real. It's a fantasy world. He gets it. He's a smart kid."

"Yes." She studied Reale's angular face. He looked happier and younger this morning, and it warmed her heart. "Well…" She fought for some way to protest, but he made perfect sense. And if she had the ability to make this one vacation fabulous for Johnny, shouldn't she do it? She cleared her throat, adopting her best adult persona. "Reale. We can't—you know, do anything *adult* around him. Hold hands or, uh, kiss." Her cheeks heated. "He doesn't know what he's seeing. He's never seen me with anyone."

Reale pulled back, studying her. She closed her eyes and took a deep breath, praying he wouldn't ask about Johnny's father. When she opened her eyes, he was smiling. His full lips were parted, exposing white teeth, and despite the hardened eyes and short hair, he looked like the sweet, caring young man she had once loved…and still did.

"Well. You'd better get a robe then, 'cause as much as I would enjoy it, it's going to be tough to explain something so 'adult' as Mommy eating breakfast naked and wrapped in a sheet."

"Oh, ha, ha." She turned away, and he slapped her butt, playfully. She turned back, giggling. "Keep your hands to yourself today, Reale. I mean it."

He held up his hands in a peace offering. "I promise, I will not touch you in front of John. But in exchange, tonight you're all mine." He grabbed the corner of her sheet and pulled her to him. He wrapped his strong arms around her waist and held her tight, gazing into her eyes.

"Tonight?" She raised her eyebrows.

"Tonight. Because now that I have found you again, Amanda Simmons, I have no intention of letting you go."

And that was just fine with her.

****

"A boat ride?" John squealed with delight as they stepped onto the water taxi Reale had chartered to take them across the Great South Bay and back to Long Island.

"Yup. A quick one, though." He turned to Mandy who was green. "Mandy." He leaned down and whispered into her ear, fighting his every instinct to draw her near. "It will be fine. We're on Fire Island. To get back to Long Island quickly, this is the best way."

"Uh-huh." She nodded, putting on a brave face.

Good grief, she was something.

"Tell you what. You go inside and you won't even have to see the water. John and I will hang out here. I hate to tell you this, but he loves the water." Reale chuckled. "How you have a kid who adores water, I'll never know. You've got to get him swim lessons."

"Uh-huh." She nodded again.

He tilted his head. "Mandy. Are you hearing anything I'm saying to you?"

"Yes. Of course. Death trap across Great South Bay. Praying we won't drown."

He sighed. "You won't drown. I won't let you." He went to a storage container at the back of the boat and pulled out two life vests, one child's size and one adult. He tossed the child's size one to John and handed the larger one to her. "Here."

John plopped on his vest no problem, but she stared at her vest blankly.

"Come here, silly." Reale held out his hands to her, and she walked closer to him. Inhaling her fresh, clean scent, he slipped the vest over her neck and secured it around her waist. He let his hand linger at her tummy before sliding across her back. "I promise, I'm trying to be good."

She turned to him with the tiniest smile on her face.

"Okay." He nodded. "I guess that's as good as it's going to get. Come on, let's get going."

Jack, the lone man who was serving as Reale's security detail, climbed on board and took a seat inside. Daniel wasn't there; he was back in the Hamptons, believing Reale was going to stay hidden and out of trouble for the next few weeks. Did he know Reale at all? An unpleasant feeling washed over Reale then, like the worst whiskey heartburn coursing through his veins. Right here and right now, he didn't want to be the bad boy punk rock star. He didn't want to destroy anything or be a drunken jerk. Right now, he wanted to be a better man. And he would be, because he was with Mandy again—exactly where he was supposed to be.

Yes, he would stay out of media trouble. He glanced at Mandy who was adjusting John's life vest for about the hundredth time. Any other trouble…well, that he couldn't promise to stay clear of.

As the engine of the taxi idled, the driver came back and stood toe to toe with Reale. He nodded to John who was standing with Mandy. "That your boy?"

The question took Reale by surprise. "A friend. I'd appreciate it if you wouldn't mention it to any of the rags. And we had an agreement—no pictures." He stood taller, doing his best to be intimidating.

Jack rushed to Reale's side, standing by.

The driver shook his head. "I'm not taking your picture. I'm not a fan. Not in the least." The driver looked down his pointed nose at Reale. "But I am responsible for this boat. I'm gonna tell you one time— don't do any crap to it." He patted his protruding gut.

"I've got this, Jack." Reale excused Jack who stepped back and made his way to the covered seated area. Reale turned to the driver of the water taxi. He tensed and stepped forward into the driver's space. "Excuse me?"

"You heard me." The driver chewed a toothpick in the corner of his mouth and adjusted his hat emblazoned with the logo of his company. "This is my company. My rules. No drinking on board. No rough stuff. No destroying property. Be a normal human being until I deliver you to the other side. Then you can do whatever it is you do."

The driver turned in a huff to go to his station at the helm, and Reale did his best to push away his anger. His hands balled into fists and his face grew hot. Who the hell was that guy to treat him like that? He was Reale Lynxx. Freaking New York. In LA that never would have happened. LA knew how to kiss up to a celebrity—at least to his or her face. New Yorkers were so jaded they felt like they could talk to anyone in any way they wanted. Who the hell did he think he was?

With ire rising through him, Reale turned and caught the eye of Mandy who was standing close by. She had seen—and heard—it all. Crap. Thankfully, she had sent John to sit with Jack, so at least Reale didn't have to explain the confrontation to a child. Embarrassment washed over him, replacing the anger he'd felt just minutes before. He didn't want her to have to see that. He didn't want her to see what people thought of him. He wanted Mandy to know him as the man he used to be. Was it too late now?

He walked to her. He couldn't run from this. And he didn't want to. "Mandy…"

She took his hand and squeezed. "We all do things we're not proud of, Reale. All of us. All we can do is go forward the best we know how. If you don't want to be the man who shows up at a children's charity event and drives the train ride drunk, then don't be anymore."

He squinted. "You know?"

"Of course I know. I read everything I can about you. I don't believe most of it, but I knew this had happened."

"I could have killed those kids."

61

She held her eyes on his. "Probably not. The train wasn't going that fast."

"It toppled."

"What?" She pulled back and her eyes narrowed.

"My press team got it covered before it was released, and the parents were all too panicked to even think about filming the crash, so it never got out on social media." He shook his head, reliving every horrid detail. "I thought it would be fun to show the kids what it means to have a good time, so after a half bottle of bourbon I floored that little train and crashed into the side of the barn full speed. It was a damned lawnmower engine, not made to go any faster than a crawl, so it toppled. Rat that I am, I crawled out without a scratch, but a couple of the kids got pretty bruised up. One went to the hospital. It was one of the two worst days of my life, and I'm sorry every second of every day that I did it. Thankfully no one was seriously hurt."

"Is that why you're on Fire Island and not in the Hamptons?"

He swallowed hard, looking deep into the eyes of the woman he loved. The woman who could save him from who he'd become. "That was the plan set up by Daniel, my manager. But—"

"But?" She stepped closer.

"But… I know it sounds crazy, but I believe I was there to find you again."

She nodded. "It may be crazy, but that's what I think too." She lifted onto her toes and kissed him on the lips.

He held her at arm's length. "Wait. You kissed me. What about John?"

She shrugged. "I'll tell him you had a boo-boo, and

I was kissing it better." She smirked.

"I can think of a few other places I'd like to have a boo-boo." He grinned at her, and then his face fell. He felt the dire need to explain. "Mandy, this guy driving the taxi, he's not an exception. A lot of people hate me and what I've done. What I do. It's not just that one isolated incident."

She sighed, her chest rising and falling gracefully with her breath. "Reale. I've never given a damn about what people think of you, or me. I care about what you think of you. You could donate every organ of your body to children in need, and there will still be people who think you don't do enough or are a lousy person because of your celebrity. We always knew we'd have to prepare for the ugly side of fame."

We always knew. *We'd* have to prepare. Them. As a couple. Together. How many nights had she spent helping him prepare for his career? And here they were again, speaking as if the last six years never happened.

"What about the guys in your band? Matt, Dylan, and Pete? I was glad to hear you all stuck together through the years."

"Yeah, well." He looked out over the water and back to her. "We're together for the band. We've grown apart. Mostly because I've been a first-class asshole."

"Reale." She shook her head delicately. "You can always apologize. They love you. They'll understand."

Was an apology enough? Could a few words heal all the pain? He gazed at her beauty that warmed him from the inside. Maybe an apology was enough. He inhaled deeply, a rush of lightness flushing over him.

The water taxi moved from its docking spot, and she closed her eyes. "I think I'd better find an inside seat with Johnny."

He chuckled. "Can I take John with me? Over there?" He pointed to the back of the boat. "You can see him, and there are two layers of guardrails. This way he can feel the water spray his face. It's cool. I won't let anything bad happen to him, Mandy."

She nodded, her eyes glistening. "I know."

She walked inside the covered area of the boat, sending John out to meet Reale. Reale smiled when John ran up to him and slipped his hand into Reale's. Without thinking, he squeezed John's hand and lifted it. Together, with their hands intertwined, they waved to Mandy, and she smiled the most dazzling smile he had ever seen. Yes, somehow they had found each other again. And in all this damned craziness, this—the three of them together—was…right.

Chapter Six

"A rollercoaster! Can we ride it?" John bounced up and down as he spoke, unable to contain his excitement. He turned his giant blue eyes up to Reale.

Reale chuckled as he led Mandy and John through the deserted amusement park. "Of course we can ride it. It and everything else in the park. It's all yours until five o'clock this evening, John."

"What do you mean all his?" Mandy stopped short, turning to Reale.

"I mean he can ride whatever he wants without worrying about lines."

"Reale?" She crossed her arms before her chest and raised her eyebrows. "Did you rent the entire amusement park for Johnny?"

"It's not just for him. I don't think being in a place with a bunch of little kids is the most strategic career move I can make right now." He shrugged, sheepishly. No, no one would want him anywhere near his or her child right now. Except Mandy. She always saw the good in him, even when he didn't.

John grabbed Reale's hand and pulled him forward. They all began walking in the direction of the balloon-shaped Ferris wheel.

"I've never been on a Ferris wheel!" The pitch of John's voice rose higher and higher, and Reale smiled. It felt so good to be with Mandy and John.

"Okay." Her word was soft. Too soft.

Reale pulled back on John's hand. "Hold up one second, little man. Tell you what, go on over to the dart game and give it a try. We'll be there in a second."

Her eyes glistened as she watched John walk to the nearby game.

"Mandy? What is it?" He reached out and brushed a stray piece of hair off her face as he spoke.

"What about all those kids who were planning a day at the park today?"

"I had my team post the closing on all social media. Anyone who shows up today gets free passes for tomorrow and lunch and an afternoon at the children's museum on me."

"Sounds like you've covered everything." She looked off around the park.

He studied her. Why didn't she sound happier about this? "Mandy, if you want to go somewhere else…"

She turned to him, sharply. "What? No, of course not, Reale. Of course not. No, no."

"And yet why do I feel as though the lady doth protest too much?"

She sighed, making eye contact. "Reale. It's wonderful. All of this. Thank you. But you don't have to buy your way into our good graces. We want to be with you. I hope you know that."

"Of course I do."

"'Kay." She nodded as she looked at John who was struggling to hold a dart.

Reale's gaze followed hers. "You'd better tell me what else is going on in that beautiful mind of yours before John throws that thing and impales the booth worker." He chuckled.

"I guess I'm thinking if you hadn't been there yesterday…" She shuddered.

"Mandy, baby, I think maybe this is PTSD. Maybe I pushed too hard too fast. You had a terrifying experience yesterday. I guess I thought this would keep your mind off it. I should have asked. I'm sorry."

"It's not that." She looked away before making eye contact once again. "If you hadn't been there yesterday, despite the accident, we wouldn't be here today. We live only a half hour away, but I don't know if Johnny would ever get to come to a place like this." Her face clouded over.

Damn, all he was trying to do was to make them happy. He nodded. "Yes, he would. When he got older, if it meant that much to him, you'd make it happen."

"You think so?" Her face brightened.

"Absolutely."

"It's just…he really doesn't have any friends. And sometimes I worry I'm not enough for him."

Her confession stung his soul.

"Hey." His voice was sharp, and it snapped her attention back to him. "Don't ever say that. Ever. He is so lucky to have you." Reale knew firsthand having a mom who cared was everything when growing up. No, he and his mom hadn't had a lot either, but they were happy—most of the time. Yes, when he turned twelve, he'd begun to grow angry at his father for abandoning them, but John still had a long way to go before he could begin to put that together. And who knew? Maybe by then someone else would step up to be a father to Johnny. Reale stood tall and squared his shoulders. Father. He liked that word.

"So what do you say? A day at the amusement park? You up for it?"

She smiled, brightening his world. "Yes, Reale. I'm up for it."

****

"How can you even look at food?" Amanda turned away from the greasy chicken tenders and French fries piled onto their food trays.

"Not feeling great?" Reale teased.

"No, not particularly." She sipped her cold bottled water that felt heavenly going down. "I think it was the seventh rollercoaster ride that was enough for me. Honestly…" She ruffled Johnny's hair. "I…" Her words fell away when Johnny looked up at her. Sitting there with his hair sticking up like that, he was the spitting image of his father. She glanced at Reale. How was it possible he didn't see it? Quickly, she smoothed Johnny's hair.

"You were saying?" Reale popped a fry into his mouth.

"Uh…" She fought to collect her thoughts. "Oh. I don't know how you two aren't exhausted."

Reale smiled. "I've got to tell you. You're way more of a daredevil than I remember."

She swallowed hard. *More of a daredevil than I remember*. There they were—those last six years. Changes had happened. They were both different people than they once were, no matter how much they wanted to pretend otherwise.

"Well," she approached it cautiously, her belly churning with desire. "What do you remember?" She blinked lazily at him.

He sat straighter. "Everything." He reached out and

stroked her hand.

Fighting her desire, she slid her hand away. No, she didn't want Johnny to see this—she couldn't have him get his hopes up—but being with Reale felt so good. Reale smiled a sexy, lopsided grin, with one corner of his mouth turning up cockily. His eyes held hers. He knew how sexy he was. He knew what was happening. No, Johnny could not get his hopes up. It was bad enough she had.

Johnny shoved another huge bite of chicken tender into his mouth. He was going to get a bellyache if he kept eating like that.

"Hey, Johnny, slow down, please."

Johnny held the chicken tender in his hand and glanced at Reale.

Reale nodded. "Yeah, buddy. You don't want to get sick when we tackle the music machine later."

"Music machine?" She raised her eyebrows, ignoring the fact that for the first time—ever—Johnny had looked to someone else for an answer. Even after she had given him one.

"Yup. We sit with different cartoon characters and spin around until we feel like we have whiplash, while the D.J. blasts music until we think our eardrums will bleed. It's like being onstage during a concert without ear protection."

She glowered, and Johnny looked up wide-eyed.

Reale smiled, pacifying her. "It's not that loud. Promise." He winked and turned to Johnny. "You do know all the Saturday morning greats, right? Cats with lisps, birds that repeat themselves, scared dogs that go into haunted houses."

Johnny shook his head while he munched on a fry.

"What do you *do* on Saturday morning?" Reale turned to Amanda, his voice filled with playful scorn. "Amanda Simmons, your son doesn't gorge on junk TV on Saturday mornings?"

There it was. Johnny finally had the male influence he desperately needed, and all she had to do was sit back and play along. It took no time at all to decide. She shook her head. "Nope. No junk food, no violent, classic cartoons, and no Saturday morning binge watching. He obviously has huge gaps in his education."

"Obviously," Reale teased. "So." He turned to Johnny. "John, what do you say tomorrow we spend some time learning all the 'greats.' " He used air quotes when he spoke and then turned to her. "I'll handle the screening room. Can I put you in charge of popcorn? Or will it be some air popped, no salt, no butter health stuff?"

"What other kind of popcorn is there?" Johnny looked at Reale expectantly.

Amanda couldn't help but smile.

"What other kind?" Reale turned his head to her and feigned disgust, looking back at Johnny. "Well, to start there are the classics: butter, extra butter, movie theatre style, kettle korn, caramel—"

"There's caramel popcorn?" Johnny placed both hands on the table, bracing himself for the answer.

She sat forward, ready to correct Johnny for interrupting when someone else was speaking, but the look of awe on his face quelled her. She put a hand to her mouth to hide her grin and turned away.

Reale slapped his hand on the table, playfully. "That's it. Amanda, your son has never had caramel popcorn?"

"Actually, Reale. He's never even had fried food before." She leaned in like a conspirator, resting her sore, scraped forearms on the table, enjoying the game way too much. The banter felt normal…and nice. Like a happy family enjoying a day out together. She picked up a fry off her son's plate. "He's never had a fry before. I made an exception because it's vacation. Then once we're back home…"

Johnny nodded. "I know. Trips to the health food store for all-natural fruit-flavored cereal."

She nodded and took a bite of the fry, chewing and swallowing hastily. Damn, she had forgotten how good this kind of food could be.

Reale turned away in mock disgust then faced her again. "All-natural fruit-flavored cereal? Wow. It's a good thing I showed up when I did."

She sat back, taking a long swallow of the cold water. *You have no idea, Reale. You have no idea.*

****

Reale balanced John over his shoulder as he carried him up the path to Mandy's little cabin. It was just past nine thirty at night, and the cool night air sat heavily on them like a moist blanket. He wrapped his other arm around Mandy, drawing her close, and she placed her head on his shoulder. He leaned over and kissed her on the top of her head, feeling like he was caught in a photograph, or even more, in a Norman Rockwell painting. Here he was, Reale Lynxx, the epitome of bad boy punk rock, in the most simple, normal setting. And he liked it. He liked it way too much.

Quietly, they tiptoed into the house, and as he laid John on his bed, sliding off his sneakers, Mandy tiptoed out of John's room. She was probably going to the kitchen to grab some wine. He stood over John's bed, looking down at the boy, while crazy emotions raced through him. Why did it feel so good to be with Mandy and this kid? How many years did he fight to make it big so he would never get caught in some simple, average life? And now that he had *everything* he realized he had nothing.

John stirred, moving his head, and Reale started at the flash of blond hair on the pillow. It was much lighter than Mandy's hair and curly, like Reale's hair when he let it grow. And John's eyes were a certain shade of blue you didn't see that often—except every time Reale looked into a mirror. He took a deep breath and rubbed away the unease in his gut. Yes, John looked like him, and some of his likes and dislikes were similar to Reale's, but that was because they were both male. Right? It had to be. C'mon, his Mandy, the woman he had always loved more than anything in this world, could never have done something so awful as to give birth to his child and keep it from him for all these years. No possible way.

He shook away the unsettling thought and stepped out of John's room, shutting the door behind him.

"Mandy?" he whispered as he walked through the dark house. The only light in the entire house came from the small light over the stove. He walked into the kitchen and found a note on the table.

Meet me in the hot tub. :)

Damn. *In* the hot tub. Not at the hot tub or near the hot tub. She wrote *in* the hot tub. And there was a smiley face. No one bothered to draw a smiley face unless they were anticipating a really good time. One thing was for sure: he didn't need to be asked twice. Yanking off his T-shirt, he rushed from the kitchen through the living room. Quietly he burst through the front door, and bending to pull off his shoes as he hurried, he passed the picnic table where they had eaten last night. Standing, he tossed aside a sneaker and caught a glimpse of her in the hot tub, her hair pinned up on top of her head. She smiled at him, and he placed a hand to his bare chest, overcome. She reached up, took a wine glass in her delicate hand, and sipped, all the while staring at him. Two fluffy white towels hung on a hook on the wall, and three white candles in votives flickered on the shelf beside the hot tub.

"Damn, Mandy," he growled as he walked to her, his hand on the button fly of his jeans.

Her jeans were laid out on the lawn chair nearby, as was her soft pink T-shirt and lacy pink bra and panties. He stalled by the bra and panties and raised his eyebrows to her. She tilted her head in response, chewing the corner of her lip. He nodded, walking toward her like a man marking his territory. Which was exactly what he was.

He stalled again as he stood next to the tub, suddenly in a compromising situation. If he were to undress completely, she would see how ready he was for her. As if she could read his mind, she lifted onto her knees in the deep tub, her body still submerged and hidden from view. She waved him forward with one hand, and he stepped closer. Reaching out, she placed both hands on the top of his button fly and popped open the first button. She looked up at him with her giant green eyes and smiled. That was all the encouragement he needed. He popped open the rest of his buttons and pulled off his jeans and boxer briefs.

She smiled as he climbed in. Sitting opposite her in the warm tub, he took her hands in his, bringing them to his chest. Then, lifting them, he kissed each of her fingertips before turning her back to him and drawing her near.

Chapter Seven

"Hey, Buddy." Reale was so happy he whistled a new tune he was working on as he walked into the living room. Sure, Mandy had beaten him out of bed this morning, and he'd wanted get up first to make coffee, but after last night, damn… A man couldn't help but sleep in. He spotted John in the kitchen hunched over a bowl of his twigs and grass cereal. "She's got you back on the healthy stuff, huh?"

"Shh." John put a finger to his lips, motioning to the couch. "It's a sick day." He kept his voice a whisper.

"What?" Reale spun around and found Mandy in her T-shirt and worn, blue plaid pajama bottoms. She was curled up on the couch, her hands pressed against her head. Damn. He knew this position all too well. "Migraine?"

"Yes." She choked out her word. "I was so stupid to be out in the sun all day yesterday, and then I drank wine last night. Ugh. It's my fault."

He squatted down next to her. "It's not your fault, Mandy. You know that. It's hormonal."

She nodded, her face blanching. When they were together, she'd faced these demon headaches once a month like clockwork, and nothing could stop them. The last time they were together she'd had a migraine. He inhaled sharply, the memory of that horrid night banging through his skull like a bass drum.

"I'm sorry I pushed yesterday. Maybe it was too much."

"No, no." She patted his arm. "Yesterday was perfect. Oh." She dropped a hand to her stomach and sat up fast. "I need…" Putting a hand to her mouth, she rushed past him and to the en suite bathroom of the bedroom.

He chased after her, then knocked on the closed door gently. "Mandy? What can I do?"

He knew what he used to do—when the migraine first hit and the aura was at its worst, he would close all the shades and turn off all noise. Even the hum of their window fans was too much for her. Then he'd give her painkillers and climb into bed with her, holding her while she sobbed or screamed until her sight returned to normal, but the already debilitating pain would intensify. Finally, after she rolled around in agony and he'd placed dozens of cold compresses on her head, she'd begin to throw up, and after hours of vomiting, she'd be well enough to sip ginger ale until she began to feel better. Once those first twelve hours of hell passed, he'd prop her up in bed and they'd watch home shows together, and he knew she was getting stronger when she began chatting about how she would decorate the houses on the show. Then the conversation would inevitably turn to the house they would one day share.

He smiled as he remembered how the house would change from month to month. Sometimes it was a big farmhouse in Kansas with a sprawling front lawn, sometimes a penthouse on the Upper West Side of Manhattan. The only thing about their fantasy that had remained the same was that they would always be in the house together…with their children.

An overwhelming feeling of nostalgia washed over him, not for her illness, but for the way things once were. Or at least the way he'd thought they were. He stood taller, perspiration dotting his forehead as he pushed up the short sleeves of his black T-shirt. Was it possible he had been that wrong about her? Was it possible this woman he loved more than life itself had left him for some guy she just met at the bar? Or even worse, had been sleeping with another man while they were together? It didn't make sense. He wasn't a bad judge of character. Not then and not now that he had pretty much seen—and done—it all. And Mandy, his Mandy, would never do that. Ever. He knew it in his soul. That's why when he saw her again for the first time in six years, he hadn't been as angry as he anticipated. Because none of it made sense. She hadn't left him that night because she wanted to. Something else had to have happened, and now, after six years of wondering—he would finally find out. Not this second, of course, not while she was unimaginably sick, but tomorrow, after the twenty-four-hour mark passed on her migraine, he would find out what had happened, once and for all.

****

"Mandy?" He knocked on the bathroom door again.

"Just a sec." Ugh. She gagged on that horrible vomit that burned her esophagus time after time. It was because her stomach was empty. Soon enough the dry-heaving would begin and then the stomach cramping. But at least all that meant the pain would begin to subside. But today the vomiting hurt even more because of the cuts and bruises on her cheeks. Although the injuries were healing, the pressure of the vomiting made them throb as if they were fresh wounds. But the sharp ache at the root of her tongue and back of her throat was the absolute worst.

She flushed the toilet again and sat back on the chipped, old, black-and-white checkered tile floor. The busy pattern wasn't helping her eyes focus one bit, and the bright yellow bathroom walls were nauseating. But still, she was so grateful to Jess's family for allowing her to vacation here—free of charge. And even more grateful that since they'd been here, Reale had been living with them. "I, uh, I think I'm okay." She stood on shaky legs and unlocked the bathroom door.

He pushed the door open, and she tried to smile. "I'm sorry, Reale, this isn't what you needed to deal with on your vacation. Please don't feel the need to have to babysit us. This will pass by tonight and—"

"I want to be with you." He nodded toward the door. "Both of you." His smile told her he was sincere. "I've seen you sick before, Mandy. If you think some vomit is going to deter me now that I've finally found you again…"

She sat down on the cold tile.

Finally found you again. What did he mean by that? Now that he was settled and reached the crazy stardom he'd worked so hard to achieve, did it mean they'd have their chance? Did her ultimate sacrifice work? She had done what she had to do. She'd left him that night so he could and would fulfill his every dream, but now, after six years, was it time for her dreams to come true as well? And more importantly, what about the unknown dreams of her growing son? One day she wouldn't be enough. One day—sooner rather than later—Johnny would want to know who his father was. Was this their chance at a happily ever after?

She smiled through her pain at the only man she could ever imagine being in love with.

"How long ago did it start?"

"Three a.m."

He sighed. "Why didn't you wake me?"

"I had already done enough damage for one night. You were sleeping pretty soundly." She tried to grin, but her jaw hurt when she smiled. "Ooo, ow."

He shook his head. "Easy, killer. Let's put it in neutral for a bit, okay?" He leaned down, wrapped his arm around her waist, and pulled her to her feet.

"Oh, Reale, no." She turned her head away. "I haven't even brushed my teeth yet."

"If you think your little girl vomit is going to gross me out, you haven't been reading all my press. Didn't you read that I bite the heads off live mammals onstage or some such crap?"

"That's Ozzy. Not you."

"Seems I emulate him. Want to be like him." He chuckled as he walked. "Truth is he's an amazingly talented guy. I've met him a couple of times. I would like to be like him—as a musician."

She smiled and winced at the throbbing in her skull.

"Hurts?"

"Yes." Her teeth chattered, hurting her jaw, as chills settled on her.

"Cold?"

She nodded.

"We're getting you tucked in. You've got to get

better for movie night tonight."

"Reale, there's not even a TV."

"I took care of it, don't worry."

She dropped her head and attempted to raise her eyes. "Ow."

"Why not keep the facial expressions to a minimum until you feel better. Come on."

Keeping his arm around her waist, he half-carried her into the bedroom. He pulled back the blanket and helped her into the bed. He tucked the white comforter and a few light blue throw blankets around her before climbing in next to her, drawing her near. He was careful not to jostle the bed or try to lay her head on his shoulder. He must have remembered how much that would hurt.

"Need a bucket?"

"No. Thanks." She was careful not to shake her head. It felt good to be taken care of. Sure, Jess dropped off soup when Amanda had a cold, but the last time someone really took care of her was Reale—six years ago. Since then, every single month she went through these migraines alone, and even after her C-section she had to fend for herself while breastfeeding a newborn. But she wasn't complaining, knowing what had become of Reale—how he'd achieved superstardom—it was all worth it. Every second of it. Staying upright and as still as she could, she attempted a smile.

"Nice to see that smile." He raised his eyebrows.

He smoothed the blanket on her lap, and she reached out, grabbing his hand. She sighed, staring at his strong, capable hands, the hands that would assure his induction into the Rock and Roll Hall of Fame. The hands that touched her with so much kindness and care that she could feel his love for her.

He reached up and stroked her scratched cheek gently. "The scratches are much better. Using aloe?"

She nodded best she could.

"Tell you what. You get rested up, and John and I are going to take a walk into town to pick up our supplies for movie night. We're going to grab you some ginger ale too. Anything else?"

"Reale."

"I seem to remember candy helping after the migraine. Sugar opens up the blood vessels or something like that, right?" He winked.

"It does." She crossed her arms and tried to pout, but it still hurt too much.

"Uh-huh. So anyway, we're hitting the town. Going to take him to lunch if it's cool. I'll rent us some bikes. I promise we'll wear helmets."

"Reale. You don't have to do all this."

"What's the poor kid gonna do all day, sit around the house? There isn't even a TV."

"He has books and crayons."

"And yawn." He put his hand to his mouth, pretending to yawn. "This is vacation, Mom. And he's going to kindergarten this fall. Full day, remember? He needs to get some time away from you. You said so yourself. I promise we'll behave. Unless..." His face fell, and he squared his shoulders to face her. "Are you worried about him with me?"

Then it hit her. She wasn't. Not the slightest bit. She was always worried about Johnny—even when he spent time with Jess. Worry was what she did. It felt right to worry about Johnny; she was his mother after all. But for the first time in five years, she wasn't worried about him. Not at all. It had never entered her mind that her son wouldn't be safe with his father.

"No. No, Reale. Of course not."

"Because I understand I haven't been an exemplary human being lately, but I promise, Mandy, that's not who I am. It's not an excuse, and I know I have to take responsibility, but I've been going through some stuff."

"Reale." She put her hand on his, and he stopped blabbering. "I always worry about Johnny. It's my job. It has nothing to do with you. I feel safer having him with you than with anyone else." For so many reasons she'd love to tell him but couldn't. "I appreciate you wanting to spend time with him today, but he's not your responsibility. He's mine." She heard it as soon as she'd said it. He should be Reale's responsibility, every bit as much as he was hers.

"It's not a responsibility, Mandy. He's a cool kid. I like him."

A crushing pressure on her heart fell away, and her headache lessened the tiniest bit. "He is a cool kid, huh? No matter how much of a worrywart geek I am. He still seems to be holding his own." She was relieved Reale thought Johnny was cool. She was worried having no father and a female-only influence would make Johnny softer than the other boys at school, and he'd be picked on. Especially since their school system wasn't the best. It was okay, but she hated they had to walk through two sets of metal detectors to enter an elementary school.

"He's the coolest. You don't need to worry about him. You're doing a great job."

"Thank you." He could never understand how that one little statement warmed her to her core.

He ran his hand across her cheek before sitting up.

"I'm going to rescue John from the healthy cereal, and we're going to hit the town. We'll shoot you a text every few hours, okay?"

She nodded.

"Good." He hesitated. "I, uh. I hate to have to do it, but I need to bring Jack along."

"I understand." And she did. This was one of the prices he needed to pay for celebrity.

"Okay." He stood. "Let me see if John's ready to tackle the day."

"Reale?" She did her best to make eye contact. "Why do you call him that? John instead of Johnny?"

"Same reason I call you Mandy. Everyone else calls you Amanda." He shrugged like it all made perfect sense. Like he was the man of their house, talking about what he did with his family. "Calling him John sounds more mature. Makes him tougher and ready for the terrifying world of 'full-day kindergarten.' " He used a mocking tone like he was doing a voiceover for *The Twilight Zone*.

"Very funny. You don't know what that school is like. Ooo, ow." She placed a hand to her head. Despite her pain, she wanted to hear what he had to say. "So you call him John…"

"To make it something just I do, I guess."

She nodded, swallowing hard. "Thank you, Reale. For everything."

He pulled up her blankets for her to snuggle down. "Try to sleep. He'll be fine. I promise to use helmets and sunscreen. I cannot promise to eat healthy or do anything educational."

She smiled, wincing.

"You need a bucket?"

83

"Un-unh. Thanks. As long as I don't eat or drink for a while, I think I've got it under control."

He kissed her on the forehead. "It's not always about control, Mandy," he whispered into her ear. "Feel better. We'll be home by five, or I'll expect the National Guard to hunt us down."

She attempted a grin as he walked out.

****

Reale peddled his bike slowly, letting John stay right at his side. The kid was obviously getting tired, but he had no quit in him. Reale chuckled. That was pure Mandy. She would fight for whatever she believed in—a refrain she felt wasn't working in his song or the health benefits of the wheat grass she forced him to drink. Sometimes their battles would last for hours—yelling, screaming, throwing books and CDs—until one of them would burst out laughing. And then they'd fall into each other's arms and make love until the sun came up the next morning. But still, she'd never admit she was wrong. Not his Mandy. His Mandy never gave up on anyth— His thoughts stopped short. Well okay, she gave up on one thing. The biggest thing in life. But still, there must be a reason he couldn't fathom, and soon enough he would get to the bottom of it all. Yes, his Mandy was still brimming with tenacity. She wasn't a quitter.

He stopped and placed his feet on the sandy path. John stopped alongside him. He reached over and adjusted John's new helmet, making sure the sun was off his face. They had been out all day, riding, playing miniature golf, climbing to the top of a lighthouse, eating hotdogs and mint chocolate chip ice cream. They were both exhausted, but it was a perfect day—except for the fact that he couldn't reach Mandy like he had promised. He'd left without getting her cell number, assuming John would know it, but try as they might John couldn't recall the number.

"Hey, John. Let's try your mom again." He just wanted to shoot her a text—the last thing he wanted was for her to be woken by a call or for them to barge in to tell her they were fine before leaving again. No, let her sleep if she could. Sleep was the only thing that could help the migraine lessen. Poor kid.

"Um, nine—one—seven…" John scrunched up his face. "I'm sorry, Reale."

"Hey." Reale held up his hand for John to high-five him. The boy stretched onto his tiptoes and then jumped high to make contact with Reale's hand. Reale smiled. "It's cool. When we get home, I'll tell Mommy you did a great job trying to remember."

Johnny nodded, smiling, the tip of his nose and cheeks pink from the strong sun.

Reale turned over his shoulder to check in with Jack who was on a bike, hanging back from them. "Does he need sunblock?"

"No." Jack shook his head. "You did it less than an hour ago."

"Thanks." Reale nodded to Jack, then turned back and smiled at John. "You're clear." His gaze dropped to the training wheels on John's bike. "How much time do you get to ride?" He nodded to John. When they rented their bikes this morning, he never expected John to use training wheels. Was that normal for a five-year-old kid? What was the age most kids mastered two wheels? He racked his brain trying to remember how old he'd been when he was on a big-kid bike, but try as he might, he had no recollection of age. He just remembered getting up one day and knocking a secret code on the front door of his best friend Alex's apartment, the two of them hustling downstairs to the basement of their building to steal Alex's father's bike to try it out. Reale smiled at the memory of Alex's father standing there guarding his bike, arms folded, staring at the two boys. In one hand he'd held a wrench.

"I'm guessing you two boys are ready to ditch the training wheels?"

"How did you know?" Alex asked his dad with awe and admiration.

Alex's dad smiled. "I heard you two dopes on your walkie talkies last night. If you're going to make covert plans, you've got to be quieter about it." Then Alex's dad had stepped forward and ruffled Alex's hair.

Reale kicked the sandy path beneath him, grounding himself, as some sand bounced into his high-tops. The memory of that simple father-son touch still sat in his very essence. His body still reacted to that moment on a cellular level. That touch between father and son—that bond—was something he had craved and never had. Alex's dad was awesome. He had been the building manager for their apartment house, and he did his best to include Reale in everything. But the truth was, he wasn't Reale's dad. And no matter how great he was to Reale, Reale knew it.

John gazed up at Reale. "Ride? Whenever Mommy can. Did we stop for a reason?"

Reale snapped out of his memory and glanced at the boy. No, John wasn't his by blood, but did it matter? Could he be the man in John's life anyway? Yes, it was fast, ridiculously fast, but these feelings he had toward Mandy were feelings based on years of love for her. Could they—the three of them—make a go of it? Sure, like a kid learning to ride without training wheels they would wobble a bit, but just as soon as they found their balance and their footing they would take off—together. John smiled at Reale, and something stirred deep in Reale's soul. If he could, if Mandy was ready, he would make sure John didn't go through what he had, learning how to be a man without anyone to guide him. Reale had become the man he was today— for better or worse—by instinct. How great it would be to teach John all those things no one had ever taught him. And in John's case, Reale would start with the most important rule: don't ever act like your stepfather had for those years he was apart from your mom.

Stepfather. Crap. He had thought it. Once that word had been released to run free through his brain, it couldn't be harnessed. He actually considered becoming John's stepfather. He wanted to give John a name—something he had never had. Yes, his mother had given him the name of his father, Lynxx, but without a man to match it to, it meant nothing. How many times in his life had people accused him of having made up the name Reale Lynxx? Yet ironically, his name was the only real thing about him. But John, he didn't even have that. He was a Simmons. Mandy never even gave John his father's name, and there had to be a reason. Something he would ask Mandy about later.

He sighed. It was time to consider what it would mean to be John's stepfather—it would mean making Mandy his wife. His heart raced with expectation and fear. Making Mandy his was something he had wanted to do for nearly the past decade, but it hadn't worked out so great last time he wanted to try. But maybe they'd come back together for a reason? Maybe fate had a plan for them after all?

Sure, there was a hell of a lot to sort through, and yes, he had a lot to make up for, but with Mandy and John with him, he was certain he could come out on top after all. That is, *if* he had Mandy and John with him. How could he know? The last time they'd been together, he would have bet his most prized possession, his silver band ring—the one he had hidden away in a specially made pocket of his guitar case—or his most monetarily valuable possession, his custom-made guitar, that they were solid. And then... How could he have been so wrong? He took a deep breath, standing tall. Could he let go of the past and trust her again? Could that be possible? Could he forgive the woman who'd ripped his world out from under him?

John smiled at Reale, flashing a full grin. A lot had changed in six years. A hell of a lot. For one thing, Reale was rich and famous, and for another, Mandy was a mom—to a darned great kid. Yeah, a hell of a lot had changed, for the better.

Filled with newfound hope and energy, he smiled at John. "What do you say we get rid of those training wheels?"

John's eyes widened. "I don't know. Mommy may not like it." He used his serious voice—the same one Mandy did—and Reale fought back a chuckle.

He approached this carefully. "Your mom is incredibly smart, and she takes good care of you. Like she always took good care of me."

"Yeah?" John dropped his chin when he spoke.

"Did she say you couldn't take off the training wheels?"

"No." John gripped his handlebars until his knuckles whitened.

"Do you want to get rid of them? Ride home later and show your mom when she's feeling better?"

John nodded enthusiastically.

"Well come on, then. Let's go back to the bike shop. Buy you the perfect big kid bike. We won't bother with these rentals anymore."

"Buy? A new bike?"

The simultaneous sound of disbelief and enthusiasm in John's voice hit Reale in the gut. Hard. Was it that difficult to believe he was going to buy something? How broke were Mandy and John anyway? She said she worked in a diner. They rented a house on Long Island, he knew that. But were things that tight for them?

Well, her finances were something else they would discuss before their vacation time was over. And if everything went as he hoped, her vacation wouldn't end. She would never again need to stay in a vacation leftover of a friend or work in a diner. They could move into any one, or all, of his homes and travel anywhere they'd like. Over the past five years or so, he had more money than he knew what to do with, until now. Now he knew what to do with it—use it to spoil Mandy and John rotten.

"Yeah, buy you a new bike. C'mon." He tossed his head and pointed to a town up ahead. "I'll bet there's a shop there. Let's go get you an awesome two-wheeler."

John jumped off his bike and rushed to Reale. He threw his arms around Reale's hips and hugged him, tight. Reale smiled before reaching down and ruffling John's hair.

****

Five forty-seven. Amanda paced the living room of her tiny beach house until she practically wore holes in the old wood floor. "Come on. Come on." How was it possible she didn't have Reale's cell number? She'd been sick this morning and hadn't thought of it. And when she'd woken up two hours ago, she'd expected to see texts from him—but there wasn't a single message. Not one. He had promised to text every couple of hours, but there was nothing. For all she knew, he could have kidnapped Johnny and run—all to get even with her for six years ago. Damn it.

Faster and faster she paced as she again considered calling 911. Taking a deep breath and mentally counting to ten, she calmed. Instead of dialing 911, she called Jess again.

"Still no sign of them?"

"No." Amanda's voice was shaky. Her racing heartbeat thumped in her already sore head. Where were they?

"Look." Jess's voice was calming.

In the background Amanda heard the din of the diner and a crotchety voice snapping at Jess. Old Man Howard the Grump no doubt, the meanest, orneriest regular the diner had. Jess was at work, but Amanda was too panicked to wait to call.

"Amanda, you said yourself he was a good guy. Always was."

"Yes. But what if—?"

"He's getting even with you?"

"Yes." Amanda's word was a whisper. She hadn't

told Jess that Reale was Johnny's father, but Jess knew of their past and present relationship.

"Amanda. I need you to take a deep breath and think. There is no way...that *person*"—she avoided using Reale's name—"would kidnap your son."

Despite her anxiety, Amanda was thankful for Jess's tact. Now when she went back to work, she wouldn't have to explain this to a diner full of her regulars. That is, if she went back to work. Assuming everything was okay. If she ever saw Johnny again. She sucked in a deep breath, hyperventilating.

"Breathe, Amanda. Think about it. Even if he is livid and has been disguising it all week, which is unlikely, he's a huge celebrity with a horrible rep. Do you think it would be in his best interest to kidnap a child? Now? After that train wreck horror story?"

"No." What Jess said made sense, but why didn't Amanda feel any better? "But I'm scared, Jess. And—"

"Mommy!"

She wheeled around to face the front window, certain that was Johnny's voice. She rushed out the door, her feet burning on the hot wood planks of the tiny landing, and glimpsed Johnny coming down the path. He was riding toward her with a giant smile on his face.

"Oh, thank God." She doubled over at the waist, tears rushing from her eyes. She stood straighter and took in her son, riding toward her. "Jess." She swallowed the lump in her throat. "He's home. I'm sorry I upset you."

"Amanda, don't worry. We're friends. We're here for each other. Thank God he's okay. Call me if you need anything."

"Like to bail me out after I rid the world of one more asshole rock star?"

Jess chuckled. "No one would blame you, but let's try to give him a chance, okay? You've been having a great week with him. He may have a legitimate excuse. Try to go easy on him."

"I make no promises." Amanda hung up her call and stuffed the phone into the back pocket of her pajama pants. She rushed to Johnny and pulled him off his bike. She dragged him to her.

"Mommy, look! See my new bike? Watch what I can do!" He spoke in a muffled voice into her chest as she embraced him, her arms heavy with relief, tears streaming down her cheeks. She took a deep breath, drying her eyes on the sleeves of her rumpled T-shirt before turning to look back down the path.

Then she laid eyes on him.

Releasing her son, she glowered at Reale as she walked toward him, the sound of Johnny's squeals of delight falling away behind her. She'd listen to Johnny later. Right now, she was too angry to focus. Instead, she marched up to Reale who was straddling his bike with a stupid, cocky grin on his face. His arms were crossed before his chest, covering the label on the expensive T-shirt he wore hanging over a pair of lightweight athletic pants. It was everything she could do not to plant her hands on his chest and push him off his bike—rocking his world like he had rocked hers.

Instead she crossed her arms in front of her chest and spoke in the lowest voice she could. "How dare you."

"What?" His eyes flashed with confusion as he released his arms and laid his hands on the handlebars.

"You said you would be back at five. It's…" She glanced at her oversized plastic watch. "Five fifty-two. And you said you'd text every couple of hours." She dug her phone out of her back pocket and held it up, waving it. "Not once. Not one single text." She stepped back, fighting the mounting tears in her eyes. It was too much to expect him to be responsible.

"Mandy." He leaned forward and reached out with his hand.

She darted back before he touched her cheek. "Don't call me that," she hissed.

The look of surprise in his eyes was evident. "Fine. Amanda. I didn't have your cell number. And although we tried several times, John couldn't remember it." He tossed his hands up. "I'm sorry I worried you."

"Worried me?" She took a step back and turned to Johnny. "Johnny, please go into the house and wash your hands for dinner."

"But I want to show you—"

"Johnny!" she snapped without meaning to. She took a deep breath and pushed it out as a sigh as Johnny stared at her, his eyes glassing over. "Johnny, you're not in trouble. I'm sorry I snapped. But Mr. Reale and I have some grownup things we need to discuss. Please go in now, and you can show me what you want to show me tomorrow."

"But—"

"Johnny."

His little cherub face fell as he turned and walked away. Once he was inside, she glanced at Jack.

Reale nodded. "Jack, I've got this. You must be exhausted. Thank you. Why don't you take off for the day? I'll text you if I need you."

"Sure." Jack adjusted his sunglasses before turning his bike and walking back down the path from Amanda's house.

If she wasn't so pissed, she would have giggled at the absurdity of it all. In his dark khaki Bermuda shorts, black polo shirt, and black sunglasses, Jack looked like a secret service man leaving the house of the seven dwarves. Ridiculous. Which is how she'd been acting all week—like a ridiculous, out of control, schoolgirl groupie. Well that ended now.

She glared at Reale.

"You feeling better?" He smiled again.

"I—" She shook her head at his audacity.

He sighed. "*Mister* Reale, huh? I must be in trouble."

His attempt to smooth things over infuriated her all the more. She turned her gaze away and ran a hand down her pajama bottoms, collecting her thoughts. After a moment, she looked at him. "Do you have any idea what you just put me through? Do you? I thought…" She shook her head.

Reale dismounted from his bike and put down the kickstand. He walked to her and stood just before her. She shielded her eyes from the sun as she gazed up at him. She shouldn't be outside without eye protection, especially not while she was getting over a migraine, but she'd rushed out so fast to get to Johnny she forgot her dark glasses. She studied Reale's face. Despite the harder features, he looked like her Reale. But was he really? She breathed him in—he smelled like fresh air and sunblock. The tiniest bit of her anger dissipated.

She took a deep breath and spoke calmly. "You don't know what it's like to have a child, but every second he is away from you, you worry. Is he okay? Is he happy? Is there anything upsetting him or bothering him? Is he hungry or thirsty? Does he need you and you're not there for him?" She choked on her last words, and again Reale reached out to touch her. She pulled back abruptly. "This is a thirty-mile island," she snapped. "You could have stopped back to get my cell number, so you could text me to say you were running late."

"I didn't want to disturb you. You used to sleep after migraine attacks."

"I used to do a lot of things I don't anymore." She tilted her head, looking into his eyes. "I was terrified, Reale. And what's worse, I was afraid he might be scared too."

Reale recoiled, stepping back. "He was with me."

"I know. But you've been in his life for all of, what, a couple of *days* now? He doesn't know you at all."

"He could."

"Not if I can't trust you."

Reale scoffed. "You've got a hell of a lot of nerve talking about trust."

Her eyes filled with tears again. "Really, Reale? We're getting into this right now?"

"When, then?"

She turned, exasperated, before facing him again. "I don't know. Maybe never. What difference does it make? It was six years ago. We are who we are now. You're a mega rock star, and I'm a waitress in a diner." She shrugged.

He stared at her, his jaw tight, his brow knitted.

"Reale. If that had been anyone else. Anyone at all,

I would have called the police."

"Why didn't you?"

"Because I didn't think you needed more bad press. What, after that train fiasco you need to be accused of kidnapping a child? I would never do that to you."

"No? *That* you'd never do to me?" He chortled, making a dark, ominous sound. She stepped back. "Honestly, Amanda, I think I would prefer being dragged into a police station accused of kidnapping a child than living through what you did to me."

She waved him away, swallowing the lump in her throat. Oh, God, had she hurt him that much? "You don't know what you're saying."

"Don't I?" He raised his eyebrows. "Maybe I've never been picked up for kidnapping, but you have no idea how much crap I've done these past few years that has landed me in police custody until my..." He stepped forward waving his peace fingers in the air like he was Richard Nixon. "My incomparable legal team has bailed me out. Destruction of property, disorderly conduct, drunken—"

She put up a hand, silencing him. Her stomach ached again as another wave of nausea washed over her. But this time it wasn't because of the migraine, it was because he sounded lost. She placed her hand to her stomach and took a deep breath. "Reale."

"But that wasn't me." He shook his head, looking off and back to her again. "I mean, yes, I did most of those juvenile, asshole things I was accused of, and I need to take responsibility for them, but it's not who I am...who I want to be." He took a step closer and raised his hand, letting it come to rest on her cheek.

This time she didn't pull away. She closed her eyes

as his thumb caressed her cheek.

"I like who I am with you. With John. That's the man I want to be. I'm sorry, Mandy. Really. I thought I was doing right by you today."

She sighed, looking up into his eyes—so bright and smart. No matter what she had heard or seen, those eyes were trustworthy. She would bet her life on it. And that's the reason she had trusted him with Johnny today. The corners of his eyes crinkled when he smiled, and the area just outside the sunglass line looked dry and burnt. He'd had too much sun.

"Did you remember to reapply your sunscreen?"

"Not as often as I did John's, no." He held her gaze.

She nodded, growing lightheaded from the migraine and her relief. Looking over that face she knew better than her own, she suddenly questioned her reaction over the past hour. Was she really worried about Johnny? Or was it that she had smacked up against a complete loss of control which terrified her more than anything? Johnny out with Reale—a place he should be—meant he wasn't with her while she kept him safe. She had to trust someone else would do that, and it wouldn't necessarily be the way she wanted. No, he wouldn't feed Johnny seaweed chips and roasted kale, but he would show him a good time, and he would keep Johnny safe. She knew it in her gut. That was the real reason she hadn't called the police. Because when it came to her son, she would have called the cops on Jesus Christ himself. This was her issue, not theirs. Would she ever be able to relinquish enough control to co-parent? Even if it were the best decision for Johnny? The tiniest seed of worry began festering in the deepest regions of her mind. Was it possible her great selfless act was actually incredibly selfish? Had she done the right thing to keep Johnny away from his father for all this time…or at all?

She sighed. "You need some aloe around your eyes. Your skin looks dry and burned."

"Okay."

"I have some inside if you want to pop in for a minute."

"I'd like that."

She nodded, turning toward the house, and he reached out and grabbed her by the elbow gently.

"Mandy…"

She fought to calm her racing breath as she glanced at his hand on her elbow.

"I am sorry I worried you."

She nodded. "I know."

He released his grasp on her, and she shuddered. "You cold?"

"A little."

"I'm gonna grab you a sweatshirt, because I think you should hang out here for a bit and let John show you something before we all go in for our health cleanse."

He darted into the house as he spoke, and she turned, watching him go. He moved easily and quickly, his body always completely under his control. She closed her eyes, envisioning him onstage, his body swaying as he played his guitar. He was so sexy and strong and talented. She opened her eyes again, waiting for him to reemerge from the house. Waiting for the only man she had ever loved, one of the biggest rock stars in the world, to reappear from her house with their son in tow. How was this happening? After all this time? Was he able to put all that hurt aside to love her again? She tilted her head, plopping her hands on her hips as he reemerged carrying her old, gray, zip-front sweatshirt with Johnny right beside him.

She took a deep breath, smiling at Johnny. Reale draped the sweatshirt around her shoulders and turned her toward him, zipping her jacket. Having him this close was almost too much. She fought the urge to glance at her watch to see how much longer it would be until Johnny went to bed. She smirked as he grasped the strings of her hood and pulled her closer. She rocked onto her toes, their bodies smashing together. She pressed her hips forward, gauging his reaction.

"Easy…" He pulled back a tad.

"You mentioned a health cleanse?" Even though her head was still throbbing, she raised her eyebrows, enjoying the happier turn this conversation had taken. "Did you eat that much junk?"

"You don't want to know." He grinned and kissed her lightly on the nose before releasing her and stepping back. He nodded to her, stuffing a hand into his pocket, before he leaned down to whisper into her ear. "You are a bad girl."

Her entire body—from her scalp to her toes—tingled. She hummed in response.

He raised his eyebrows. "Those little sounds you make—not helping." He shook his head before turning to Johnny. "John, buddy, helmet first." Reale tapped his finger to his head, and Johnny gave him a thumbs-up.

"Got it, Reale!"

Her heart swelled at the interaction between the two. It was natural and fun; exactly as it was supposed to be. Johnny was beaming, and she could feel the grin spreading across her face.

Reale wrapped his arm around her waist and pulled her to the side of him. "That's a pretty big smile."

"I just…" She shook her head, feeling so much love for them both she could burst.

"Yeah." He nodded, squeezing her waist tighter. "I get it. Now get ready, 'cause you're in for the surprise of your life."

Amanda glanced up at Reale. *That would make two of us.*

Chapter Eight

Amanda snuggled up against Reale on the outdoor couch, her feet tucked beneath her, inhaling the cool night air. Her headache was down to a dull roar, and she could see clearly. Johnny lay on a blanket on the lawn before them, engrossed in the cartoons playing on the giant screen Reale had had set up for them. Johnny's new bike was perched just off his blanket—no doubt he'd want it to sleep in his room with him tonight.

"I can't believe you gave us an outdoor screening room." She sighed happily.

"I was going to bring you two to my place tonight, use the media room there."

A tiny cramp formed in her aching belly. His place. It was inevitable. At some point they would all have to break out of this little fantasy world they had created; a world that was some hybrid of past and future, but she wasn't sure she was ready to face who Reale was now. "Media room?" She raised her eyebrows, questioning him.

"Full-sized theatre." He nodded. "I thought John would love it. Popcorn machine, surround sound, everything." He shrugged, pulling her closer. "But since you had a migraine today, I thought this would be better. We can watch a movie there tomorrow."

"Tomorrow?" Was it possible there could be a

tomorrow and tomorrow after that?

"Sure. I promised John a screening room. I don't make promises I don't deliver on. I'm a man of my word." He picked up a red licorice string and popped one end into his mouth, chewing.

She froze. A man of his word. Her jaw clenched, and she ground her teeth, a habit she was trying to break. Her head still ached from the migraine, and her jaw hurt even more.

He turned to her. "It's an expression, Mandy. I wasn't making a grand statement. I would never be that passive-aggressive. We both know we need to talk—about a lot—but we've both been good at finding reasons not to."

She nodded.

"Although I've gotta say, there are less dramatic ways than with a migraine."

She rolled her eyes. "Ooo, ow." She placed her fingers to her temples, rubbing gingerly.

"Not a great idea to roll your eyes, huh?"

She shook her throbbing head. "Ooo…" Her head thumped in response. "Ow." She placed a cool hand to her forehead.

"Mandy, relax. Please." He placed his hand on her shoulder and caressed gently. Her tension fell away.

"More licorice?" He held the opened bag out to her.

"No, thanks. I have gorged myself on junk food. No more." She snuggled against him tighter and caught a whiff of the sweet, artificial cherry scent. "But I guess since it is vacation…" She grabbed one last red licorice string, and his relaxed body tightened beneath her. She sat up and placed her hand on his tummy. She tilted her head, looking into his eyes. "What?"

"What, what?" He furrowed his brow and looked away the way he always did when he was avoiding something.

"Why did you tense up?" She slid the uneaten licorice back into the bag.

"I didn't."

Obviously, he tensed because she mentioned vacation—and all vacations were finite. Eventually this little fantasy they created for themselves would have to end. And unfortunately, it would be sooner rather than later. But right now, she was going to enjoy every second of it.

"Reale, this is me. You did tense, and I can prove it. I saw your tell."

"What tell?" His voice was deep and playfully incredulous.

"The way you furrow your brow so seriously and drop the pitch of your voice." She mimicked his position and did her best impression of him. " 'No Mandy, I didn't tense up at all. So what if you could bounce quarters off my amazing abs? I'm always this tight.' " She grinned, and he leaned forward, tickling her.

"Amazing abs, huh?"

"Oh!" She squealed as he moved his hands from her tummy to her sides, working their way to her underarms.

Johnny turned around. "Mommy, Reale, you're too loud. I want to see what the rabbit is going to do. He's trapped."

"Sorry, little man. Mommy needs some serious tickling." Reale turned his attention back to Amanda. "I seem to remember you were ticklish here…" He tickled her under both arms as she kept her head as still as she could while laughing. "And how about…" He lifted her onto his lap and reached out for her bare feet, tickling the soles of her feet until she didn't think she could breathe.

"Momm-my," Johnny whined at her.

"Wait, wait. Stop, Reale, please."

He stopped tickling, and she stayed sitting sideways on his lap. With one hand stretched out long across her lap, his hands came to rest on her hips.

"I have to catch my breath."

"I'm letting you off the hook because John can't hear his completely non-educational show. And because you're getting over a migraine. How is your head after all the tickling?"

"Better, thank you." And it was. Everything felt better when she and Reale were together.

He smiled. "You remember when we used to sit in bed and watch home shows as your migraine lessened?"

"Of course." She shifted uncomfortably. Was he referring to their last day together? Was there any way to avoid thinking about that night? She changed the direction of the conversation. "I never thought you paid attention to those shows."

"I didn't."

He flashed a smile as he toyed with the drawstring at the waistband of her freshly changed pajama bottoms. She had to get out of the ones she'd been wearing when she'd thrown up, but even attempting to get dressed in real clothes was impossible. In typical Reale fashion, he'd insisted she stayed in PJs, and he and Johnny were both in pajamas as well. Reale had on a pair of dark blue plaid bottoms that looked like they'd never been worn, and a white V-neck T-shirt. He'd had them delivered when the outdoor screening room was set up. Johnny was wearing his usual dinosaur bottoms with one of Lynxx's concert T-shirts on top. The shirt hung down to his calves. It was all so perfect.

"I didn't watch the shows. I listened to you when you told me about how you would have designed the homes. How you would design our home one day."

"Oh. I, uh…" Her gaze dropped down to his abdomen wedged between them. Crap. It was inevitable. It wasn't his fault, but what a way to bring down the evening. Yes, he'd brought up the past, but everything that had gone wrong since those good days of the past was her fault. Everything.

"Hey." He smiled sweetly. "Since we're stuck with cartoons, why don't you tell me what you'd do with this place?"

She brightened, sitting taller. Maybe he understood her head wasn't clear enough for this discussion tonight. Or…ever. "Here?"

He nodded.

"Well…" She started off timidly. This wasn't like the old days when they had twenty bucks—if they were lucky—for the weekend, and since their imaginations were free, they let them run wild. This man had all the money in the world, and she could only imagine what his houses must look like. Intimidation washed over her. No doubt he hired the best designers in the world. She wasn't going to talk about adding a throw rug or new comforter.

"Mand? What would you do? 'Cause I can tell the wood paneling drives you crazy."

"How do you know?"

"I'm not the only one who has tells."

She crossed her arms, playfully. "And what, exactly, are mine?"

"Like hell I'm giving up that info." His eyes sparkled as he teased her. "Come on. What would you do? I know it wouldn't be an underwater theme."

"Oh, ha, ha."

He reached out and stroked her cheek, and she nuzzled against it, giving over to the warmth and strength of his hand.

"Well, those beautiful beach houses I see on the home shows, I don't like the ones that are all chrome and stark white. They look cold to me, and I'd want it to be warm and inviting. A place where Johnny would be happy." Oh, damn. What if he had a house that looked like that? "Not that those houses aren't beautiful. They are. Gorgeous. So if you have a house that looks like that—"

"Mandy. Relax. Please. I promise not to take offense. I don't even remember what most of my houses look like."

"Really?"

He nodded.

"Most of your houses? How many do you have?"

"I have no idea. I have a team that handles all that for me."

Worry washed over her. "And that's okay by you? You trust them? They are doing right by you?"

The smile he gave her then was indescribable. Condescending? Sweet? Loving? Her cheeks flushed in response as he reached up with both hands and placed them on her face. He held her while he gazed at her.

"Mandy. My Mandy. Always worrying about me."

He pulled her to him and held her tight. His face was at her neck, and her breasts were pushed against his strong shoulders. His arms rested around her waist. His body was so hard but felt so right. She glanced over her shoulder to see Johnny was glued to his show, so she took the opportunity to swing her leg over Reale's lap and straddle him. His eyes widened with surprise as she let her weight press down against him.

"What would you do with the house?" he whispered.

In his arms she felt so safe and protected. She knew he would never laugh at her—not about this or anything. So what if his world of parties and yachts and world travels made her small life of working in a diner on the South Shore of Long Island seem sad? He wasn't going to judge. He honestly wanted to know. He always cared about what she thought. Besides, the longer she could postpone talking about that fateful night, the happier she was.

She smiled. "Without changing the floor plan, I'd get rid of the dark mustiness. I'd tear down the wood paneling and add windows anywhere and everywhere I could. I'd make the rooms all a light pearl gray and leave the exposed beams on the ceiling, staining them cherry. I'd replace all the wood grain with white, horizontal shiplap walls and put brightly colored, giant bins in the deep recessed corners—made of some interesting texture, like basket weave—filled with toys for Johnny. I'd decorate with soft, inviting, pearl-white, puffy couches covered with dark gray throws, and the low wooden coffee table would be the perfect place to sit around and do puzzles together." She was lost in her world, as she created the home she would love for the three of them. "Ooo." She wiggled on his lap, and he pressed his lips together.

He steadied her by her hips. "Careful."

"Oh, sorry." She bit her lip and smirked.

"What else?" he prodded her.

"The kitchen would be all white with a huge farmhouse sink and stainless appliances. One of those big fans over the stove and a huge, handmade, dark wood kitchen table. The kind of table Johnny would sit at eating cookies with his friends, or people could gather around at a dinner party. Stoneware jars lining exposed shelving…"

"Sounds beautiful."

"Yeah?"

"Oh, yeah." He nodded. "How about the bedrooms? John's?"

"Johnny's would be classic boy—light blue walls, big bed with dark blue comforter, baseball mitt hanging on the wall."

"And my poster, I hope." He grinned.

"Of course."

"How 'bout the master?" His eyes glazed when he asked, and he adjusted her again. Pressure mounted in his pajama bottoms.

"I, uh…I've never thought about the master."

"Well, think about it now."

"Same idea I guess. Open, bright, big bed, picture windows…oh! And French doors leading out to a garden." She shrugged. If she was going to have a fantasy, why not have it all the way? Including Reale lying in a king-sized bed, strumming his guitar. "The master bathroom—whoa." She whistled, shaking her hands like they were hot.

"You are a geek, you know that, right?"

She smiled. "Why's that? My house design?"

"No, I love your house design. Whistling and shaking your hands? No wonder your son has so many mannerisms of an old man."

She giggled, but her stomach flip-flopped. She was a bit concerned her son was a geek. "Maybe you should help him become more rock and roll?"

"Un-unh." He shook his head. "He's perfect just the way he is."

She smiled. "He is, right?"

"Yeah."

She glanced back over her shoulder at Johnny. He was laid out, one arm under his head. "I think he's out." She turned back to Reale.

"I hope so, because these pajama bottoms don't offer much camouflage." He smirked. "And with you straddling me…"

"Well, what do you say we relieve some of that pressure you're feeling?"

"No way." He shook his head. "You're getting over a migraine. Not tonight."

She turned away, collecting herself. The final day they were together she had pretended to have a migraine, and they missed their last opportunity to be together because of it. Here in Reale's arms, she couldn't imagine letting another chance slip away.

"Mandy." He lifted his hand and placed a finger under her chin. He turned her to face him again. "I want to be with you more than anything. But I don't want to hurt you."

"But I don't want to waste a single moment with

you. I don't want to lose our chance."

"Hey." He shook his head. "It won't happen. I won't let it. Not like that. Not again."

"No?" She scanned his eyes, looking for the answer.

"No."

And just like that there was an unspoken promise to do better this time. This time, it would be different.

"Let's get John into his room and hop into that tiny bed you've got. I want to pull you close and feel you against me. I want to hold you all night. What do you say?"

"I say it sounds perfect, Reale."

He nodded, and scooping her into his arms, he stood, kissing her on the lips.

****

"Are you kidding me?" The look on Mandy's face was priceless. It was shock and awe and pride. She was proud of him. Not for the asshole things he'd done, but for how successful he'd become from his music. She moved from the massive entryway of his beach house into the open concept living area, shaking her head. "I—I'm speechless." She crossed her arms before her and turned to her left. "That gorgeous cherry wood spiral staircase." She pointed over her shoulder. "The kitchen. Good grief! With all the copper pots and pans over that giant island with the gorgeous, dark gray granite. Forget chef's kitchen, it looks like it belongs in the world's finest restaurant."

"Thought you were speechless," he teased, his own grin spreading wider. How many times had he fantasized about this scenario? About bringing Mandy into the dream house he provided for her?

"I am." She laughed, tossing her head. She walked closer to the wall of windows. "And these floor-to-ceiling windows overlooking the private beach and ocean." She turned to face him again, her brow furrowing. "But I don't understand. Why were you on the same beach as me if you have a private beach? Why were you...? It doesn't make any sense."

"These beaches are all private but all connected. And I don't know, I felt like walking." He had asked himself that question every day this week. Why had he forced Daniel to take a walk off their immediate beachfront? It made no sense. None at all. But they had done it, and because of it, Amanda Simmons was in his life—again. He dared a glimpse at her stunning smile. Was it...fate? Then his eyes found hers, and her gorgeous green eyes searched his; no doubt she was wondering the exact same thing.

"Wait 'til you see the upstairs skylights and rotunda for stargazing. We'll go up after the movie. Let's go catch up with John in the screening room. I got him the new plastic people movie a week before it opens."

She shook her head, the look of joy in her eyes nearly overwhelming. "Thank you, Reale. This is spectacular."

"Well I don't own it." He reached out and took her hand. He pulled her closer. "But if you like it, I could."

She tensed, her hand tightening in his. She tilted her head. "What are you saying?" The tone of her voice deepened, and she dropped her chin, looking up at him through her lashes.

"What do you want me to say?" He wrapped his arms around her, holding her close.

"Reale." She spoke softly. "I don't know what's happening. I don't know what's real and what's not. This has been overwhelmingly wonderful. But…"

"But?" He leaned down, trying to read her eyes.

"But Johnny and I—we could never live in this world. This is amazing. Fantastic. But it's not real. A child needs a steady home. One steady home. And sure, having a brand-new bike is special, but he doesn't need—and shouldn't have—everything."

He lessened his grasp, leaning back. How much subtext was in this one statement? Was she telling him when this week was over they were out of his life for good? No. No way. He couldn't lose her again.

"Fine. Then I'll buy your place, and we'll vacation there."

She placed a hand to her mouth, giggling. Her eyes danced with happiness. "Well yes, I suppose that would be an excellent compromise." She laughed. "Except lucky for you, it's not for sale, been in Jess's family forever. They'll never sell."

"Everything's for sale, Mand." He reached up and stroked her hair lovingly, before letting his hand cascade over her cheek, careful of her scratches. "Everything."

She bristled, pushing back from him. "There it is."

"What?" He furrowed his brow, trying to understand.

"We've been in your world for fifteen minutes, and already I'm seeing a man I don't know. Everything's for sale?"

"It's just an expression."

"Is it?" Her eyes searched his.

"Mandy." He released his grasp on her waist and

took her hands in his. "You want me to be the man I was six years ago, but that's not fair. We've both done some growing and changing. And truthfully, Mandy, you've got no business expecting me to be the man I was then. You were the reason everything changed." Damn, that was harsher than he meant, but he had more anger bottled up inside than he realized.

She broke free and stepped back, placing a hand to her head. "So we're here. It only took us three days."

"What did you expect? That we'd never talk about it? That we'd never discuss why you walked out on our life?"

Tears flooded her eyes as she stepped back. She ran a hand through her beautiful, long, blonde hair before focusing on him again. Her shoulders deflated, and she looked three inches shorter and ten years younger. His heart ached for her.

"Look. Reale. Johnny and I are leaving in a couple of days. Sunday afternoon. We have ferry tickets. Yes, you and I have to talk—I mean, if you want to." She gazed down at her feet, shuffling. She looked up at him again. "But can we please do it when he's asleep? I don't want him involved in this."

"Isn't he?"

She turned her head sideways, reading his eyes. "What do you mean?"

"I mean, if there's a man in your life, doesn't it directly impact him? For the better?"

She sighed. "Depends."

"On?"

She shook her head, the bone in her angular jaw popping. She was tense. "Let's watch the movie." She stepped forward, slipping her warm hand in his. "We'll talk after. Later." She smiled, tentatively. "You have plenty of wine?"

He chuckled. "Enough. But I have no intentions on drinking tonight. I don't want to miss one moment of it. I have waited and wondered about this for six years, Mand."

She nodded. "I know." She bit the corner of her puffy lip. "The wine is for me."

Chapter Nine

Reale was sitting behind her, hunched over the tiny table in the kitchen of Amanda's vacation house. Even though her back was to him, she could feel his eyes on her as she fussed about, moving around the kitchen, filling a kettle with water and placing it on the stove, grabbing some organic gingersnaps from the cabinet, arranging them carefully on a red decorative plate she found buried in the back of one of the cabinets, and anything else she could think to do to stall. She took a deep breath. Okay. It was becoming obvious. She needed to turn around and face him, but in doing that, she'd have to face the past six years of her life.

Breathing deeply and mustering every ounce of courage she had, she turned toward Reale. She walked slowly toward him, placing two mismatched, heavy ceramic mugs on the table. She twirled the mug before him nervously, and he reached out to grab her hand, steadying her.

"Mandy."

She nodded, forcing a smile. He sounded so confident and in control. Things he always was—or used to be, anyway. Would he stay calm when he learned she had kept him from his son for the past five years? She sucked in a jagged breath. Why was it so hard to breathe at times like this? She hurried away to retrieve two chamomile teabags from the cabinet.

Maybe it wouldn't be so bad after all. Maybe he would realize why she had done it. Maybe he could understand, forgive her, and they could move forward together. The three of them. Just as it was meant to be. And who knows, maybe in a year or two they could have another baby—a girl this time—and Reale could be there for every diaper change and two a.m. feeding. Her tense shoulders dropped as she thought about a baby daughter. Their baby daughter. With his gorgeous blond hair and her giant green eyes.

Feeling a little stronger, she waltzed closer to Reale, and his gaze followed her as she plopped the two herbal bags into their mugs. She raised her eyes to his and was lost. Those eyes she had stared in so many times. That man who had calmed her and cared for her and loved her…he was here. And tonight, six years after she'd left Reale Lynxx—purposely walked out on their life—it was time to confess and beg for absolution. It was time to explain herself.

Whhiizzzz! The kettle whistled behind her, and she jumped, placing a hand to her racing heart. Reale took a deep breath and stood. He put his hand on her forearm as he walked past on the way to the kettle. He turned off the burner and brought the steaming kettle to the table.

"You think that woke John?" He spoke as he poured hot water into their mugs and replaced the kettle on the stove.

"Un-unh." She shook her head. "He's usually tough to get to sleep, but he sleeps soundly once he's out. I make a lot of late-night tea. He's used to the noise."

"Mandy…" He plopped down into a chair and took

her arm, gently guiding her to the chair next to his. He leaned forward and rested his forearms on the table.

She took in every bit of his handsome, masculine face, his full lips, and piercing eyes.

"You've got to start, babe. Because I don't know what happened that night or any of those nights leading up to it. As far as I know and knew, we were happy. Really happy. We loved each other."

She pulled the sleeves of her light sweater over her hands and grasped the hot mug. She stared into her tea like an old fortune teller reading tea leaves. Only there were no answers in the teacup—the answers were in his eyes. She gazed up at him, forcing steady contact. "We did love each other, Reale. And I never stopped. I have loved you every second of every day since that first time I saw you onstage. I think about you more than you could possibly know."

"Then why, Mandy. Why?"

She sighed, stretching her arm long on the table. His hand found hers, his grasp warm and strong. He held her hand purposely, his grip just tight enough to prove he was as scared as she was. She swallowed hard.

"I don't know how to start." She searched his eyes for the answer.

"At the beginning." His already strong grip tightened. "Did you leave me because your mother convinced you to?"

"Is that what you think? You think I would let anyone come between us or turn me against you? I couldn't care less what that old woman thought. She was cruel and senseless. I'm sorry for any moment of grief she caused you."

"Mandy." He sat straighter. "Obviously someone

came between us."

She shook her head and allowed it to drop to the side. Her gut ached and her heart hurt. "It's not what you think."

"Then tell me what to think. Tell me what happened. Start with that night. If it wasn't your mother, then what?" He shifted in his chair. This had to be awful for him. "Did you know that guy? That guy you…you kissed?"

"No."

"Why the hell did you kiss him, then?"

"I had already overheard the record executive. I knew you were going to be offered a contract. He had already seen how amazingly talented you are."

"So?"

"So I knew the only way to leave you for good was to do something so shocking and jarring. Something you couldn't forgive me for." She dropped her chin. "Although, I'm hoping maybe someday you could forgive me for it."

"Why did you want to leave me? That's what I don't get. Because I was poor? Because we were broke?"

"Of course not. I loved you, Reale. I didn't care about that. I knew someday you'd get your break, I'd be a nurse, and the times we spent scraping by would be a happy memory."

"I don't get it, Mandy. I'm sorry, but I just don't get it."

She nodded as a deluge of memories flooded over her, burning her from the inside out. "That day, the day your record company came to scout you, I didn't have a migraine."

"What?" He sat back, letting her hand go. His eyes dashed back and forth, trying to make sense of a senseless situation. "You did. You were vomiting all morning."

"It…it wasn't from a migraine."

His eyes narrowed. "Morning sickness?"

She nodded.

He pushed back from the table and ran his hands through his hair. "Jesus." He stared up at her. "I don't understand, Mandy. Why? Why would you? Weren't we happy together?"

"Of course we were, Reale. I was happier with you than I've ever been in my life."

"Then why would you…?" He leapt from his seat and paced around the tiny kitchen. "Why, Mandy?"

The look on his face crumbled her heart.

"Because I loved you so much. Everything I did, Reale, you have to know it nearly killed me. Leaving you was the hardest thing I have ever done."

"Wait. You're telling me you screwed some other guy while we were together because you loved me so much?" His demeanor toughened. The angles on his face hardened, and he crossed his arms before his wide chest. "I'm sorry, Mandy. I don't get it. Then what, you screwed some other random guy you picked up at a bar during my show—during the biggest night of my professional life? And then? You run off to Mommy because your failure of a rock-and-roll-wannabe boyfriend couldn't support you like you wanted? Is that what happened?"

Disgust flipped her stomach. "Of course not. How could you even think that?" This was beginning to spiral out of control.

"How could I think that? How could you *do* that?" His voice rose, and he threw up his hands in exasperation. "Mandy, you were my entire world! We lived together like a married couple who really loved each other. We were a team. You were always the smarter one, the one who kept us grounded while I was free to dream. And I loved you ferociously, not for what you did for me, but for whom you were." He stepped back. "For whom you are." He dragged a hand through his hair and dropped it in a defeated move. "That night—we had spent weeks preparing. You helped me get ready for the music executive, and then you annihilated me." His voice grew softer, and the tears flowed freely down her cheeks. "You walked up in front of the stage and…and kissed that preppy asshole. Why? Why would you do that? Weren't you happy?"

"Yes. Happier than I'd ever been."

"Then why? And why would you fuck some other guy while we were together?"

She shook her head, tears falling fast and hard. "I didn't."

"Didn't what?"

"I didn't…I wasn't."

"What, Mandy?" His voice was deep and hollow.

"I kissed that guy so you would leave me for good. I did it all for you, don't you see?"

"No, Mandy. I don't."

"I didn't sleep with that guy, Reale. I walked out of the bar and went to Grand Central and hopped a train to my mother's. When I got there, I told her I was pregnant, and she gave me an ultimatum—get an abortion or be gone. So I left. I went to Long Island and did the only thing I knew to do—give my son a life."

"Mandy. Please."

"I never cheated on you, Reale. I loved you. I love you."

His eyes widened, and he shook his head. "But you just told me you had morning sickness the day you left me. You had to have been with someone else, or else…"

Her heart thumped in her throat. "Or else what, Reale?"

"Or else John is mine."

She took a deep breath, staring at him. He had a right to know. Now please, God, let him understand why she'd done it.

"Mandy? It doesn't make sense. You either slept with someone while we were together, or John is mine."

She stared up at him, her chest heaving in time with her hurried breath.

"Amanda. Answer me right now. Did you sleep with someone else while we were together?"

His eyes were wild with emotion. She bit the inside of her cheek and swallowed back her tears.

"Amanda Simmons. Answer me."

She shook her head slowly. "No, Reale, I didn't sleep with someone else while we were together. I loved you."

"Then…are you telling me…?" He straightened up tall, and his eyes flashed to the door of Johnny's bedroom. "He's *mine*?"

"Yes." Her word was a whisper.

He glanced at the door and back to her. He repeated his action over and over. "That boy…John…that's why he looks just like me. But

Amanda, why? What in God's name were you thinking?"

"The record executive was coming to see you. Your career was just starting. I overheard his conversation on the phone. I knew he was going to sign you, and you needed your chance."

"You made that decision based on overhearing the phone call of a drunken stranger?"

"Of course not. I went that night knowing I had to leave you. Knowing you would never get your chance if suddenly you had a pregnant girlfriend."

"What?"

"You would have given it all up to support us, Reale." She rose to her feet. "I couldn't let you go work in a department store or sell computers for minimum wage so you could feed a wife and child. Don't you see, Reale? It was the only way." The desperation in her voice was palpable.

"The only way?" He shook his head. "Amanda, you of all people know what it was like to grow up with no father. You know how much I hated my father for that. You know that was the one thing I carried with me like an oozing, festering wound. I hated my father, and yet I missed him every second of my childhood. How could you do that to John? How?"

"I didn't do that to Johnny. I did it for you."

"For me? And what about him? That boy you say you care for so much? What happens when he asks about a father? Was he going to grow up with no father figure at all? Or were you going to marry some other guy and let *him* be John's father? Damn it, Amanda!"

"No, no, Reale. You're seeing this all wrong. I did what I had to so you could become the man you are."

"The man I am!" He marched in a circle and landed a foot or two away from her. "The man I am is a louse. A mostly drunk, insensitive, half-assed musician with a hell of a lot of money. What gives you the right to make that decision? Huh? Who said you can have that power? He's mine too, Amanda."

"Yes." She stepped backward, shame washing over her. "At the time, Reale, all I could see was your future. Your rise to stardom. Your talent. I wanted you to have it all."

"Except the woman I loved and my son. What do I have, Amanda?"

"Your career." Her voice cracked as she spoke.

"My career. And what makes you think that would have been better than working somewhere to support you and John until you finished school? Then you could work and I'd get my chance."

"But your talent…" She placed her hand on his, and he shook her away forcefully.

"Yeah, what about my talent? How dare you? You think the best I'd ever get was that one shot?"

"No, Reale, no." Damn, this was going all wrong.

"I would have found a way somehow. With you and John with me. So what if we played in small clubs forever? Then I would have had my music and my family. But you robbed me of that, Amanda." His voice was desperate. "How could you?"

"Reale. Please. Please listen. I really thought I was doing the right thing. How many times have we heard about people's careers ending because they suddenly have a family to support?" Why couldn't he understand she'd done this for him?

"But you kept my son from me. Do you have any

idea how that feels? I've missed five birthdays and five Christmases and his first steps...and damn it, Amanda!" He stormed off, pacing again. "I would have supported you. Both of you. Even if you didn't want to stay with me...you didn't have to be with me. I still would have taken care of him. Given him the best of everything. How would you feel if you were kept from John? Huh?"

She gasped as if she had been punched in the gut. Nothing in the world could ever be worse than being without Johnny.

"I did want to be with you, Reale. It's all I ever wanted. Maybe now we can give this a try—"

He wheeled around. "Give this a try? Give what a try?"

Heat overtook her face. "Okay, I understand if you don't want to be with me anymore, but we can arrange..."

"Arrange what? How can I trust you? I have no idea who you are. I thought you were my soul mate, the person I would go through life with. Grow old with. But I never knew you at all. You're just some cruel, sick woman who'd keep her son from his father. Why? Is it because of my image? Because I never did anything back then."

"Of course not." The tears fell fast.

"You, Amanda. All these years you preached how horrid your mother was. But here's the truth, you're no better."

"Reale." Her throat ached as she choked back a sob.

"Your mother never thought I was good enough for her daughter, and apparently you didn't think I was good enough for your son."

"That's not fair, Reale. And it's not true."

"No? Then why not contact me. Huh? I get a thousand paternity accusations thrown at me a year. It's not tough to find me. My management knows which ones to offer a paternity test. It would have been you."

"Your *management*? You'd pass me off to your management?"

"You have no business getting self-righteous."

She sucked in a deep breath, anger swirling in her core. "You want a paternity test? That's not a problem."

"Damn right I want a test. Now. Immediately."

Her stomach flipped.

He stood still, his shoulders slumping. "You have betrayed me far worse than I ever thought. All those years I wondered what I had done. And in fact, it was you. You lied. And you kept my son from me."

"No, Reale. You don't understand." She took a deep breath and focused on him through eyes burning with tears. "We'll work something out so you can spend some time with him."

"Some time with him?" Reale raised his eyebrows. "Oh, I'll be spending more than some time with him."

"Okay. Well, as soon as we both cool off, we'll talk to Johnny, and you and I can work out a visitation schedule."

"A schedule?" He scoffed, tossing his head. "You think I'm going to settle for a visitation schedule? After keeping him from me for five years?"

Her stomach clenched, and her body trembled with fear. "What do you want, Reale?"

"I want John."

"What are you saying?"

"I'm saying you've had him to yourself for five years. Sounds like it's my turn."

"Your turn?"

"Yeah. My turn to take him for five years. You can see him when he's ten. How's that sound?"

"Reale!" Sobs poured out of her, and she clutched her stomach, her gut aching. She drew in her breath, collecting herself. She had to stay in control. "Stop saying that. There's no court in the land that will take a child from his mother."

"They will if the father has my money and my legal team." His eyes flashed with cruelty. "Think about it, Amanda. I can do more for him than you ever could. Private schools, French tutors…a…a horse, anything and everything he's ever dreamt of."

"He needs me, Reale."

"He needs me too, Amanda. And damn it, if it takes my last dying breath, that boy will know his father." Reale turned abruptly and back again. "I'll be here first thing in the morning for a paternity test. You can expect to get a court date within two weeks."

He stormed out the door, and she fell to the floor, sobbing.

Chapter Ten

"Hey, buddy." Amanda roused Johnny more forcefully than she meant to. "Let's go."

"What? Where?" Johnny rolled over in his sleep.

She glanced at the clock—eleven thirty-seven. It had taken her less than thirty minutes to get their things packed, even while she continually looked over her shoulder and glanced out the window. Even though she ran to the door time and again to check Reale wasn't coming up the path. Her nerves were frayed, and she was terrified and shaking as she hustled around the house. She did her best to clean up as fast as she could—stripping the bed, tossing the opened food in the fridge, taking out the garbage—but she couldn't take the time to wash the sheets or sweep up. Jess would understand. She cleared her throat and focused on her son. "It's time for a special trip."

He yawned. "With Reale? Are we going somewhere cool?"

Damn it. All it took was a few days for Reale Lynxx to completely win over her son. She sighed heavily. She needed to go, tonight. She couldn't wait for Reale to show up at her door tomorrow morning demanding a paternity test and God knew what else. For all she knew, he'd have the police with him and somehow convince them she was an unfit mother. A chill washed over her. It was horrid to think she would ever be without Johnny, but so much worse to imagine Johnny being without her.

"No Reale. Just us. Like it usually is. We're taking a special ferry ride." She couldn't afford a private water taxi across the Great South Bay, but she couldn't afford not to take one, either.

"Home? I don't want to go home." Johnny flipped over in bed, his tiny body rattling the old, wooden four-poster bed.

"Johnny, come on." She shook him a tad more vigorously. "You've got to get up." It wasn't possible to carry Johnny and their bags, and since there were no cars, her only option was to tuck him into a wagon and pull him to the water taxi. She glanced at the clock again, and her stomach ached. She was terrified taking her son out of his sleeping bed at close to midnight would qualify her as an unfit mother. Oh, God, would this be every second of her life now? As if she didn't worry enough. Now she would be living under a microscope, knowing one false move could get Johnny taken away from her forever. She drew another deep breath. They needed to leave—fast.

She roused Johnny again. "Listen, we're going to take a walk to the water taxi, you and me. You get to ride in a wagon, and I'll pull you."

"But at the parade last year you said I was too big to ride in a wagon."

"Well tonight's an exception."

He sat up in bed. Thankfully the idea of a wagon ride piqued his interest.

"Come on. Take a trip to the bathroom, and let's get going."

"'Kay." He yawned again. "Is Reale going to meet

us at the ferry?"

Her shoulders slumped. "No, Johnny. Reale won't be there." God willing.

****

Like a thief in the night. That's what she was as she stole away from Jess's house at midnight with her son tucked into a tiny wagon and her bags tossed over her shoulder. The path to the ferry was dark, and she had only the flashlight from her phone to guide them. As she walked, the ominous sound of the ocean's waves crashing assaulted her ears. That should have been a sign. That accident…it should have told her only bad was going to come from this trip. Without thinking, she let one of her bags slide up her arm as she touched her fingers to her bruised and battered cheek. She winced from the contact but less from the healing pain and more from the memory—of him.

She turned to look over her shoulder, listening to the sound of her hurried breath. Would he be there at the dock, waiting? Would he stop her from taking Johnny—*their* son—from him again? Faster and faster she walked. She glanced back at Johnny, half-sleeping in the wagon with a bow and arrows tucked in next to him. If anyone stopped them, how would she ever explain this? The faster she moved, the more he was jostled, but she couldn't slow down. In fact, she walked even faster, her heart racing like a kid on Halloween certain ghosts and goblins were chasing her. She looked up at the dark sky, the wetness of the damp air falling heavily over her. She was barely able to breathe. She forced a deep breath and another, not able to fill her lungs completely. "No, no…" she murmured. "Do not hyperventilate." She repeated this mantra over and over as she walked the path. Thank goodness there was only one way back to the dock, or she would have been lost for sure.

Bump, bump, bump. The wagon jostled along, and without stopping, she rearranged the bags on her shoulders. She peeked at Johnny once again. What would happen when he woke up tomorrow morning—she glanced at her watch—correction, later this morning, and realized his bike was back on Fire Island? Okay, he'd have the bow and arrows, but he couldn't use those often, and as much as he loved the archery set, he loved the bike more. It was his most prized possession and the facilitator of his greatest accomplishment yet. Oh, he would be devastated. She bit the corner of her lip, determined. She couldn't bring the bike with them. They needed a clean break from Reale—if that was possible. Maybe Johnny would eventually forget where the bow and arrows came from as well. She'd find him another bike. Maybe it wouldn't have all bells and whistles of the bike Reale had purchased for him, but he didn't need all that. She and Johnny didn't need all that. They were doing fine on their own. Perfectly fine.

Oh, thank goodness. She glanced ahead at the dock and the water taxi waiting for her. She pulled harder and faster, rolling the wagon and Johnny onto the wood planks of the dock. He woke up, startled.

"Mom?" He sat up, looking around as he gripped the sides of the wagon.

"It's okay, Johnny. We're at the boat. I need you to walk on for me."

He yawned and stretched as she pulled the wagon to a stop, and the driver bounded from the water taxi to the dock to meet her.

"Johnny, I need you to move a little faster." Her heart raced and her palms grew sweaty. She was close. Could she make it across the bay and forget this ever happened? Was it possible Reale wasn't the man she knew but truly a spoiled rock star who would lose interest in the scenario by morning and leave them alone? Her stomach clenched. No. No way. Deep in her soul she knew Reale was the same man she had loved all those years ago—and somewhere, deep inside, still did. He was a man who would never run from his responsibilities, a man who would want to know his son.

With one final glance over her shoulder, she abandoned the wagon at the dock and climbed on board after her son.

****

"Wanna talk about it?" Jess leaned across the banquette of the diner, grabbing another ketchup container. They sat in a window banquette looking out over the parking lot as they refilled half-full bottles of ketchup, getting ready for the dinner rush. Jess's long dark hair was pulled back off her face, and her sharp, pointy features softened when she looked at Amanda. She smiled, flashing polished teeth framed by a hideous, neon-pink lip color. Jess abandoned the ketchup to grab a deep plum lip liner from her apron pocket. Even without a mirror, she applied it expertly.

Amanda half-laughed, shaking her head. "That lip color? Really?"

"Helps me get into character. This character I'm playing is a waitress. I figure I've got that down." Jess glanced about the empty diner. "With a real nineteen-eighties Loung Island edge. The lip color is perfect."

"Please don't say 'loung.' " Amanda shook her head. "Not while we're talking."

"You mean, 'tawking?' " Jess wiggled her eyebrows.

"Oh, ha, ha." Amanda gazed up at Jess. "You don't want to tone down that lip color?" She struggled with the gummy cap of a red squirt container.

"Why would I?" Jess shrugged. "I've got tons of regulars who know I'm an actress and love me. I make a boatload of tips. Even Old Man Howard the Grump gave me a second glance."

"Yeah, to see if you've lost your mind. But…" She leaned forward, abandoning her squeeze bottle, ready to argue.

"But what?" Jess cocked her head.

But what exactly? "But what if, you know, a man comes in? Someone who doesn't know you're playing. You could lose a chance."

"Wait, wait, wait." Jess held up her hand and laughed. "A man? Like a guy?"

"Well you haven't been on a date with the type of man you should be."

"Oh, Jesus!" Jess sat back in the booth, snorting. "What are you now, my muth-a?" She grinned as Amanda winced. "Amanda. Is that what this is going to be? A lecture on the type of man I should be dating? 'Cause I gotta tell you something, you had much more credibility in this department before you spent the week screwing bad boy rock star Reale Lynxx!" She giggled and covered her mouth with her hand, flashing her long, multicolored press on nails.

"Shhh!" Amanda sat forward and reached out to

grab her friend's hands. She pulled them back across the table. "You promised you wouldn't say anything."

"Oh, please. It's only you and me." Jess glanced around the empty diner. "And a bunch of empty bottles that need refilling and napkins that need folding. Come on, before Old Man Howard the Grump comes in for his split pea soup with—"

"—fourteen octagonal shaped soup crackers on top. No crumbs, and none—"

"—broken." They giggled and Jess settled her gaze on Amanda. "And don't forget the fourteen-cent tip he leaves every time."

"Forget? That's my retirement plan. Isn't it yours?"

Jess smirked. "Come on. Please? I need the distraction from this monotony. It's just us. Mom's got Johnny. Spill. I want the gory details on your week with rock and roll's hottest grungy bad boy. What's the big deal?"

It wasn't a big deal. Except…she wanted to forget this week. As soon as possible. "That was really nice of your mom to take Johnny for the afternoon."

"Oh, please." Jess waved her hand. "She loves Johnny. Thinks he's the closest thing she's going to get to a grandkid so…"

"He doesn't have to be." She raised her eyebrows, finally freeing the cap from her bottle. She was grateful to have the conversation off her.

"Okay." Jess placed her bottle on the table between them and gripped the sides of the table with her hands. "Once and for all. I am in school in the city, studying to be an actor. I live out here—home—to save money, and I work at the diner to make money to take my dream trip to Greece. I want to see the Parthenon, the ancient theatres, and then I want to go directly to London—to immerse myself in theatre. To gorge myself on everything playing in the West End. And aside from you who is not available, there is no one else I want to go with." She sat forward, twirling her ponytail. "What is it with you and Mom? Why can't you understand that I want to take this trip on my own terms? I don't want to wait for the 'right' man. Okay, no, the guys who come in here don't know I don't have a Long Island accent, and this character I play is just a character, but does it matter? You think any man is gonna look past this hideous, chick-colored uniform we wear with the little white lacy apron? And even if he did, you think my dream man is going to come walking through those thick-paned, fingerprint-smudged double doors? Is yours?"

Amanda dropped her head, shaking it. "No. I don't think our dream men are finding us here." She tugged at the neckline of her uniform. It was tight and claustrophobic.

"Then let me play my character to prep for my showcase and have some fun while I do it. Hey." Jess took her hands. "Are you really going to tell me having a man is the only way?"

She looked into her friend's gorgeous brown eyes. "Of course not. Right now—short of having Johnny—if I were to do it all over again, I wouldn't get caught up with a man either."

Jess nodded. "What's really going on?"

She sighed. She ached so much inside she was desperate to tell someone, and Jess was always that someone. "I, uh…what I have to tell you…it's big news. And Johnny doesn't know. And I have to be the one to tell him. You have to promise not to breathe a word."

"Amanda…" Jess's voice was low and clear. "Did you get yourself knocked up by Reale Lynxx?"

"Not recently."

"Excuse me? What do you mean, 'not recently'?"

Amanda nodded.

"Holy crap!" Jess was out of her seat before Amanda could speak.

"Jess, wait." She jumped up after her friend and placed her hand on Jess's forearm, trying to calm her down. "We were a couple. We were close. We were young and in love."

"And the answer was to keep his son from him?"

She flopped down in a chair at a table in the middle of the empty diner. "I didn't keep him from Reale. I just didn't tell Reale about Johnny until this week."

"But this week was a chance encounter. Would you ever have told him?"

And that was the question she asked herself over and over again. "I don't know."

"Damn, Amanda. This is big." Jess slid into the chair opposite Amanda. She toyed with the edge of the lace doily placemat on the table. "He's got to be pissed."

"He is." She swallowed hard. "He refuses to see I did this for him."

"For him?"

"Yes, for him. I left him and raised Johnny on my own so he could get his shot at his career. And he refuses to understand I did it all for him."

Jess sat back. She picked up the fork before her and placed it down gently.

"What?" Amanda nodded to the fork.

Jess raised one shoulder and dropped it again. "Nothing, it's just…if I were a guy and a girl I was in love with got pregnant and kept it from me so I could have the acting career I wanted…"

"What?" She glared at Jess.

"Well, I maybe wouldn't be too thrilled about it."

"What?" She stood. "But I don't understand. What if that choice gave you Emma Stone's career? Wouldn't it be worth it then?"

"To never see my kid? To not know I had a child walking around out there?" Jess looked away and back again. "I don't want kids, Amanda, but even so, I don't think that tradeoff would be worth it."

"What?" Amanda shook her head. She was so certain. Certain in her gut she had been making the right choices. That's the only way she'd gotten through the tough times—the fevers, the nights with no sleep followed by a day with no rest—how could none of them understand this?

Ding-ding! The bell rang as the door opened, and the first patron of the dinner rush came walking in. Jess glanced at the clock. "It's only four forty, but the diners are coming." She smiled sweetly at Amanda. "I'll take the counter and the front quad."

Amanda nodded and swallowed back her rage. Did they all think she'd been on a picnic for the past five years? Didn't they know what she had sacrificed to raise Johnny on her own? Her eyes ached as she watched Jess seat the lone diner at the counter and offer him a menu. He placed his brown leather briefcase on the counter and waved away the menu but took the coffee she was pouring. He added cream and stirred, never taking a sip.

An ache hit Amanda in the gut. He was no regular patron. He was here for her. She knew it. She glanced at the door. Why would her instinct be to run? She had done nothing wrong. She was certain she had done right by Johnny and by Reale. The heck with what everyone thought. Steeling her nerves, she took a deep breath and marched up to the counter. Jess glanced at Amanda, her eyes as big as saucers for a giant's coffee cup. She nodded and turned to the man.

He glanced up at her. "Amanda Simmons?"

"Y-yes." Her voice squeaked, and she cleared her throat. "Yes. I'm Amanda Simmons."

The man reached into his briefcase and pulled out an envelope. He pushed it toward her. "You've been served." He stood up and dropped a five-dollar bill on the counter before casually strolling to the door. *Ding-ding*! The doorbell rang as he exited.

"Amanda, I'm so sorry." Jess rushed around the counter to stand next to her.

"I—uh…" The envelope was heavy in her grasp.

"Whatever it is, we'll get you the best attorney around."

"I can't afford the best attorney."

"I'll help. I've already got nearly five grand in my trip fund. It's yours."

Amanda snapped out of her daze. "Oh, no, Jess. No way. You've worked too hard and too long. I will get legal counsel. Thank you, though."

"But Amanda. You need someone good. This man probably has a legal team—"

"He does. Told me himself. The best there is."

"That's why we have to get you someone really

137

good."

"No matter what we can afford, even with your parents' help, it will never be enough. It won't matter, Jess." She glanced up at her friend and spotted the look of worry etched on her forehead. "He'll win. He always wins."

"Well, let's see what that says."

Amanda slipped her finger in the tiny gap at the corner of the envelope and whisked her finger along the edge to open the envelope. "Ooo, ow!" She stuck her finger into her mouth, nursing a paper cut. If his paperwork made her bleed, she could only imagine the litigation.

"You okay?"

She nodded. "It's a court order for a paternity test." She folded the paper and placed it back in the envelope. "I'm sure his legal team wants to be positive. Although, anyone can tell just by looking at the two of them..." Her words fell away. "Anyway, it will come back that Reale is Johnny's father. And then Reale will do everything in his power to take Johnny from me."

"Because he's a bastard."

She shook her head. "No. Because he's angry and hurt." A shudder washed over her as she glanced up at her friend. "He'll file for joint custody. To make a point. He knows I would set a schedule for him to see Johnny—he knows that. But he feels betrayed. I kept his son from him for all these years. He doesn't trust I won't do it again. But deep inside he's most angry with himself. This bad boy image he has isn't him. And without a court saying he has legal rights to his son, he's terrified sometime in the future something might happen that'll force me to make a parental decision to keep Johnny from him. This is his insurance policy. Not just against me, against himself and his behavior."

"Oh, Amanda."

"Jess, would you do me a favor?"

"Of course. Anything. You know that."

"Would you cover for me tonight? And call your mom to please bring Johnny back?"

"Are you sure? Maybe you need some time to process what's happening?"

She sighed. "I know what's happening. And I know I'd better spend every second I can with my son."

"Oh, Amanda." Jess reached out and took her friend's hand, squeezing.

She nodded as she fought back her deluge of tears.

Chapter Eleven

"I can't believe we saw that new superhero movie!" Johnny was beaming as they walked through the crowded parking lot outside the old movie theater in Babylon. "And while it was in a real movie theater!"

Over the past three weeks, Amanda had taken Johnny out for these "special treats" almost nightly. One night it was pizza, another bowling on the discounted night, and tonight, superheroes in a real, albeit rundown, movie theater. Johnny was definitely getting used to this constant entertainment, but if it weren't for these extenuating circumstances...

Amanda lifted her hand to her stomach and rubbed away a burning feeling. Still holding Johnny's hand, she fished open the top of her bold patchwork, nearly-worn-through, oversized mom bag and pulled out a half roll of antacids. She popped in another two as Johnny held her hand tighter. He picked up speed as he walked, and soon the two of them were skipping along together toward the car. She glanced back at the theater, laughing to herself. It was an old theater, straight out of the nineteen-sixties, without a single update. In one theater the ceiling was caving, and in another, people had claimed mice scurried up and down the aisles. But the theater charged less per ticket, and it was convenient. It was an "experience" she told herself. As far as seeing first-run movies, that was an extravagance usually reserved for birthdays only. But tonight, well, in a way it was an odd sort of birthday. Three weeks had passed since she'd received the court-ordered paternity test, and she had only one week left to comply. Tonight she would have to tell Johnny that Reale Lynxx was his father.

"What do you say to some ice cream?"

"Ice cream too? Yes!"

Johnny jumped higher as he walked, and despite everything, she grinned. All she wanted was for her son to be happy. To have everything he needed. To have everything. Could she do that without Reale? Sure, she'd provide for Johnny as best she could, but without Reale, Johnny would never have a father. Her grin fell away, but she forced a smile.

"Come on. Let's head back to that little place that makes homemade ice cream."

"I love that place! The one with the tiny, old-fashioned music players on the table?"

"Jukeboxes. Yes, that's the one."

"Cool. I love flipping through the music." He stopped still in his tracks and turned his big, beautiful blue eyes up to his mother. "Do you think they'll have Reale's music?"

"You really like him, don't you? Reale."

"Yeah. Why? Shouldn't I?" His face contorted as he struggled with her question.

"No, no. I mean, of course you should like him. Very much."

"But you don't like him anymore."

"Why would you say that?" She shifted from foot to foot, glancing around the busy parking lot. She had been so careful not to let him in on anything that was happening between her and Reale, but he sensed it anyway. "Johnny, we're in the middle of the parking lot. Let's go to the car and head over to get our ice cream. We can talk there."

She pulled him forward toward their old car, a dark red, nineteen eighty-seven imported wagon. No, it wasn't a fashion car, but it was safe and reliable, even at close to one hundred thousand miles. She kept it clean and took care of it as best she could, and it just kept going. She liked that about the car—it reminded her of her in a way. No matter what came up, she just kept going.

She unlocked the doors and held open the rear door for Johnny. He climbed into his car seat and buckled, still not looking at her. She glanced up at the sky as she manually locked his door. It was a clear night, but the air felt oppressively heavy, as it often did on Long Island. That was another reason she couldn't understand why people loved the water—the humidity was ridiculous, and because of that, the bugs were unbearable. Just walking from the house to the car, Johnny would sometimes get two or three mosquito bites. She was forced to invent a game to see who could run to the car the fastest, and many a stubbed toe and bruised knee were the consequence.

Sighing, she walked around to the driver's side. Unlocking her door, she climbed in and tossed her bag to the passenger's seat—the seat that was always empty. She glanced at Johnny in the rearview. He crossed his arms before him.

"Johnny? Are you mad about something?"

He turned his cherub face stubbornly to look out the window. He looked serious and angelic.

She suppressed a giggle, collecting herself. "Johnny? Please tell me. Why do you think I don't like Reale?"

He uncrossed his arms and leaned forward as far as his restraints would allow. "Because we left without saying goodbye. I fell asleep one night with him there, and then we left. I never saw him again. And you wouldn't let me go back to get my bike!"

Oh, damn it, the bike. He had said he'd understood the countless times she'd explained it since they got home, but did he, really? Did she? Why didn't she ask Jess's mom to retrieve the bike on their next trip out? Why didn't she allow her son that one luxury? She caught a glimpse of herself in the rearview and started. Was it possible she was being the petulant, insensitive child? Was she trying to erase Reale from their lives? Well she sure as hell wasn't successful. Because the thing was, he was about to come charging back in. In a big way.

"Johnny." She turned and looked at her son over the back of her seat. She craned her neck to see better. The last thing she wanted to do was to get into this in the busy parking lot of a strip mall in the middle of Long Island. But looking at her son's glassy eyes, she knew she had no choice but to get into it here. "Oh, the heck with this." She unsnapped her seatbelt and climbed in back. She sat next to her son.

His eyes widened. "You've never sat with me back here before."

"No?" She tilted her head, thinking. But he was right. She'd never before had anyone drive the two of them anywhere so she could sit with him.

"Un-unh." He shook his head.

143

"Well." She settled back against the seat. "Looks like I've been missing out. Pretty swanky back here. What with the plastic superheroes"—she picked up a superhero doll and flew it past a chuckling Johnny—"and these cool stickers on the door."

He giggled, the sourness of the moment before long forgotten. She gazed lovingly at her son. If only adults could forgive and forget like children could. She ran her hand out to his soft blond hair, combing it over to the side. He needed a haircut. Every day since they got back from vacation, his hair was rumpled and out of place.

"Mommm…." He wiggled about and brushed his hair the opposite direction.

She drew her hand back. "You're doing that to your hair on purpose?"

"It's cool. Like Reale." He shrugged and dropped his chin, looking back up at her with his giant blue eyes that weren't sure if he was in trouble or not.

"It is cool." She swallowed hard. "Tell you what, before school starts in the fall, why don't we make an appointment for a trim so we can make it spiky on top just like Reale's hair?"

"Really?" He gazed up at her.

"Really." She nodded, letting out an exhausted sigh. "Johnny, listen. I need to talk to you."

"Yes?"

"You know how some of your friends have a mommy and a daddy?"

"Like Lenny next door?"

"Yes, like Lenny. Well, all babies come from a man and a woman. You can't have a baby without. Sometimes babies are adopted…"

"Like Wei-Ling at the diner."

"Yes." Thank goodness they lived in such a multi-cultural place. "Wei-Ling who comes into the diner, she's adopted from China. Her parents knew she was there and went to get her."

"Am I adopted?"

"What?" She covered her mouth with her hand, fighting a smile. "No, no. Of course not." This was going all wrong. "You came from me. But to make you, I needed someone else. A man."

"A daddy?"

"Well, uh, yes." Her mind swirled with all those things she wanted to say. How a daddy isn't a man who drops a seed, but a man who's there for his child…but it wasn't time for that.

"I have a daddy?" His voice was a mere whisper.

Tears formed in the corners of her eyes as she watched her son process this. No, she didn't want to have this conversation in the back of a car in a parking lot, but they were this far now. "Yes, Johnny. You have a daddy."

"Who is he?"

"He's um, Reale, honey."

"Reale Lynxx is my dad?" He unbuckled his restraints and burst off his seat. He turned to her, the small back of the car barely able to contain him.

"Johnny, shhh, please. You need to listen."

"When will he move in? When can I see him? Will he walk me in to kindergarten with you?"

"Johnny." She shook her head and took her son's hands in hers. "Reale is your daddy, yes. And I'm sure you two will do lots of fun things together, but you need to understand something—Mommy and Reale are

145

not together. We won't live together like some mommies and daddies do."

His face fell. "Oh." He searched her eyes. "But what will you do when I'm with Reale?"

She smiled. He always worried about her. "I'll be working."

"But we did all sorts of fun stuff together. Like the rollercoasters and the outdoor movie. You like him, don't you?"

"Yes, Johnny. I do. I like him very much."

"Well then why can't we do things together? Lenny does things with his parents all the time."

"I know, Johnny, I know. But think how special this is. You get to do things with your dad sometimes and your mom other times." God willing. Because the other option—that she couldn't even consider. The fact that Reale had threatened to gain custody of Johnny and keep him away from her…no. No person on earth could be that cruel to a child.

"I don't want to do anything without you."

She moved in her seat, her gut aching. "But it will make me happy to know you're happy."

"Really?"

"Of course." She reached out and touched his soft porcelain cheek. "That's all I've ever wanted, Johnny. For you to be happy."

His face scrunched up again.

"And Johnny. If it should ever happen that you're away from me longer than you expect to be, you have to know I'm thinking of you every second of every day, okay?" A sob ached in her throat, but she had to stay strong. In the back of her brain sparked the thought she hadn't wanted to face since Reale had threatened to keep Johnny from her. With Reale's means, he could take Johnny and disappear.

"But I can always come home, right? To you?"

She nodded, forcing a smile. "Of course, Johnny. Of course."

He fell against her and held her tight. "I love you, Mommy."

"I love you too, baby."

She held him for seconds more until he pulled away. Then, as nonchalantly as she could, she slid out of the back door and vomited on the blacktop next to her front wheel. She stood tall, inhaling deeply. *Dear God, help.*

Chapter Twelve

Amanda sat across a long conference table in a legal office in a high rise in Manhattan. On the left of her sat her attorney, Keisha, a young woman with thick black hair pulled into a low bun and a light-gray pants suit with sensible gray pumps. She had recently graduated law school but came highly recommended from Jess's mom who knew Keisha's parents from the country club. On the right side of Amanda sat Jess, who was busy scowling at Reale Lynxx sitting opposite them. Flanking him was his legal team consisting of five attorneys, three male and two female, all wearing some version of an expensive, charcoal-gray suit. At the head of the long mahogany table was an empty chair, and on the table before the chair, a gavel and sound block sat waiting for a family court judge.

Amanda could feel Reale's stare, so she turned to gaze out the window. Johnny would love this view from the thirtieth floor. Oh, Johnny. What if…? No. She shook her head. She had to be strong. She adjusted her navy-blue suit jacket and white shirt and toyed with the string of pearls around her neck. She smoothed the lap of the knee-length skirt she wore. Everything was on loan from Jess's mom, who also took Johnny for the day. That woman was a saint. Amanda's hair was slicked back into a low ponytail, and Jess had done a simple, clean makeup on her. Jess was dressed similarly, in a tight white suit with her hair pulled up in a beautiful French twist. Long gone were the press-on nails and phony accent. When Amanda needed her, Jess was there, with every bit of her expensive New York education and breeding shining through.

Amanda's attorney shuffled some papers before her. She was young, but she was strong and confident. She truly believed Amanda would walk away from this the winner because they had the ace in the hole. Reale's bad boy image was hurting him, and all Amanda had to do was say she was worried about the safety of her son, and she could annihilate any chance Reale had at custody. Problem was, she wasn't worried about Johnny when he was with Reale. Even that night he had come back late, that night on the beach after her migraine—even then, deep in her heart, despite all the crazy thoughts running through her brain—even then she knew Reale would take care of Johnny.

Amanda stole one more glance out the window as the door swung open, and a short man with a balding head and a dark beard hurried in. Like Reale's attorneys, he also wore a plain gray suit. She fidgeted, chipping at the clear polish on her nails. Was there some dress code she wasn't aware of? She glanced at Reale dressed in a steel-blue suit and white shirt with a dark-blue tie. His hair was combed to look more professional and less rock star. Okay. There were other colors to wear. She relaxed the tiniest bit. But damn it, he looked gorgeous. She sighed wistfully. The attorneys stood as the man approached the table, cueing Amanda that he was the judge. She and her group stood as well, and so did Reale.

"You may be seated." The judge nodded to them as

a group. He glanced at the papers before him. "Because of the nature of Mr. Lynxx's celebrity, I understand we have all agreed to meet here in lieu of a courtroom. But in doing so, we all agree that my ruling and decision of custody over Jonathan"—he glanced at a paper in his hand—"no middle name, Simmons, is binding in the state of New York and in all of the states of the United States of America. Are all in agreement?"

"Yes, Your Honor."

The lawyers spoke in unison as Amanda mumbled after them. The judge turned to her and raised his eyebrows. She swallowed hard.

"Ms. Simmons, I understand you have had sole custody of your son, Jonathan Simmons, since his birth. Is that correct?"

"Yes, Your Honor."

"How old is your child?"

"Johnny is five."

"And just now you have decided to tell Mr. Lynxx of his paternity?"

"Yes, Your Honor."

"Why did you wait?"

She cleared her throat, and her attorney scribbled something onto her legal pad before sliding it on the table toward Amanda. She glanced at the note. *He wasn't trustworthy.* She shook her head. "It was a chance encounter, sir. I didn't expect to see Mr. Lynxx again. When I did, I believed it was the right thing to do."

"It was the right thing to do now. Why not earlier?"

She turned to her attorney who nodded. She faced the judge and spoke clearly. "We—Mr. Lynxx and I— we were very young when I became pregnant with

Johnny. I made a conscious decision to keep the news from Reale because he was just beginning his rise to superstardom and at a critical moment in his career. He needed to stay focused, and I was afraid if I told him he would have given up music for us."

"Amanda," her attorney whispered, shaking her head. Murmurs rippled around the table, and Reale sat back, crossing his arms. The judge banged his gavel to quiet the room.

Amanda glanced at the attorneys and back to the judge. "If Mr. Lynxx hadn't had the option to pursue his music—all of us would have lost. His music is a gift." She made eye contact with one of his attorneys who looked away. Why would no one understand her? "He, Reale, his music is breakthrough. Before him, no one else did this new form of punk. There's no doubt he'll go down in history as a pioneer in his field—like Prince."

Another one of Reale's attorneys, a tall man in a well-fitted gray suit and heavy gold watch, sat forward. "If I may, Your Honor?"

The judge nodded, sitting back in his oversized chair.

"Since Ms. Simmons brought it up, wouldn't you agree, Ms. Simmons, Mr. Lynxx's recent increase in income would benefit you greatly? Wasn't that the reason to tell him now? To demand reparation?"

"What?" She sat back, flummoxed.

"Ms. Simmons." The judge nodded to her.

"I'm not demanding anything from Reale. I'm not the one who asked for this custody suit."

The judge shifted in his seat. "Let's get back on track. At the time you first found out you were pregnant, could you argue, however, that a better partner would have known you were pregnant? Was he simply caught up in his self-obsessed rock and roll persona?"

"Truthfully, Your Honor, I don't know how he could have known. I hid the vomiting the best I could. That morning when he saw me getting sick, I told him I had a migraine. He'd been with me through lots of migraines. He knew I vomited when I had them. It would be impossible for him to know morning sickness from a migraine."

"I see." The judge sat forward, steepling his fingers.

Jess looked up at Amanda, clearing her throat. She spoke in a hurried whisper. "Don't make him sound like such a good guy."

Amanda nodded. No, she didn't want to lose Johnny, but she wasn't going to lie about Reale. Aside from this horror story, Reale had been nothing but kind and loving to her. To them.

The attorney with the gold watch leaned forward. "If I may, Your Honor, Ms. Simmons is establishing a pattern of lying. She lied about the pregnancy and lied to my client for all these years. This goes to show her character and the poor choices she makes."

Reale shifted in his seat as the attorney went on. "Because Ms. Simmons is not trustworthy and has kept Reale from his son for five years, we are moving for Mr. Lynxx to gain full and complete custody of Jonathan Simmons."

"What?" Amanda stood up. "Full custody? What are you talking about?"

"Ms. Simmons, please sit." The judge banged his

gavel.

Amanda's attorney pulled her down, forcing her into her seat.

The attorney continued. "Of course, Jonathan Simmons will have visitation rights with his mother on an agreed upon schedule."

Amanda stared at Reale. "Reale, what are you doing? I know you're mad, but don't do this to Johnny. You can't. You were with him for one week. *One week*. You have no idea what to do for his nightmares or on sick days or what he likes to eat—"

"You're right, Amanda, I have no idea. And whose fault is that?"

The judge sat forward and banged his gavel again. "Mr. Lynxx, Ms. Simmons, kindly respond only when given permission."

She turned to the judge, sweat pouring off her body and dripping down her spine. "Please, Your Honor."

The judge nodded.

"You can't let this happen. Please. I thought I was doing right by everyone—Reale and especially Johnny. I never meant to lie."

"Your Honor, when was Ms. Simmons going to tell my client?" Reale's attorney pushed her.

"I would have when the time was right! When Johnny was ready." She looked back and forth from person to person.

"And then, after telling Mr. Lynxx and giving him no time to process the information, you took your son and stole away in the middle of the night!"

The judge sat forward, resting his forearms on the table.

She settled her gaze on the judge again. "He is my

son. I was doing what I thought was best for him. It was my decision to make. Please, Your Honor."

The judge sighed. "I am not in the habit of siding with a father over a mother or of keeping a child from his mother. Especially when the mother is the only parent he knows. But the reason you're the only parent he knows is your doing, Ms. Simmons."

"Yes, yes. I'm sorry, Your Honor. Please."

Gold Watch sat forward again. "Your Honor, what about her financial situation?"

The judge sighed again, spinning back and forth in his chair, tapping a thin black pen against his chin. "There is the matter of your financial situation. Mr. Lynxx will now be required to pay child support, but aside from that, will you be able to care for your son and his needs as well as yourself as he grows older?"

"Yes. I can. I do."

"Your Honor, she's a waitress in a diner." Gold Watch pushed some papers back and forth and glanced at Amanda. "Don't you work for tips?"

"Yes. Primarily." Good God, if looks could kill, that jerk would have been dead twenty times over. She took a deep breath, calming herself.

"And what happens if the tips run dry? Could you secure a mortgage on your income? Cover out of pocket health care? Be certain to always have the means to take care of Jonathan?"

"That's true of all people, Your Honor." Amanda's attorney sat forward. "Any one of us could be out a job tomorrow. And Jonathan will now be receiving child support from Mr. Lynxx, so I do not understand how any of this is relevant. And even if it were relevant, which it's not, there are many excellent parents who do not have the financial means to support a lavish lifestyle—"

"But those aren't the children of Reale Lynxx."

Amanda's attorney glared at Gold Watch. "No, they're not, but child support will more than handle—"

"Which means without Mr. Lynxx, Ms. Simmons is an unfit parent."

Unfit parent. Those words had haunted her days and nights for the past month. She was going to be ruled an unfit parent.

Amanda's attorney pushed forward, raising her voice. "A lower income hardly qualifies someone as an unfit parent. And in addition, I think you will find, Your Honor, the reason my client kept the information of his paternity from Mr. Lynxx is because of Mr. Lynxx's reputation. Mr. Lynxx endangered the lives of dozens of children."

"My client was cleared of all wrongdoing." Gold Watch put up his hand. "That's inadmissible. But to be clear, that was an accident made to seem much worse by the media. The lives of children were never, at any time, threatened. They were never in any real danger. It was a small fender bender. Nothing more."

The judge turned to Amanda. "Ms. Simmons? Do you have anything to add?"

"I—uh…" She glanced at Reale, and he cast his eyes downward. Of course those children had been in danger. Reale had driven drunk and toppled the train, and she knew it. And so did he. She had, in her hands, the power to get her son back and obliterate Reale all in one breath. She could force Reale to admit to what really happened during that accident, and once it was out there, it would ultimately destroy him. She had the power.

Reale turned his gaze toward her. Yes, she had the power to destroy him…but not the ability.

She shook her head lamely.

"Your Honor," Gold Watch went on, "my client can afford a lifestyle Jonathan will benefit from. The best education, tutors, world travel…"

"But I'm his mother." She sat forward.

"Amanda." Her attorney leaned over, whispering, "You've got to destroy this man. It's our only chance." She cleared her throat and spoke loudly. "Your Honor, if I may, I'd like to address my client on the record."

"Proceed." He lifted his eyebrows, dropping his chin.

"Tell me, Ms. Simmons, that day Mr. Lynxx kept your son out past your agreed upon time. Weren't you worried?"

"Yes."

Her attorney nodded. "Were you concerned for Johnny's safety?"

Amanda glanced at Reale, and he made steady eye contact. She could see him in there, in those eyes, somewhere behind the pain and anger. Those bright blue eyes held the answer. She was damned if she did and damned if she didn't.

"I wasn't worried about Johnny with Reale."

More murmurs filled the room, and her attorney leaned over to speak in Amanda's ear. "You're going to lose Johnny. You need to shoot the bullet right between Reale's eyes."

She nodded. "I know." She glanced back at Reale. "I didn't tell Reale about his son all those years ago because I thought it was the right thing to do. But I'm not a liar. And I'm not going to start lying now. I have always trusted Reale with my life. And if I tell you I was worried about my son with Reale, well then, you'll question my judgment as to why I let him go in the first place. But if I don't tell you that, Reale looks like a good guy, and I potentially lose my son except for court-ordered visitation rights. Like I'm a *criminal*. Well, I'm not a criminal." She faced Gold Watch. "Or a liar. What I am is a woman who made a decision I thought was best to protect the man I loved. But the truth is, he is a good guy. And he would never hurt our son. He's just angry. But there's no winning here. So I'm taking this out of the hands of strangers."

She looked into Reale's eyes, holding him rapt. "Reale. I have loved you for as long as I've known you. I am sorry I kept your son from you, but I swear, I swear I thought I was doing the right thing. For both of you. You're going to win today. You have all the cards. But I'm begging you. Please. Let's make this as easy on Johnny as we can. Don't turn his world upside down."

She swallowed hard and raised her eyebrows. "As angry as you were growing up, don't do that to Johnny over me. Don't make him feel his mother is suddenly gone except for a short meeting every other weekend. Please." As she stared at him, she saw all those things he could give Johnny that she couldn't: an expensive education like those rich kids who came into the diner on Fridays after school, world travels, the best health care.

Gold Watch cleared his throat. "There's nothing more, Your Honor. It's clear this woman is abdicating her parental rights."

The judge turned to her. "Have you, Ms. Simmons?

Have you decided to give custody to Mr. Lynxx without contesting?"

She faced the judge. "Are you asking me if I'm giving up Johnny without a fight? Hell no. I would die for that boy or anything else I had to do. He is my life. But I refuse to have his childhood marred by warring parents. It's clear Mr. Lynxx is winning. But I will not lie and say Reale is unfit to be a parent. And I will not say I was wrong in what I did. Because in my heart, I truly believe I was right. All I want is the best for Johnny, and if Mr. Lynxx thinks he can supply it—then do it. But Your Honor, you need to understand Mr. Lynxx can take Johnny and disappear, and someone with the limited means I have will not be able to find him. And by the time the courts intervene and someone locates them, months will have gone by. Whatever the court decides, this is really between Mr. Lynxx and me." She turned to Reale. "It's in your hands. Make the right decision, Reale. Be the man I know you are—the man you want to be. Don't be that asshole rock star they force you to be."

She fought back the tears in her eyes and breathed deeply to calm her racing heart.

"We'll take a recess for lunch, and you'll have my decision shortly." The judge stood and left the conference room, and quietness fell over the remaining group of people.

Amanda stood, and Reale's gaze followed her.

"Where are you going?" Her attorney stood with her.

"To call and check on my son." She looked around the room and focused on Reale. "That's what you do when you're a parent." She shook her head, grabbing her cell phone from her brown leather bag, and left.

****

She was standing next to the water fountain by the elevators. Her back was to him, and she was leaning against the wall. She had the phone tucked between her shoulder and her chin, and her hands were fumbling with something. He walked as close as he dared, and she shifted then, revealing a small bag of potato chips she was struggling to open. Damn. Was that her lunch? He would have taken her to a restaurant or ordered something in. She used to love those pastrami sandwiches from the deli on Eighth. It would be no problem to have a couple of sandwiches delivered, and they could eat on the terrace on the opposite side of the building...

He dropped his head, shaking it. What was he thinking? This was a *date*? What the hell was wrong with him? They were here as enemies. This was an antagonistic meeting. She wasn't going to eat with him. She wouldn't do anything with him, ever again. It was better that way. *Fool me once, shame on you. Fool me twice, shame on me.* Leaving him the way she did all those years ago was horrible. Keeping John from him was unforgiveable. Yet...she hadn't ratted him out when she could have. And frankly, should have. She should have told the judge he had endangered the lives of all those children on the train. That he drove drunk. That he toppled the train. That lives were in danger. And his legal team had covered it and he ran like a coward—like a damned dog with his tail between his legs. No one would ever consider giving him custody if they knew the truth. It would be entirely up to her as to whether or not he saw his son. And the press...Christ.

They'd have a field day with that story, destroying any tiny bit of a good reputation he had left. His fans would grow sick of it too. Allegedly biting a head off a tiny mammal was one thing; nearly killing a trainload of children was something else entirely. But she hadn't outted him. She wouldn't do that to him. He owed her for that. And way more than a sandwich.

She laughed into the phone, her voice higher and lighter. "Yes, I have had Mrs. VanDyke's grilled cheese. Yes, they are the best. How many did you eat?"

He didn't want to eavesdrop, but he couldn't help it with the echo in the empty hallway.

"Three? Go easy there, friend. No, Johnny, you don't have to save any for Mommy. It's okay. Thank you. I'm having a big fancy lunch in the city. No, none of your favorite foods, that wouldn't be any fun without you. But delicious grown-up foods. Fancy salad. I've got a big bowl in front of me right now." She bit into a potato chip. "Crunching on a carrot. You love carrots, right? You're still eating too? Well it's like we're having lunch together. Yes, I promise I'll come to school to eat lunch with you whenever I can."

She turned and started when she saw Reale. Her face came alive with shock and happiness, before clouding over with disappointment. Damn. That's the last thing he ever wanted her to feel—disappointed. And yet that's what he was feeling as well.

She focused on her phone call. "Um, Johnny, could you please put Mrs. VanDyke on? Thank you. And Johnny, I love you. I'll be home soon." She turned away again. Now it was impossible not to hear the conversation. "Thank you so much, Lynda. Are you sure? With the commuter train, I should be home early evening." She moved just enough that her gaze flashed to Reale's again. "I don't know, Lynda. I don't know. Thank you. Please kiss Johnny for me. Yes, thanks, Lynda." She took the phone from her ear, then clutched it again, juggling it and putting it back to her ear. "Lynda? Yes, thanks. Sorry. He—Johnny—he needs his multivitamin. Would you mind? They're in the corner cupboard opposite the stove. Yes. Thank you. See you soon. Bye."

She turned off her phone but didn't turn to face him. As they stood there with awkward silence blanketing them, all he could wonder was what her house was like. The vitamins in the corner cupboard opposite the stove. What did her kitchen look like? Incredibly neat, no doubt. She was always a stickler for keeping things clean. And she sounded organized, that didn't surprise him at all. One of the million reasons she would have made a great nurse. But that was the Mandy he used to know. Before him stood a woman gazing into her half-eaten bag of potato chips like it held all the secrets of the universe—a woman who'd kept his son from him. And although it ached in his very soul, she was a woman he did not know.

He turned away, leaving her to her lunch of broken potato chips from the vending machine.

"Reale?" One of his attorneys poked his head out of the conference room. "You hungry? We ordered in, Thai, from that place just written up in the *Times*."

Reale stared at his million-dollar attorney blankly and then gazed over his shoulder at Amanda. She stood there, unmoving, watching as everything unfurled around her. This had to be hell for a control freak like her, and although he was livid with her, he didn't want her to suffer. He wasn't cruel. No, maybe she was no longer the woman he knew, or thought he knew. He couldn't do anything about that, but he sure as hell wasn't going to be a man he didn't know. Not knowing who she really was, was a mistake. Not knowing himself was a tragic flaw.

"No, thanks. I'm grabbing lunch from the vending machine."

"The vending machine?" His attorney glanced over at Amanda and back to Reale. "What are you, poor?" He laughed, raising his briefcase in the air in a victorious move. "You rock stars. Lunch cost a grand, and you'd rather eat stale food from a vending machine? Whatever. Rock and Roll!" he yelped before playing his briefcase like an electric guitar on his way back into the meeting room.

Embarrassment washed over Reale as he stared after his attorney in disbelief. Without looking, he could feel Amanda's disapproving gaze on him. And who could blame her? He hired an asshole who was going to destroy her life, and then that same asshole bragged about the cost of lunch in front of her. When he knew Mandy had nothing. Why would someone be that insensitive?

The sound of rustling plastic caught his attention, and he turned to her. She had emptied her bag of chips and was crinkling the bag. Slowly and purposefully she tossed the bag into the nearby garbage, and licking her fingers methodically, one at a time—not sexually, more calculating—she strode past him and yanked open the door to the conference room, walking in.

And he was all alone. Again.

Chapter Thirteen

"Are we moving?" Johnny turned his giant eyes toward Amanda as he watched her rush about his room, putting stuffed animals and superheroes into an overnight bag.

"No, Johnny." She forced back the bitter bile taste in her mouth. "You're going to visit with Reale for a bit, you know that." She spied his archery set in its safe spot on the top of his closet. Should she send it? Hell yeah. Maybe with some luck he would accidently shoot Reale in the eye. She balanced on her tiptoes, pulling it down from the shelf. She stepped aside so it would drop to the ground and wouldn't fall on top of her.

"But it's so much stuff."

She nodded. "I'm making sure you have everything you need." This was the only way to have some grasp on a situation that was otherwise completely out of her control. She shuddered. No way in hell was she going to forget a superhero or a stuffed toy that could bring him peace or happiness in the uncertain world he was about to stumble into head first. How did this happen?

Damn. She glanced about Johnny's tiny bedroom as she stuffed the last of his favorite toys, including Peanut, into one small, dark-blue overnight duffle with a Yankees emblem on it. The bow and arrows didn't fit, so she stuffed them into his superhero backpack. Her gaze found Johnny. Sure, he thought he was taking a lot, and that's because it was everything he owned. How was it possible she had never before considered how little he had? One small duffle with toys and one adult-sized backpack stuffed full of superhero T-shirts, loose tie-front shorts that wouldn't cut in at his waist, super-soft pajamas, socks, and seven pairs of faded superhero underwear. Plus a spin toothbrush that played a superhero theme song he had begged for while they were shopping at Target one day, and a small blue hairbrush. Now that he had his cool new "Reale haircut," he needed the brush to take care of it. And the last of it was the archery set sticking out the top. But that was it. Everything this kid owned was in two bags. Damn.

She glanced about the empty bedroom, surveying the worn bedspread tossed across his toddler bed and the tiny dresser pushed tight to the wall. Had she been doing right by him? She had always assumed because he had her—a mother who loved him and cared for him so very much, a mother who would love him no matter who he grew up to be—he had everything he needed. But did he, really? Or was he better off in Reale's multimillion-dollar houses with a wait staff and indoor pools? She shuddered at the thought of Johnny in a pool without her. She resumed her pacing as she opened and closed the empty drawers time and again. She'd have to triple remind Reale to keep Johnny's swimmies on him tightly. She stopped her frenetic moving and glanced at her son. What was there left to say? To do? Reale had won custody, and her legal rights only gave her the opportunity to see Johnny every other weekend. She had done her best to make it sound like he was going on vacation with Reale, but that was just to ease the blow.

As he spent more and more time with his father and was more and more secure with him, then she would explain everything to Johnny. And then, maybe, she would be able to face the truth as well.

She sat down on Johnny's superhero toddler bed, his bag falling open on her lap. She was suddenly immobile, unable to do one more thing or to worry about one more thought.

"Think of it as a much-needed vacation," Jess had said to her back at the conference room/courtroom when the judge ruled on Reale's behalf. "Think of it as some time to get some things done for yourself."

But what could she do without Johnny? And then they started—the tears she'd promised she would not shed until Johnny was tucked safely in Reale's car.

"Mommy? Why are you crying?" He climbed onto her lap. He pushed the bag onto the old wood floor as he wiggled to get closer.

"I'm not." She kept her voice light, trying to laugh it all off.

"You have tears coming from your eyes." He reached up and wiped one away, softly and carefully, the way his father used to do all those years ago.

"Oh, Johnny." She clutched her son to her tightly, allowing the forbidden tears to drench them both.

"Why are you crying, Mommy?" His voice was pained and filled with fear. He clutched her tighter as his tears fell. The two of them held onto each other, sobbing, as she fought for her breath.

"No." She sat taller and held him at arm's length. "Johnny, I am crying because I will miss you. But I'm thrilled you are going to see Reale and you're going on this little vacation with him."

Little vacation. It was the statement she made as much for her as for Johnny.

"But I'll be back soon." He was trying to stop her tears with logic.

She reached out and wiped away his tears with the sleeve of her blue and white baseball shirt. "Yes, you will. And I will see you soon. Okay?" She gazed at her son lovingly. "All I want is for you to have a wonderful time. Write me a letter and tell me all about the fun you're having."

"I will." He scrunched up his face, dropping his voice to a mere whisper. "You know I don't write very well."

She laughed. "Johnny. You write beautifully. Just draw a picture if that makes you happ—"

Bam. Bam. There was the knock she had been dreading since the day she found out she was pregnant with Johnny. The knock that meant someone was coming to take him away from her. *Bam. Bam.* It was Reale. She felt it in her bones. She took a deep breath and stood. Lifting the corner hem of her T-shirt, she wiped beneath her eyes.

"Come on." She placed her hand out, and Johnny slipped his in. A natural move they both made and had been making forever. But now that would change. Now, whenever she would put out her hand for him—out of habit—she would find nothing but cold emptiness. And what's worse, whenever Johnny lifted his hand for guidance or security, hers would no longer be there for comfort. So *his* better damned well be. *Damn you, Reale Lynxx. Damn you.*

Bam. Bam. Her head grew hot and her eyes ached. No. It was time to be strong. Being a mess when

Johnny was leaving would confuse him and make it worse for him.

"Let's go answer the door."

He nodded, his eyes wide. He was trying to be strong for her, but underneath it all, she could see his confusion.

She got down on her knees and smoothed out his damp T-shirt. "Should we change that shirt? It's a little damp."

He shook his head. "No. It's my favorite."

She glanced at the red superhero T-shirt, making a mental note to remind Reale to have his housekeeper use the gentle, fragrance-free detergent she wrote on her list to wash Johnny's clothes so his skin wouldn't get chafed—or worse. Most detergents gave him a terrible case of the hives.

"Okay then." She looked down at the ground and back up to him. "I'm happy, you know. That you're getting to know Reale. He's your dad, and you should have some guy time." She nudged his shoulder with hers, smiling. "I will be fine. Busy. Very busy. And before we both know it, you'll be back."

"For good?"

She bit the corner of her lip and drew in a deep breath. "I'm always with you, Johnny. Even when you're with Reale, and if you guys take some fabulous trip somewhere." She placed her hand on his heart. Sure, whenever she'd seen it done in movies it looked cheesy, but right now it felt right. "I'm always here. Home is always here. And I promise, I will see you soon."

He nodded, falling against his mother. She grasped him and held him as hard and as long as she dared.

Damn you, Reale Lynxx.

****

Peeking into the bedroom window, Reale swallowed back the lump in his throat. He didn't mean to spy on them. It's just when she didn't answer the door…well, maybe she'd taken off again. Like she had that night on Fire Island. But this touching moment between them—he shook his head. What was he doing? Pulling a child from the only parent that child had ever known? What was wrong with him? How much better this could have been, if only he had known she was pregnant, all those years ago.

He slunk around to the front of the house as the door unlocked.

"Reale?" John's eyes lit up when he looked up at Reale, and it warmed Reale to his core. It had been a long time since someone had looked at him like that, with admiration and…love.

"Hey, John!" He did his best to sound happy and lighthearted, despite the fact that he was destroying his son's mother in the process. He held up his hand for a high-five, and John slapped it.

John stepped back into the house, awkwardly.

"John? Everything cool?" He tried desperately to read the boy's face. Was it possible he had been the caretaker of this child for about thirty seconds and already he was blowing it? It was possible. He was an expert at screwing up.

He stepped through the double glass door with silver, faux iron scrollwork and into the small but warm kitchen. It was as he had imagined—clean and organized but dated. The kitchen was tiny, only a square with white appliances and dark blue Formica countertops, and no room for an island. The cabinets were raised, paneled, light wood, and two dishtowels with what looked like handprints on them hung from the stove handle. Opposite the stove was a tiny, round, dark-brown-stained table with two ladderback, matching, brown chairs pushed tightly to it. A square table would have given them much more room, but that was Amanda. She probably thought this looked homier for John. Or…she got it for a deal.

From the kitchen he gazed past the half-wall, taking in the living room. This room carried the homey feel, with a tan microfiber couch and matching chair, a multicolored, mosaic coffee table, and a couple of woven high baskets that—best he could tell from this distance—held games and puzzles. Monopoly sat on top. Wasn't that a game John loved to play? Seemed to him that was what John had said he wanted to play that first night on Fire Island. The house looked very much like what Amanda had tried to do with the sitting area of the kitchen on Fire Island.

She leaned against a counter, watching Reale take everything in. "I wanted to paint the cabinets white"— she nodded to the far wall—"but since we rent I wasn't able to."

"No, it, uh, looks great like it is."

She smiled a small smile, and Reale cleared his throat. She made no effort to show off the rest of the house. Why would she? This wasn't a social visit.

"Do you have the upstairs as well?" Why the hell did he ask? He knew the answer.

She scrunched her face. "No." She waved it off. "This is plenty of room for the two of us." Her face dropped. Well, what was the two of them. Now it would be mostly only her. Christ.

He caught a glimpse of John standing perfectly still, looking down at the ground. God knew Reale was not an expert on children, but it seemed to him a five-year-old boy never stood still this long.

"John?" He shook his head, trying to understand why John was suddenly closed off and shy.

Amanda stepped toward John, holding out her arm, and he attached himself to her leg. She inhaled sharply as her gaze found Reale's. She patted John's back and somehow unattached him from her body while squatting down next to him, smoothing his hair. That was a good move, squatting down next to him—John must have felt like the grown-up was his equal. *Yes, good move, Amanda.* Reale would have to remember that if he ever needed it.

"Johnny?" She held her son at arm's length and smiled at him. "Are you wondering about what we discussed about Reale's name? Would you like me to ask him?"

John nodded.

She turned her gaze to Reale but stayed tight next to her son. Their son. "Reale, Johnny understands you are his father. He's wondering if he should call you Dad."

"What?" He took a step back, running his hand through his spiky hair, and John turned confused eyes to his mother. Reale leaned in toward her. "He wants to call me Dad?"

She cleared her throat. "He wants to know what you would like him to call you." She widened her eyes until they appeared to take over half her face. She tossed her head toward John. "He's confused."

John reached out and took his mother's hand, squeezing until his knuckles turned white.

"Reale?" She cocked her head, waiting for his answer.

"I—uh…" A tiny drop of sweat dripped down between Reale's shoulder blades. How the hell was he blowing this already? "Would he like to?"

Dad? He'd only been in his son's life for about a month—and the boy wanted to call him Dad? Wasn't that awkward? How had he never considered this? All he thought of since the moment Amanda had told him John was his son was how she had slighted *him*. Had he considered what this was like for John? All of a sudden being told he had a father? He gazed at John's blond hair that looked exactly like his. Hell yeah, Reale knew precisely what that was like. It was like suddenly being told he had a son.

But *Dad*? What would his managers say? Suddenly he had a kid. Given his rep, people would just assume he was a dad who had abandoned his son at birth. Unless…unless they told the truth and explained that she kept John away from him. Damn. The press would question why, and they'd deduce it was in the child's best interest. And he'd probably lose custody again. She would never allow him to see his son after the way he had treated her…after what he had done. The press would crucify him, and he'd have to go back to her and beg for her help. No one would care that six years ago when she found out she was pregnant, Reale hadn't yet become the asshole he was today. No. None of this would be good for either of them—or any of them.

She exhaled audibly. She stood tall, still holding her son's hand, swinging it between them. She turned to

John. "Tell you what, Johnny. I think you should call him Bud."

John turned bright eyes up to his mother. "Bud?"

She gave an exaggerated nod. "Yup. And Reale, I think you should call Johnny Buddy. This way you both have a name for each other that is only yours." She knelt down by her son. "No one else in the whole world calls you Buddy, and no one calls Reale Bud. What do you say?"

His face flashed with happiness as he glanced up at Reale. "Reale? I mean, Bud? Do you like it?"

"Yup, Buddy. I think it's great. Except…"

"Except what?" John's face clouded over again as she stood, crossing her arms before her chest.

"Except, what if I decide to call him Bananahead?" Reale glanced at her who dropped her arms, smirking. "Would that be okay?"

"Hmmm…." She placed a finger to her lips, tapping playfully as she pretended to ponder the question. "Bananahead… Well, I guess that's okay, but only if he can call you Picklejuice."

"Picklejuice?" John slapped his knee like a little old man.

Reale chuckled.

"If I call him Picklejuice, what can he call me, Mommy?"

She smiled. "I think you'll have to take this game to the car and come up with names on your ride."

John nodded happily, and fifty pounds fell off Reale's shoulders. Well at least they'd have something to get them as far as the Long Island Expressway without too much awkwardness. He and Amanda had come to an agreement that John would come out to

Reale's Southampton house. That would be the closest house in proximity to the only home John ever knew, and therefore, it would be easiest on him.

She turned to John. "Johnny? Would you give me a moment to talk to Reale?"

"You mean Prunehead?" John giggled as he walked into his bedroom.

She smiled, but her face hardened when John closed his door, and she turned back to Reale. She held her hand out to the small table in the back of the kitchen. Reale strode over and sat. He stretched his legs long in front of him and smoothed his hands down his jeans.

"Something to drink?" She walked to the fridge, yanking open the door. The bottles of condiments shook as she bent forward, peering in. "I have water, juice, milk…"

She stood up and sighed, her shoulders slumping. The look that crossed her face was one of concern—for him. Was it possible she still cared? After everything?

Without a word she pulled a half-full bottle of wine from a shelf, and holding it in her grasp, walked to the far cabinet. Balancing on her tiptoes, she reached up and flicked open the lattice trimmed door of the cabinet over the stove. Still stretching, she retrieved two long-stemmed wineglasses and held them expertly upside down in her fingers so they wouldn't clang together. He watched, mesmerized. He wanted to jump up and help her, but his body was immobile.

She ambled to the table and placed a glass before him on the blue woven placemat and at the setting across from him. Methodically, she pulled the cork from the bottle and poured a light-smelling chardonnay into his glass, filling it a third of the way. She did the same with hers before falling into her chair.

"Chardonnay?" He raised the glass, questioning her.

She shrugged. "Beggars can't be choosers. Jess was over last night and brought this." She leaned forward, resting her chin in her hands. She looked tired but beautiful. "Any Bordeaux or Merlot, or heck, anything red is long gone." She raised her eyebrows, taking a deep drink from her glass. She placed the glass down and spun it in her lean fingers.

He shuffled in his seat. It was his turn, but what the hell could he say? He cleared his throat. "Mandy…"

Her eyes shot up to his and narrowed. Hardness and ice replaced the languid but friendly complacency he detected moments ago. "Do not call me that." She shook her head deliberately. "You lost the right to call me that when you took my son from me."

He nodded. She wasn't being nice. This was all her strength, keeping it together for their son. "Our son."

Her eyes narrowed again, and she picked up her wine, taking another long drink. She placed it down, stood, and then walked to the cabinet opposite the stove. She retrieved a small white bottle from the high shelf and tossed it to him. He caught it in one hand.

"Johnny's vitamins. Take these because it's not easy to find the superhero ones, and that's all he'll take. He gets one a day."

He nodded.

She pulled a yellow legal notepad from the drawer next to her and flipped through a couple of pages. She stood stiffly.

"This will tell you what he does in a day. You're

his father. You do what you think is best, but I'm going to advise if all you feed him is junk, he'll feel awful and his growth will be negatively impacted."

"I understand. I already told the cook to create a healthy menu for John."

She nodded, her eyes softening. "This list has the name of his pediatrician, his dentist, and all his favorite shows, books, and foods. I've mentioned it before, but I can't stress it enough. He has incredibly sensitive skin. You need to use the laundry detergent I have listed here, or he'll get welts all over his body. And he's the kid who gets wired from the allergy medicine, not sleepy. I'm telling you, after going all night without sleep, you'll only make that mistake once."

He suppressed a smile. "I think I've stayed awake all night once or twice before."

"But never with a sick child. It's not the same, Reale." She held the list tightly and inhaled sharply. "Reale, I am asking, please, if he gets sick, tell me. He'll need me if he—" The tears fell fast, drenching her beautiful face, and she shoved a hand to her mouth, stifling a sob.

He sat motionless, desperate to hold her and help the pain to pass. Instead he looked down at the placemat before him, once again having no freaking clue as to what to do.

She took another few deep breaths and grabbed a napkin from a nearby holder. She dabbed beneath her eyes, wiped away her tears, and then turned from him and walked to the sink. She leaned over and splashed water on her face, before grabbing the same napkin and dabbing at her face again.

"I don't want Johnny to see me cry." She spoke

while facing the sink.

"I understand." He nodded, daring a glimpse at her.

She turned abruptly. "Do you, Reale? Do you really understand what you're doing?"

"He's my son too, Amanda."

"Yes, he is." She clenched the sink behind her. "But all you've done since you've found out is to blame me. I understand you don't agree with my reasons. I know you think I made a mistake. And yes, keeping him from you was my doing. But damn it, Reale, you're not the victim. That boy is. So grow up and take responsibility for what you're doing here and now. As a grown-up with a child. Because what I did six years ago, I did out of love for you and our unborn baby. Whether you believe it or not. But what you're doing, you're doing out of spite and anger. It's time you face who you really are. You think I'm not the woman you thought I was? Well you're sure as hell not the man I thought you were. This"—she pointed toward the hallway and then back and forth between the two of them—"this is your doing. You are responsible for this misery befalling your son and his mother. And don't you dare try to put this blame on me."

She dropped her hands abruptly and marched past him to go retrieve their son.

Chapter Fourteen

"Milton, Spenser, Dante, Hawthorne?" Jess shook her head as she took a sip of her wine. She was sitting at Amanda's small kitchen table, flipping through Amanda's school books.

"I need the English credits to finish my undergrad." Amanda pulled healthy pizza rolls from the oven and shoveled them off a cookie sheet and onto a large white platter.

"You're really doing it, huh?"

"Getting my degree?" She shrugged, fighting with one pizza roll stuck to the aluminum foil. "I've got to do something with my time. The nights are…endless. And now that Reale pays child support…" She swallowed hard and glanced out her small kitchen window. "I have the money for community college. Thank heavens they offer summer courses. It's something." She delivered the tray to the table.

"It's awesome." Jess grabbed a roll and juggled it.

"Careful, they're hot." Amanda nodded to the platter.

Jess made steady eye contact. "Yeah. I got that."

"Sorry." She sat and grabbed the bottle of wine from the middle of the table. She poured herself another glass of merlot. "Habit."

Jess nodded. "Aren't you going to eat?"

She shook her head. "Not hungry."

"But you look so thin. When's the last time you've eaten?"

"I ate at the diner during my shift yesterday."

"Yesterday?" Jess furrowed her brow. "Amanda. You have to take care of yourself. He'll be home in a couple of days."

"Yup." She leaned forward and rested her head on her arm. "For two nights and two days." She sat up taller again, swallowing away the lump in her throat.

"Any word today?"

"No."

"Did you get the call to sing them to sleep last night?"

Amanda sat back. "I don't sing them to sleep. I sing Johnny to sleep. I'm sure Reale's not even around."

"Did you?"

"Yes."

Jess chuckled. "Don't you think it's odd that one of the most famous rock stars in the world has to have someone else sing his son to sleep?"

"I'm not someone else. I'm Johnny's mother. He misses me. And the calls won't keep coming. Johnny will get settled, and Reale's probably getting the hang of it by now. He's a smart guy."

"A smart guy who washed Johnny's clothes in the wrong soap when you expressly told him not to. Amanda, you literally spelled out what he should use."

She shrugged. "A rookie mistake. Can happen to anyone. After being up all night trying to keep Johnny from scratching the welts on his body, Reale learned."

"Yeah. But with all the money in the world, he needed you to tell him to give the kid allergy medicine and cortisone cream for the welts."

"I'm Johnny's mother. I have the answers. Reale is learning. He's doing right by Johnny. I have to keep telling myself that." She took a deep breath. "How did this happen, Jess?" She looked at her friend. "I mean, really? How? All I meant was to do right by him. By *them*. Both of them."

"I know, Amanda. But sometimes life doesn't make any sense."

She released a dragged-out sigh. "Jess, I know you believe in all that 'everything happens for a reason' crap, but what's the reason here? I mean, really?"

"I don't know, Amanda."

"We had it all, you know?" She spun her glass as she spoke. "Reale and I. We loved each other. I loved him so much I gave up everything to raise his child so he could have the life he was meant to have."

"What if the life he was meant to have was with you?"

She started, sitting back in her chair. "Well, that opportunity is gone, isn't it?"

"It doesn't have to be." Jess's voice was soft.

She chuckled, covering her mouth with her hand. "You think if Reale Lynxx came knocking on my door begging for forgiveness I would let him back into my life? You don't know me as well as you think."

"I think you love him. And I think there was a time on Fire Island when you thought maybe the three of you could make a go of it."

"Well, that goes to show how pathetically stupid I am."

"No." Jess shook her head. "That goes to show how much you love him. And sometimes the people we love the most are the people who hurt us the worst. That's the risk of happiness. When you fly that high, any hurt you feel brings you down farther than you ever thought possible."

"But this wasn't some dumb fight, Jess. He didn't flirt with another girl or even sleep with someone else. He took my son."

"His son too."

Her chest tightened. "Whose side are you on?"

"Yours, Amanda. Always yours. I just want you to be happy."

"Happy?" She raised her eyebrows, her throat constricting. "My happiness walked out of here with a backpack stuffed full of faded superhero underwear."

"He shouldn't be your only happiness, Amanda. You're a young, beautiful woman."

"Who foolishly loved the wrong man. And now, not only am I emotionally linked to him, publicly I am linked to him—forever. I'm like Hester Prynne with my own scarlet letter A on my clothing." Amanda dug through the pile of books on the table and grabbed the worn copy of *The Scarlet Letter*, shaking it for emphasis. "I kept Reale Lynxx's son from him. Shame on me."

"I see that English class is paying off."

"Ha, ha." She released the book, letting it drop to the table with a thud.

"All I'm saying, Amanda, is consider your happiness too."

"Thanks, Jess. But I can promise, thanks to Reale Lynxx, I will never be happy again."

****

"How does your mother handle this?"

Reale spoke under his breath as John, wielding a water gun, ran in circles around and around the solarium. Reale adjusted the back of his lounger, not trusting to lie back for fear he'd fall asleep.

Two freakin' weeks. He'd only had John to himself for two weeks, but it felt like ten years. Damn, parenthood was *hard*. Really, really hard. It's like nothing else he'd ever done. At least in negotiating a deal or prepping for a tour he dealt with grown-ups. And although some of them loved drama and acted like adolescents, he never had to worry about anyone's feelings—or burning some horrible memory into their brains. He wasn't complaining. He loved John and being with him, but damn, parenthood was exhausting and freakin' *hard*.

"Bud, want to get in again?" John stopped only to point to the pool.

"No, thanks, Buddy." He ran his hand over his head, getting rid of the excess water from their fourth trip into the pool that day. Wait. What about that redirecting tactic he'd read about in some parenting book he picked up? That might work. "Hey, Buddy, don't you want to go do something else? What do you say we watch a movie in the screening room? I can get something that hasn't even been released yet." He spoke with as much enthusiasm as he could muster. A movie would be perfect. He could close his eyes for a few moments and maybe grab a quick power nap…

"Un-unh. I want to swim!" John squealed, picking up his pace again.

Crap. He wasn't getting a nap today—or any day. Maybe there was something to not feeding a child too much sugar. Maybe ice cream and cookies for lunch wasn't the best idea after all. But how did Amanda always feed John healthy foods and consider what John was eating?

John ran faster and faster, shooting the water gun at the plants. No, maybe the salt water wasn't great for them, but it was the lesser of all evils. Besides, it kept the kid entertained for a moment. Jesus. How did any parent ever survive summer vacation?

"Just stay over there, please." Reale pointed away from the pool and toward the large open area of the solarium decorated with potted plants and freaking expensive white lounge chairs like the one he was sitting in. "Stay away from the slippery edge of the pool."

"*Yaa-hooo!*" John yelped as he ran toward Reale and away again. It would have been cute if Reale wasn't so dog tired. "Watch me, Bud!"

Bud. Would there ever be a time when they would get out of this awkward phase? Would the kid ever call him Dad? And would Reale ever really want him to?

"Damn," he muttered under his breath. Of course he'd want the kid to. He was his father and proud of it. He desperately wanted to make up for not being there for the past five years, whether it was his fault or not. He wasn't thinking clearly because exhaustion was taking over.

Watching John run until he must have been dizzy, Reale dragged his hand down his scruffy face. How long had it been since he'd shaved? He didn't have the time for that like he did before John came to live with him. Oh, hell—he didn't have time for anything. He'd stopped shaving because John was there every morning, watching and wanting to help. And although it was a nice gesture, when he helped, everything took at least twice as long and had to be redone. And forget working out daily. Why the hell did he imagine he and John would ride bikes together for eight miles at a time and hit the gym after? John rode for three feet and wanted to stop to examine a bug or watch a plane. Everything was interrupted. *Everything.* Christ, the kid found him while he was in the bathroom taking a crap. Every morning.

The one thing that was interrupted more than anything was sleep. Forget sleep. Seemed as if every single night John came into Reale's bedroom because he didn't have the right stuffed animal or superhero underwear. One time the housekeeper washed John's clothes in the wrong soap, and that night—just as Amanda predicted—they didn't sleep at all. Not one bit. And it wasn't at all like staying awake partying. This was *work.* He had to call Amanda that night, like he did every time John couldn't sleep. But she was always kind and patient. With both of them.

How the hell had she done this alone all these years? He shook his head. He wasn't surprised. She could handle it. She could handle anything.

But the lack of sleep... Didn't kids eventually sleep? What happened to eight p.m. bedtimes and sleeping like a baby? Christ. He would have settled for midnight bedtimes and sleeping past five a.m. Why did John wake up at five a.m. every morning?

"Bud!" John ran by, squirting Reale smack in the eye with pool water from his squirt gun.

"Ow!" Reale stood and grabbed a towel. He rubbed his eye. "That burns." It was the damned salt from the saltwater pool. Sure, it was softer to swim in, but it burned like hell in his eye. "Damn it, John." He stormed off and grabbed a bottle of water at the poolside bar to flush his eye. "You've got to be more careful. You can't squirt that in someone's eye—"

Sniff. Sniff. He turned to see John's face turn bright red and scrunch up into a scowl. John sniffed again, rubbing his nose. Damn it. Christ. Was he going to cry? Reale'd only had to deal with John crying late nights when he missed his mom, but usually a video chat would take care of that until John fell asleep. Reale was getting spoiled listening to Amanda's beautiful but untrained voice singing "High Hopes," about an ant that moved a rubber tree plant, nearly every night. But he'd never before had to deal with his son crying midday.

"Uh, John, I didn't mean to snap." Damn, his eye still burned. He wanted to flush it again, but John needed his attention. His eye would have to wait.

"*Waaaahhhhh!*" The wail that came out of that kid was louder than Reale's guitar with the amps turned up all the way.

"John?" Reale sprang to his side, but John backed away, crying louder.

"Mr. Reale?" Marianna, the nanny, materialized at the door of the solarium. "You want me to take him away?"

Take him away? No. Christ, no. John didn't need to be separated from his dad; he needed to be with him. If only his dad knew what to do. "No, thank you, Marianna. I think I scared him."

She nodded warily. "Okay, Mr. Reale. If you need me to take him to his room, let him cry it out—"

Cry it out? Christ! Had he hired Nurse Ratched when he meant to get someone happy and loving? No way. No. "He's scared, Marianna. I have it. Please."

"Fear is a sign of weakness," she mumbled and left after one final glance over her shoulder and shake of her head.

Damn. As soon as John was calm he was going to fire Marianna and yell at the woman at the service who recommended her. Damn, damn, damn. Oh, no. What if that was the way she was with John whenever Reale was away? Oh crap. Don't let her have said anything awful to John those times he left the two of them alone so he could have a moment to work... Jesus, she was awful. How could anyone be that cruel to a child? How could anyone think keeping a child from a parent was okay? "Huh—" He gasped, drawing in a long gulp of air. Damn it.

John yelled louder.

"John. Please." He stepped closer, but the boy screamed louder still. "I didn't mean to be mean. Really."

"You said a bad word," John wailed through his sobs.

"I did?" He wracked his brain. How many "bad" words had he said in his life? He was supposed to remember this one? "I'm sorry. What was it?"

John screamed, "I'm *not* going to say it!"

"Of course not." Reale put up his hands, shushing, trying to calm him. "Please John. Buddy. I'm sorry. I'm not mad. I was surprised." He rubbed at his burning eye again as John wailed louder. Christ, how long was he going to go on? Couldn't this be over? That's another thing little kids did—hold on way too long. He stood tall with a start; maybe that was a trait his son got from him. Reale was never going to forgive Amanda for what she'd done, no matter her reasons. No matter how noble and kind they truly may have been.

"*I want Mommy!*" John screamed louder than Reale had ever heard anyone scream.

Instinctively, Reale covered his ears like a coward. "I want her too, John. But she's not here." He dropped his hands.

"That's your fault!" John's face was red and his breathing jagged.

"What do you mean?"

"Mommy is always with me, so you must have said you didn't want to be with her otherwise she would be here right now! *Mommmmmm-yyyyyy!*"

Three members of the housekeeping staff hovered near the sliding glass doorway, peering into the solarium, including Mr. Jones, the groundskeeper. Their black uniforms were pristine, but their contorted faces gave away their concern. Damn. If Mr. Jones was here, that meant they could hear the disaster from outside.

Reale put up his hand. "I've got it, thanks."

Mr. Jones gave a quick nod and signaled the other two to follow him out. They left.

"John." Reale moved closer, but John backed away. "You're too close to the pool, Buddy. Please John." Sweat pooled on his lower back and dripped from his forehead. He had negotiated rights for countless record deals, and none were as difficult as this. "John, let's call her." He sprinted to the bar again and grabbed his cell. "We can video chat, and she can tell you everything is okay."

"I don't want to see her on the phone!" John lurched at him, and before he knew what was happening, John grabbed the phone from his hand and tossed it into the pool.

"*Jonathan Simmons*!" he barked, and John's eyes widened.

John's screaming stopped, but the tears fell harder and faster.

"You had no right to do that! Damn it!" That was every contact he had from his manager's private numbers to Amanda's cell. He couldn't run his empire without that phone. "What the hell did you do?" He stepped toward John, his chest widening and his breath racing. "You have really fucked up, John. Really fucked up."

"*Mommmm-yyy*!"

"Well we can't call her now because that was the only contact I had with her. It's me and you alone. Maybe I should send you to your room to cry it out!" Damn it! What was he saying?

"You're mean!"

"So are you. You ruined my phone. That phone is my life." He started, shaking his head and staring at his son. Had he really told his five-year-old son that a phone was his life? Christ. "John, listen…"

He took a deep breath, stepping closer, but John backed away again, shooting Reale with the water gun.

"John, you don't have to protect yourself from me."

But John backed up faster and faster until he broke into a run by the slick, wet side of the pool.

"John, no, it's not safe. You're going to slip and hit your head—"

Crack!

No sooner did the words come out than John slipped and fell into the pool.

"Johnny!" Reale rushed into the pool and grabbed his unconscious son. The tiniest pool of blood clung to the top of the water. *No, no, no…* Maybe it wasn't his head. Maybe, please God, maybe he'll be okay. "*Help!*" he screamed as the staff came running in. Marianna glared at Reale. "It was an accident. Call 911! *Now!*"

He carried John from the pool and laid him on the hard tile. Someone was calling 911 as he hovered over his son, listening for a heartbeat. It was there, thank God. He glanced past his son and into the pool, his phone sitting at the bottom. Why the hell hadn't he memorized Amanda's number? What was he going to do? What, what, what? Sweat dripped from his forehead as the staff gathered around him.

"Did he inhale any water?" Mr. Jones asked.

"No." Reale shook his head. "I don't think so. I grabbed him as soon as he hit the water." He turned to his son again. "John? Johnny? Come on, John. Stay here. Stay with me." He had no idea what he was doing. Amanda would know. She would have the answers. Problem was he had no ability to even call her. "How long does an ambulance take?" He spoke loudly as panic overtook his body.

"They said they were in the area. They should be here any moment." Mr. Jones was calm as he squatted next to John and Reale. "My son slipped like this once. Hit his head. He was okay, Mr. Reale."

Reale nodded, hardly able to listen or maintain a lucid thought. All he could think, over and over, was how much better off John would be without him. How much better off Amanda *and* John were without him. Damn. She had been right to keep John from him all those years. He was nothing but a fuck-up.

Sirens wailed behind him. Thank God. He turned to see flashing lights coming through the windows of the solarium.

Two EMS workers rushed in and immediately began work on John as they asked Reale a million questions.

"My son. In the water for only a few seconds. Heard a crack as he fell." He winced reliving the moment. "No allergies. No medications, just a multivitamin. No illnesses. Last thing he ate was some ice cream and chocolate chip cookies before we went swimming." He focused and fought to remain calm as he answered. The EMS workers moved John onto a stretcher, and Reale glanced up at one of them, a female. "His mom. We don't live together. John's with me. I need to contact his mom, but my phone..." He pointed to the pool feebly. Never before had he felt so weak and powerless.

"Think." The female EMS worker turned to him, giving him her attention. "Can you recall the number?"

He wracked his brain, banging his forehead with his fist. "No. I've got nothing." Damn, he could barely remember his own name right now.

"Okay. Stay calm, sir." The female EMS worker spoke slowly and clearly. "Does he have a travel bag? Your son? I always write my cell number on a slip of paper and slide it into my son's bag when he goes to his incompetent father's house. For emergencies."

"His bag. Yes." In a flash he stood.

"Tell her with a head injury he'll be sent via medevac to Cohen's. She should meet you there," the female EMS worker called after him as he ran out the solarium door.

Reale rushed down the long, sunshine-filled hallway connecting the solarium to the main house. He burst through the double doors leading to the entryway at the side of the house and ran through the living room, nearly tripping over the long, low, white leather couch. He stumbled to the main staircase and climbed the polished wooden spiral steps by taking them two at a time. John's room… He had put John into the guest room closest to his master bedroom. Christ. That was all the way on the other end of the wing. He slowed for a moment—had he really moved his son into a guest room?

He moved at top speed again, running the upstairs hallway, knocking a vase from the Asian table in a recessed crevice in the hallway. It landed with a thud—like John falling into the pool. That vase was probably priceless, but who cared? His son's life was in danger, and his son's mother had no idea. He owed this—and so much more—to her. He skidded down the shiny mahogany floor of the impossibly long hallway, sliding his hand down the muted yellow wall. He grabbed the white oversized doorframe to John's room and hurled himself inside. Where? Where? Where? He turned in a circle, taking in the mostly empty room. The bed was nicely made with a plain blue cover, and the pillow was set just so. But where were the bags? He rushed to the closet and yanked open the double doors, stepping inside. Thank God, John's duffle and backpack. He squatted down on the closet floor and tore them open, breaking the zippers.

"C'mon, c'mon, Amanda. I know you. You did this. I know you did." He pushed past John's clothes, dumping them onto the floor. Why hadn't he unpacked?

That was for another time, not now. Now, he needed Amanda's contact. Nothing. "C'mon, Amanda. You always take care of everything. You know I'll lose my cell. You must have left…" He turned the duffle upside down, shaking it. "Yes!" He pumped his fist in the air. A slip of yellow paper from a legal pad fell to the floor. With shaking hands, he grabbed the paper and opened it.

I love you! Mom. With her cell number. Oh, thank God. Fighting to steady his hands, he bolted out of the closet and stumbled across the room. He threw himself across John's bed and grabbed a house phone. He dialed Amanda's number. Thank God she answered.

"He's been in an accident."

"Is he okay?"

Her voice was calm and steady, but he couldn't squeak out one single word. Was he okay? Who knew?

"Reale? Answer me. Where is he going?"

He choked out the name of the hospital and hung up. He rushed out of the room and back to his son's side.

Chapter Fifteen

"How is he?" Amanda spoke calmly as she cornered the doctor. They were standing outside John's hospital room, waiting for test results. Reale studied the doctor intently, looking for any concern in his cool exterior, but his long white jacket was immaculate, complete with an expensive marbled pen tucked into the pocket, and not a single strand of his black-gray hair was out of place. The doctor pushed his silver wire glasses high on his nose and maintained steady eye contact with her.

"He's still unconscious, but so far the test results look promising. I expect he'll wake up soon. He has a nasty cut on his forehead, needed a few stitches, and his arm has a hairline fracture." He turned to Reale. "That crack you described. I believe it was his arm, not his head."

Reale winced.

"That's a good thing." The doctor nodded encouragingly. "We are very lucky. I believe he will recover fully."

"Thank God." Amanda sighed, wiping a tear. She placed her hand on the doctor's forearm delicately. "Thank you, Doctor. Thank you."

He nodded, patting her hand. "We're not out of the woods yet, but it looks promising."

She thanked him again, jutting her chin. How could

she be this together when all Reale wanted to do was crumple to the ground? That was Amanda.

"His tests are completed." The doctor motioned toward John. He turned back to Amanda and smiled. "He'll be ready for you in a minute." He walked away and out a swinging glass door.

She stood unmoving, and Reale was frozen by her side. They were in a private hallway staring through the glass at their unconscious son. They were close to one another, so close he could feel her next to him, could smell her scent of fresh air and sunshine. His arm ached; he desperately wanted to lift it, to drape it across her thin shoulders, to pull her to him. He wanted nothing more than to comfort her and tell her everything would be okay. But that wasn't his job anymore. His soul ached. She would never trust him again—not after what he had done to them.

He glanced at her out of the corner of his eye. She wouldn't turn to him, wouldn't speak to him, and the silence was torturous. He inhaled deeply, standing tall. He'd made this mess; he separated the three of them and was responsible for his son's accident. He was also the man, and it was his job to take care of his family, and in this case that meant Amanda too. He closed his eyes as his knotted stomach flipped. How long and how desperately he had wanted to have a life with her. And yet here they were, with a child together, and because of everything he'd done, they would never be a real family. The one thing he had always wished he had. The one thing he wanted to give his son. The only thing he had ever wanted with Amanda—to make her his forever.

He turned to her, taking in her long blonde hair

cascading down her back, her soft pink T-shirt falling loosely over her breasts and hugging her hips in her fitted faded jeans, her soft face streaked from tears. She was so beautiful.

"Amanda." He rubbed the back of his neck with his hand. "I don't know what to say to you."

She didn't turn to him.

"It just happened. No, it wasn't my finest moment. I was tired. Exhausted. He hasn't been sleeping and neither have I. I yelled at him."

She flinched, placing both hands on the light wooden chair rail of the glass partition before them.

"He shot saltwater into my eye and wanted you. I offered a video chat, and he freaked, tossing my phone into the pool, so I...I yelled at him." How cowardly and weak it all sounded. "He got scared and backed away. When I tried to get him to come away from the pool, he ran and slipped and—"

She closed her eyes, inhaling deeply.

"I'm so sorry, Amanda. I'm sorry this happened on my watch. I'm sorry I yelled at him. I'm sorry I'm not a better father." He dropped his head. The lump in the back of his throat ached. "I'm sorry I did this. All of it." He raised his head. "I'm sorry I did it to all of us. Especially to John...and you." He forced back his tears. He needed to be strong for her.

"Once..." Her voice was soft and barely audible. She cleared her throat, never turning to him or taking her eyes off John. "Once when he was only a year old, he was standing in his crib. I didn't know he could stand, but he must have pulled himself up, and I walked in with my arms filled with laundry—and the next thing I knew, he toppled head first out of his crib. Landed on his head. I thought…" She sucked in a deep jagged breath. "I thought he had broken his neck."

She turned then, her gaze finding his. "I did everything wrong. I ran and moved him. I screamed and screamed, but he didn't respond. I scooped him up, running out of the house, and"—she shook her head—"nearly tossed him into his car seat, driving like a madwoman to the hospital. I ran into the ER clutching him like he was a porcelain egg. They took him immediately, and thank God the scans came back negative. Not a scratch on him." She turned to look back toward John.

"It was an accident, Amanda. It wasn't your fault."

She glanced at him, her beautiful eyes filled with heartache and pain. "Truthfully, when I walked into his room, he was crying. I had put him in there as a kind of timeout, because he'd been throwing everything all day long"—exasperation rang through her tone—"and he never slept. Never at that age. Not that he's a great sleeper now. Vacation was a freak thing. I think the salt air tired him out. And Jesus—" She looked at the sky. "I was so exhausted that day, and I had no idea why he kept crying. His diaper was dry, he wasn't hungry, he wasn't teething, no gas. I just couldn't take one more second of the crying…" Her voice fell away. "Not one more." She placed a shaky hand to her mouth, reliving the horror. "I yelled at him to stop, and he wailed louder. So I plopped him into his crib and walked out."

She sighed, placing her hand on the glass wall between her and her son, delicately dropping her forehead to the glass. "When I went back a few moments later, he pulled himself up and fell over the edge. When I grabbed him off the floor, all I could think was, 'If these were his last moments of life—dear God—his mother was yelling at him.' " She rolled her head back and forth on the glass wall.

Reale inhaled sharply. His heart ached for her. "I think I know how you felt."

She nodded, still with her head to the glass. "All I could think that entire time was how much I wished Johnny had a dad to be there with me. To help Johnny." She pulled her head from the glass and turned to Reale. "All I could think was how much I wanted *you* there with me."

She placed a hand to her mouth to silence a sob as her shoulders rounded with grief. The hell with it. This was his Mandy, and he would never let her hurt like this again. He stepped forward, wrapping his arms around her and pulling her tight to his chest.

****

"Mommy?"

"Oh, thank God. Johnny." Amanda threw herself carefully over her son, hugging him as best she could. She pulled back and wiped her tears in her T-shirt. Thank God. Thank God. Thank God. "Oh, you scared us, mister. We knew you'd been fine, but we're really glad you're here to talk to us."

"Where was I?"

She turned to Reale. This was as much his moment as it was hers. He stepped up by her side, and she inhaled his smell of strength and clean laundry. God help her, even here and now, it was an aphrodisiac.

"Mommy? Where was I?"

Reale smiled. "You were sleeping, little man."

"Oh." Johnny glanced away and back, and Reale shot Amanda a look of concern.

She sat on the edge of Johnny's bed and tucked Peanut tight to his side. She held the hand of his unbroken arm. "Johnny. Are you okay? Does your head hurt?"

"Un-unh." He shook his head. "Nothing really hurts."

She nodded and turned to Reale. "Thank goodness for painkillers." She turned back to her son. "Is something else wrong? You seem a little upset."

Johnny tried to sit up.

"No, no." She eased him down and leaned over him. "Is it a secret?"

He nodded.

"Okay." She turned so her ear was near his mouth.

"Reale is mad at me."

She sat up, furrowing her brow. "Why would you think that, Johnny?"

"Because I shot him in the eye with my water gun."

She nodded, whispering, "Johnny. Accidents happen. To all of us. I'll bet you didn't mean to hurt Reale. Am I right?"

He nodded. "Yes."

She smiled. "And I'll bet Reale is not the slightest bit upset. Is it okay if I ask him?"

Johnny's eyes widened as he nodded.

She turned to Reale. "Reale, are you mad at Johnny for squirting you in the eye?"

He rushed to Johnny's other side and sat on the bed opposite Amanda. His plaid shirt opened as he sat, exposing his lean abdomen covered by a white V-neck T-shirt that hung over his swim trunks. She smiled.

"What? No. No, not at all. I was hoping you weren't mad at me."

"For what?"

"Well…"

Reale dragged his hand across his face, and she glimpsed the scruff. She hadn't had a chance to notice it before. She inhaled, her core warming. He'd had a similar short, scruffy beard the entire time they were dating, and she loved it. She'd loved the way it scratched her face when he kissed her, the way it tickled her neck when he nuzzled her…it was *her* Reale. The man she knew and loved.

"I'm hoping you aren't mad at me because I raised my voice. I'm sorry I did that. And I'm sorry I said a phone was the most important thing in my life. It's not. Not by a long shot."

"No?" Johnny stared at Reale with so much admiration it made her heart flutter.

"No." Reale shook his head. "The most important things in the world to me are you and your mom."

"Really?" Johnny brightened.

"What?" She sat straighter. "Reale." She shook her head. Yes, moments of stress like this could bring people together, but with their history, they could never be a couple again. And the last thing she wanted was to give Johnny false hope. "Let's be clear on what we mean and not confuse Johnny."

"I don't think I am confusing him." His gaze was locked on hers, his eyes unwavering.

"Uh…" She furrowed her brow. "Um, Reale, can we speak for a moment, please? Privately?"

"Okay." He didn't budge.

She turned to Johnny. "You okay if Reale and I step out of your room for a second? We'll be in the hallway, right there." She raised one finger and pointed out of the room and to the hallway.

Johnny nodded.

"Okay." She stood and wiped her sweaty palms on her jeans as she spoke. "Reale? Would you come with me, please?"

"Of course. See you in a second, Buddy." He stood and reached down to brush his son's hair in just the right way. Her heart fluttered again. Damn it.

Reale opened the door of Johnny's hospital room, holding it for her, letting her pass. As she walked past him, she could feel his presence. That was what it was like when Reale Lynxx wanted to make himself known. His aura was so powerful it took her breath away. *Damn you, Reale.* She stepped into the hallway outside Johnny's room, her feet slipping on the incredibly shiny floor. Reale let the door close behind him and moved closer to her. She held her breath and took a tiny step back. She needed distance and clarity.

She cleared her throat. "Reale. Times like this—accidents, terrifying moments in life—they bring people together. And people tend to forget the reasons they were angry to begin with. But then time passes and you have some distance from the tragedy, and you remember the reasons you were angry and then—"

"I don't want to do this anymore."

"What?" She looked up at him.

He hovered closer to her. "Pretend I don't have feelings for you." He shook his head. "Pretend to be happy. Pretend that any of this makes sense."

She glanced at him sideways. "What are you saying?" Her voice was low but steady.

"I want to be a couple again. To raise John together. As a family."

"As a what?" She stepped back farther, distancing herself.

"A family."

"Reale." She shook her head. "I'm starting to wonder who hit their head back there, Johnny or you. You're talking crazy."

"Am I?"

"Yes." She cleared her throat. "Yes, you are. This is fear talking. The scare with Johnny. It's natural. You're forgetting we were just at war."

He stepped closer. "You're telling me you never imagined the three of us together?"

No, she couldn't tell him that. That would be a lie. "I thought of us together. Before I ever got pregnant, I knew I wanted to have babies with you."

"How about more recently?" He raised his eyebrows in the most condescending but thrilling way.

She tilted her head. "When we were on Fire Island. When I was getting ready to tell you about Johnny. I imagined the three of us together and—" Oh, no way. She stopped short. Why was it always easy to bare her soul to Reale Lynxx? Why, after everything, did she still trust him more than she trusted anyone? But could she trust him completely? No. Not after everything that had happened.

"And what?"

She shook her head, and her chest tightened as he stepped closer.

"Mandy? What?"

He was close now. He reached up and tucked a stray piece of her hair behind her ear. Damn. It felt so good a warmth settled deep in her core. She shifted uneasily.

"Baby? What were you going to say?" His voice coaxed her with a soothing, mellow sound as his hand lingered dangerously close to her ear.

She lifted her gaze to his, staring into those eyes she knew so well. It was as if he had her under a spell, using his melodic voice to learn her deepest secrets. The hell with it. "I was going to say I imagined having more babies with you. Raising them together."

He inhaled sharply, letting the back of his hand brush her cheek. The gesture was soft and kind and intimate. She closed her eyes, breathing him in.

"I thought of that too."

Her eyes opened wide. "You did?"

He nodded. "I do."

She shook her head, stepping back. "But Reale…"

"What? Tell me why not? Why couldn't this work? We could raise John together. Maybe, when you're ready, have another baby or a boatload more babies." He smiled an unnerving grin, that same smile he flashed the first time she had met him in that club all those years ago.

She stepped back. "Reale, no. No." Her eyes searched his. "What do you think is happening here?" She walked away purposely and then turned back to him. "We were just at war. You took Johnny from me."

"I know." He dropped his head. "I'm sorry. I know now it was a mistake."

She shook her head. "A mistake? A mistake is buying blue socks when you meant to get black. Or ordering a chocolate milkshake instead of vanilla. This was not a mistake, Reale. This was a calculated move. One meant to hurt me to my very soul." Her eyes danced across his as anger welled in her belly. "And what's more, it hurt Johnny."

"I'm sorry he's here, Mandy. I'll apologize to my last day—"

She put up her hand, stopping him. "That was an accident. That was a mistake. It can happen to anyone. It happened to me. I don't blame you for that. But taking him…" She walked away and wheeled around, storming to him again. "What? Are you saying I can have him back permanently? Or are you saying I can only have him if I'm with you?" Her chest heaved as she spoke.

"No, no, neither." He fumbled for his words. "I'm saying I was wrong in what I did. I was angry, Mandy. Can't you see that?"

"But what you did, Reale. How could I ever trust you again?"

"I'm trusting you."

She threw up her hands in exasperation. "But for the millionth time, I didn't keep your son from you because of some horrible, malicious reason. I did it for you. Maybe you think I shouldn't have done it. But the only person it hurt for six years was *me*. But you…you deliberately hurt me, and what's worse, Johnny paid the price too. Yanking him away from the only parent he's ever known. Having to video chat with my own son when he's upset and can't sleep. Getting shuffled back and forth between the home of his rock star father and his dirt-poor mother. It's like the storyline for an afterschool special. Jesus, Reale." She placed a cool, shaking hand to her forehead.

"Are you saying there's no chance for you and me? But when we were standing over there, and you told me your story… And you thought of having more kids with me, Mandy."

"I told you my story to make you feel better. Because we're connected, you and I, and always will be. But the thought of having more kids with you, that was before, Reale. Before I knew how cruel you can be."

He started, standing taller.

"You had a rock star hissy fit with a rock star budget, and you played with our lives, Reale. Our *lives*. And the life of your son."

"Are you really saying there's no chance?"

She shook her head, slowly, her stomach aching. "Not for us, no." She gazed up into his beautiful eyes that were cloudy with pain. "I don't want to hurt you, Reale. But I'm not leading you on. The best thing we can do for him"—she pointed to the closed door to Johnny's room—"is to share custody. None of this partial visiting rights crap." She took a deep breath, crossing her arms before her. "I did you a solid when we were in negotiation. I could have told everyone the truth about the train and those kids. You would have lost and God knows what else."

"Yes."

"So be the man I know you are. Be Johnny's father. Enough with the Bud crap. Have him call you Dad; take him places on weekends. We'll come up with a schedule that works for both of us."

He reached out and grabbed her by the forearm. "I want more, Amanda."

"Then pay to get him an education near to me that doesn't require him walking through a metal detector every morning. I know the place. It'll be tough to get into this late, but with the right letter and your celebrity…" She shrugged. "It will cost you. Way more than tuition. We'll need to make a significant donation as a family."

"Yes, yes. Of course. Whatever he needs. Whatever you need."

"I don't need your money, Reale." She sighed sadly. "I need for you to be a father to Johnny. One who lets him live at home with his mother, no matter how meager our surroundings."

"Of course." He gazed at her, and she recognized that look on his face. It was the same pained and confused expression he wore that night she'd left him at the bar. The night she'd walked out with another man.

"I'm sorry, Reale." She swallowed hard as a tear dropped from the corner of her eye. She stepped closer to him and patted his arm. "But what you did, ripping Johnny away from me to get even…" She shook her head. "It's unforgiveable." She yanked open the door to Johnny's room and walked in, leaving Reale behind.

Chapter Sixteen

"Is that a Lynxx backpack?" Mandy pulled the backpack from a bag of school supplies Reale had dropped onto her kitchen table. She left the backpack on the table and stepped back from it as if it were laced with poison. John sat at the table munching on healthy cheese puffs and eyeing the backpack.

"We're celebrating John being out of the hospital and home for one month."

"Un-huh." Her eyes were still on the backpack, but she turned back to the watermelon she was carving on the countertop near the stove.

"And school starts in a couple of weeks."

"Yes." She put down her knife, her gaze not wavering from the table.

Reale pressed on. "And I, uh...I finalized my new tour schedule. We kick off right after Christmas."

"Oh?" She raised her eyebrows, glancing back at the half-carved watermelon.

Was she happy about it? Interested? "It coincides with John's vacation."

She glanced at him sharply. "I see."

"I would only take him along if you thought it was cool."

"I appreciate that."

His stomach clenched. He had spent all day wondering what it would be like to have her and John on tour with him, and best guess, it would be freaking awesome. But something in her demeanor didn't seem open to conversation right now.

He cleared his throat. "Well, since you had no time with school and work, and John's not getting around great with the cast, I took it upon myself to come up with the world's coolest backpack." He grinned, turning to John and back to Mandy. "Custom made."

"Sure." She abandoned her watermelon and walked the few steps back to the table. She tilted her head, peeking into the bag. "And is this"—she pulled out a black-and-red, small, insulated box—"the matching lunchbox?"

"Yup." Reale swung his hands back and forth, whistling a tune.

She turned to him. "Cool melody. Is that new?"

"Yup." He slapped one fist against the other hand. "Working on it. Hoping it'll be ready to debut this tour. I tell you, Mandy, I'm on a roll. The songs are flowing. I think it's my lucky charm here." He leaned down and ruffled John's hair.

"Dad." John fixed his hair. "You're messing it up."

Dad. The word still affected Reale to his core. He was a dad. Someone's dad. More than someone, he was this incredible little person's father. He glanced up at Mandy. And that brilliant, gorgeous woman was his son's mother. Damn, he was one lucky son of a gun. She smiled at him. She understood.

"So." She lifted the backpack and held it away from her body. "Are we sure this goes with the preppy uniform of khaki shorts and blue polo shirts with navy blazers?" She twirled the backpack, taking in its designs.

On the front of the black bag he had created a silhouette of the band in white. The sides had the Lynxx band symbol—the animal Lynx—in red. One side had a holder for a water bottle, also a black-and-red Lynxx original, and the other side had a space for John's new cell phone Reale had ordered for him. It wasn't time to tell Mandy about that one yet. The back of the pack had John's first name embroidered. He had wanted to make it read John's whole name, but that was a conversation he still wanted to have with Mandy. John didn't have a middle name, so how easy it would be to make his full name: Jonathan Simmons Lynxx. He glanced at Mandy who was surveying the backpack with a wary eye. He smiled.

"It's a little heavy, Reale. I appreciate it, but—" She bounced it up and down like she was weighing it.

"It's not the backpack that's heavy. It's the computer tablet inside."

"*What*?" John and Mandy spoke in unison.

"No way!" John jumped up and hugged Reale. He pulled away to yank the tablet out of his backpack.

"No way." Mandy shook her head and crossed her arms before her. "Reale, he's starting kindergarten. He doesn't need a computer tablet for kindergarten."

"But it's full-day kindergarten." Reale chuckled. "Remember that conversation?" He winked at Mandy, grinning as he showed John how to turn on the tablet. "And it comes complete with a waterproof custom superhero cover." He glanced at Mandy. "This way he can send you emails and can research his homework."

"Research his homework? The ABCs?"

John sat in his seat, focused on his tablet, engrossed in a game.

"Okay, there may be a few *educational* games on there."

"But you gave him a state-of-the-art gaming system to keep him busy while he recovered. He doesn't need this."

"Sure he does. And besides, this way you two won't have to fight over one tablet."

"Well, we don't fight over one tablet, because we don't own one."

He nodded to the half-opened plastic bag on the table. She had been so focused on the backpack she didn't even notice something else was inside the bag.

"What?" She turned her head to the side, appraising him warily. "Reale Lynxx, what did you…?" From a distance she peered into the bag and opened it with outstretched fingers. She moved carefully, like she was pulling off the top of a basket with a venomous serpent hiding inside. "A second computer tablet?" She pulled her hand away fast. "What?" Her jaw dropped, and she shook her head.

"For you."

"No, Reale. Thank you, but I can't accept this. I don't need a gift."

"Seems to me, Mandy, I'm behind on many, many gifts for you."

"Reale." She sighed. Everything she did was soft and graceful, even at, or maybe especially at, her strongest moments. "I don't need anything, Reale. But thank you."

"Huh." He took the tablet from the bag. "That's too bad because I had this really nice pink custom cover made for you."

He held it to her, and she ran her hand over the soft

leather finish. "It's nice."

"Mm." He nodded. "And last I checked a tablet like this is helpful for nursing school."

She laughed. "Nursing school? I have to finish my undergrad first."

"Okay. I'm sure this will help with your undergrad as well."

She glanced at the tablet in his hand. "I'm sure it will, but I can't."

"Why not?"

"Because it's ridiculously expensive for one thing."

"Mandy." He cocked his head, smiling.

Her cheeks flushed. "Maybe not to you, but…" Her words fell away as she glanced at the tablet again. "And for another, I should not be accepting gifts from you."

"Why not?"

She jutted her head forward and up again like a cartoon character whose eyes grow large when she sees gold. "Why not? Because there's no reason to accept a gift from you."

"Ah. I see. A reason. Well, aren't you and I friends?"

"Yes. Of course we are." Her gaze fell on John who was engrossed in his tablet.

"Don't you buy gifts for Jess?"

"Of course. For birthdays and holidays." She turned her gorgeous eyes back to him.

"We're friends. I'm buying you a gift."

"Reale. It's not my birthday, and it's not Christmas. There's no reason—"

"Mandy, you won't win this one. Just take it and say thank you." He took the tablet from his hands and placed it in hers, gently pushing it toward her chest.

"I…" She shook her head, glancing at the tablet. "This is…" She bit the corner of her lower lip as she fumbled for words. "I don't think…" She placed the tablet into the crook of her arm and tucked a hair behind her ear. "I can't—"

"How about, 'Thank you, Reale'?"

She held the tablet to her chest with a contented sigh. "There's no winning this one?"

"Un-unh." He crossed his arms before him, loving the banter with Mandy. Loving making her happy. This would have to suffice right now. He'd bring up the tour again later when she was more open to it.

"This is a onetime thing, though. Got it?"

"Nope."

"No?" Her eyes widened. "Reale, we can't. I can't."

"Mandy." He dropped his hands and stepped closer. "Just enjoy the tablet. I'm enjoying the heck out of giving it to you."

"Well, uh. Well…" She switched her tablet from one arm to the other, gazing up at him. "Thank you, Reale."

She looked beautiful standing in her warm kitchen…this close to him. Her eyes sparkled as she licked her pouty lips.

He inhaled deeply. "No thank you kiss?"

She cocked her head and raised her eyebrows. "Ha, ha."

"Doesn't hurt to ask." He smiled.

"Thank you, Reale. For all of it." She glanced at the backpack again.

"If the backpack is too much and you want something more preppy, then I'll get him another—"

She shook her head. "I think it's perfect."

"Really?" This he was not expecting. He'd half brought the backpack hoping it would be so extreme the tablets would become an easier sell.

"Yup. He's your son. And mine. The child of a rock star and a waitress. That backpack sums him up perfectly."

Waitress. The way she said it. "Mandy. There's nothing wrong with being a waitress. It's a good, honest living. Hard work. But you're not only a waitress."

"No. You're right. I'm a mom too." She walked to the far counter and placed the tablet down. She turned her back to the counter, leaning against it. She faced him, crossing her legs at the ankles.

"Mandy? What's up?" He walked closer to her and leaned against the counter a few feet away from her.

"Nothing." She stared at the floor.

"Mand?" He stepped before her and placed a finger under her chin, lifting. "Did I offend you in some way? Is it because you feel like maybe you can't afford to get him these things? Because I'm here now, in his life. I'm his father, and I don't make money like a normal person—"

She put up her hand, placing it on his chest. Damn, it felt good. "Reale. I'm thrilled you are in his life and able to afford those things for him. And as far as money, there is no one I know who comes anywhere near to making what you make. I'm not in competition with you. I am thrilled for you. And thrilled Johnny gets to reap the benefit of your incredible talent and all your hard work."

"Then what?" He stayed as close to her as he dared.

She lifted her head, making eye contact. "I'm sick to death of being me."

"Excuse me?" How could she be sick of being the most incredible person he knew?

She broke away from him and picked up her cell from where it was charging. She poked a code, pressed a button, and then turned the phone to him. "Take it. Go ahead. It's my email."

"Okay…" His eyes scanned down generic emails from stores and credit card companies.

"All I get, every day, is the same darned junk. Companies offering me credit cards. Stores telling me about upcoming sales. Charities looking for donations. Parent blog updates about things that will make me a better mother or about 'milestones my five-year-old should be reaching.' " She made air quotes as she spoke, shaking her head. "It's like I'm stuck in *Groundhog Day*. Same thing over and over."

"What would you like there to be?"

"I don't know!" She stormed to the fridge and yanked open the door. She stood, staring in, and then closed it with a thud. "I'm not hungry. Or thirsty." She turned to him. "You?"

"Un-unh." He scratched the scruff on his beard, and her eyes followed. "Mandy, I'm sorry. I don't understand."

"What's there to understand?" She lowered her voice, checking John was still engrossed in his game. She leaned in closer to Reale. "I'm nearly twenty-eight years old, and my entire existence is being a mom." She breathed heavily. "I haven't had any grown-up fun in…I don't know how long." She walked in a circle and stopped before him. "I am so grateful he's home and healthy and that his arm is almost healed, but sometimes…"

"Sometimes what?"

"I miss going out. I miss museums and concerts. I miss your concerts. I miss seedy bars and watery drinks. I miss Manhattan and life. I miss being around people. I miss having an identity that's not just 'Mom' as much as I love it." She shook her head. "I know, I sound so spoiled. I should count my lucky stars."

"Not spoiled, Mandy. You are grateful. The most grateful person I know. What you are is burnt out. But lucky for you, I am just the man to help with this. Come on, call Jess and ask her to babysit. I'm taking you out."

"Reale, you don't have to. You just brought all these gifts. I can't afford a night out, and I don't want you to have to pay." Her body leaned toward him.

"Mandy, please. Don't insult me." He handed her cell back to her. "When, in all our time together, have I ever allowed you to pay? I'm not going to start now. Call Jess and then go get changed."

She smirked at him, and her sexy little smile warmed him to his core.

****

"You sure you don't want to keep the car?" Reale was holding her hand as they walked the streets of the West Village at night.

"Un-unh."

She turned to him, flashing the biggest smile he had ever seen. Damn, she was beautiful. Damn, this was fun.

"I haven't walked the streets of Manhattan in years. And the Village at night…" She stopped short and inhaled deeply. "It smells divine."

"It smells like urine." He covered his nose.

She tilted her head back and forth. "Maybe a little, but mostly it smells like magic and freedom and excitement. Possibility." She threw her head back, laughing, and he was transfixed. "I haven't been out like this in…" She shook her head, her thought falling way.

"Me either."

She plopped a hand on her hip and turned to him. "Please. You party all the time. I read about it in the papers."

"Not all the time." Why did he feel sick thinking about the past few years of his life?

"You party enough. Who was that girl you used to live with? You two were always in the papers, getting drunk and causing havoc at three in the morning. Savannah something."

"I don't know." He turned away, rubbing a pain in his esophagus. This was something he would just as soon forget.

The city lights reflected in her gorgeous green eyes. "You don't know the name of the woman you were living with?"

"I wasn't living with her." He swallowed hard. "That was the media creating stories. We both had our own places. I've never lived with any woman but you."

Her eyes widened. "Really?"

"Yes."

She stared down at the sidewalk, shuffling her feet in her high-heeled boots. He took a moment to let his gaze travel up her not-too-tight jeans and onto her ever-so-slightly low-cut, black T-shirt that clung to her breasts perfectly, not overtly. On her wrist she wore a single, black leather bracelet, and her hair fell loosely down her back. She wore hardly any make-up—she didn't need any. Maybe some mascara and a nude gloss on her luscious lips. Damn those lips. Watching her mouth move when she spoke or when she chewed on that lip from nerves or excitement... Damn, damn, damn. He stepped aside and adjusted himself as inconspicuously as possible.

She shuffled from foot to foot again. She was uncomfortable, but why? He didn't want her to be uneasy, and whatever she had to say about this he sure as hell didn't want to hear. He rubbed at a knot the size of a truck in his gut.

"How 'bout you?" He kept his voice as cool and casual as possible. Thank God his voice would always obey him.

"How about me, what?"

"You live with anyone else these past few years?"

She laughed, placing a hand to her mouth, turning away and back again. "Live with someone else? Just Johnny."

His tense shoulders dropped as he relaxed. "Good. That's good."

"Why?" She searched his eyes, looking for the answer.

Why the hell was it good? She was a grown woman, and she had every right to see anyone she wanted. But... His core tingled, and his breathing deepened as he looked at her. She may not still be his, but at least she wasn't anyone else's.

"Reale? Why is that good?"

He cleared his throat and stepped closer. "How about boyfriends?"

She raised her eyebrows and looked to the ground. "I tried dating once. A couple of years ago. Right at the time I had read Savannah Whatever Her Name Was moved in with you."

"And?" This stung his soul, but he had to know.

"And nothing. He was a nice enough guy. House on the island. Office in the city. Went out with him twice. The first time we went to dinner on the island. It was perfectly bland."

"The food?"

"No." She shook her head. "Dinner was spicy Mexican."

"You hate Mexican food."

"Yeah, well." She shrugged. "He didn't bother to ask. And I do love margaritas."

"Yes, you do." He smiled at the memory of the two of them on their fire escape while he strummed his guitar and sang to her as they sipped margaritas until the wee hours of the morning. "What was bland?"

"Him. Me. The date."

"But you went out with him again. You said you saw him twice." Energy coursed up and down his veins. Had she slept with him? And why did he care?

She smiled. "The next time we went to a Broadway show."

He nodded, swallowing hard. "That's a good choice." At least the bastard came up with something decent eventually.

She stared into Reale's eyes, her face softening. "I cried through the entire first act."

"It was sad?"

"No." She scoffed. "I cried because being in Manhattan—it reminded me of you."

"Mandy." His heart ached and swelled simultaneously.

"I went out with this guy to forget you, and instead I spent the entire first act of this musical comedy bawling my eyes out."

"What happened for Act Two?"

"He took me home. Poor guy spent three hundred bucks a ticket and missed more than half the show."

"And?"

"And?" She giggled. "Can you imagine he didn't call me for another date?"

"Fool. His loss."

She tossed her head. "Yeah, I'm sure he thinks that."

"You really don't get out much?"

"Reale. This is a first for me." She looked herself up and down. "It's been so long I don't even know if I'm dressed okay."

"You look perfect. Stunning." She did. And the fact that she didn't date—that felt good. Way too good. "It's a first for me too. Walking around. No plans. Just chilling. No security."

"What?" She stepped back, her face changing from a look of excitement to horror. "Oh, Reale. I'm sorry. I didn't think. Will you be okay?"

He glanced about. "Seems so. Besides, I'm still hated. People are avoiding me right now."

"I doubt that. I'm sorry." She placed a cool hand on his cheek, warming his heart. "This was inconsiderate of me."

"Mandy." He took her hand from his cheek and placed it to his chest. He pulled her close. Their bodies were touching, and his breath raced to catch up with hers. "I am so happy to be here. With you. Like this."

"Really?" Her eyes flickered with hunger and passion.

Damn, yes. It was like old times, only he didn't want it that way. In the past. He wanted it like this always. Despite everything, he wanted a future with her. People rushed by and into a dive bar on the corner. Music spilled out onto the street.

"Margarita?" He nodded toward the bar.

"I'd love one."

"Only one?" He still held her close.

"I have to be alert when I get home in case Johnny needs anything."

"I could stay. Help out."

"Reale…" She dropped her chin, her voice a growl. "Besides, I have to be careful because of the migraines."

He nodded. "Well, let's make sure it's one hell of a drink, then."

She smiled.

"C'mon." Still holding her hand, he pulled her toward the bar.

She hesitated. "Reale. It's crowded, and you don't have security. Maybe we should go somewhere else?"

"Nah." He shook his head. "It's New York. No one will care I'm there." He held her hand tightly and pulled her gently through the door of the dive bar, happier than he had felt in years.

****

The hush that fell over the bar was almost comical. This was New York for heaven's sake. New Yorkers saw celebrities all the time—they weren't supposed to care about what was happening around them. Yet when

Reale Lynxx sauntered in wearing a white T-shirt that pulled across his chest, hanging untucked over his old faded jeans…darn. The place came to a standstill. And man, she couldn't blame anyone and everyone for staring. She'd been doing it all night.

She hesitated at the door, trying to get him to come to his senses and to go someplace less crowded, but he insisted. He made his way to the high wooden bar, and while he leaned across it, talking to the bartender, she hung back, gazing around the one big room with a few rickety dark wood tables and chairs strewn about, and walls chock-full of flyers advertising out-of-date and up-and-coming bands. The lead singer of the band playing spotted Reale and nodded to the guys in his band. The music grew louder and tighter. They were obviously trying to impress him. Then the noise level increased, and the bar full of New Yorkers ignored Reale and went back to their conversations. That was New York. She smiled. A bed of peanut shells crunched under her feet while she inhaled the smell of stale beer and sweet bourbon. Naturally he'd want to stay. Despite his millions and his swank surroundings, this place was Reale.

Her breath caught in her throat. This place was *so* Reale, in fact, it was exactly like the last bar she had seen him play in. That night she'd walked out on their life. The back of her head tingled, and her neck grew hot. Tears prickled the corners of her eyes.

"Mand?" He turned to her, oblivious to the havoc he was causing around him. "I got us margaritas on the rocks with extra salt—" His brow furrowed as he stared into her eyes. "Mandy? What's the matter? You're not happy here?"

She shook her head and bit the corner of her lip. "No, that's not it." She sighed, turning her eyes up to his. This crowded, noisy bar was the last place they should get into this, yet her body ached with the desire to apologize. She couldn't go even one second more without telling him. "I'm sorry, Reale."

"About what?" He turned to her, giving her his full attention. "You need to go?"

"No, no. I—this isn't the time or the place, but I'm sorry for walking out on you. I'm sorry for hurting you so badly." She swallowed a lump in her throat. "I'm sorry for not having more faith in you. In us. I believed in your talent so much; the last thing I wanted was for you to miss your chance because of me. Because of Johnny and me. I truly believed it was for the best. I wanted everything for you. I honestly believed I was doing the right thing." She stared up at him, his bright blue eyes sparkling.

He reached out and placed a hand on her cheek. He rubbed his thumb gently up and down. "I know, Mandy."

Tears sprang to her eyes. He understood, but did he forgive her? Could he ever? Could she ever forgive him? It didn't matter tonight. Tonight they were together, and she was going to enjoy every second of it.

He took her hand and pulled her to his side. They stood tight to one another, facing the bar, waiting for their drinks. She nuzzled against his side—he was strong and virile and oh, Lord help her, he smelled so good. The drinks were placed before them, but she didn't move. When he lifted his arm to hand money across the bar to tip the bartender, she caught a glimpse of the sweat stain in his armpit and a whiff of his scent.

Oh, damn. She closed her eyes, inhaling deeply. That scent…it was pure sex and freedom and rock and roll. It was hot summer nights on their fire escape, fumbling through the opened window, tearing each other's clothes off and making love right there on the stiff, uncomfortable rug in their tiny sitting area because they couldn't wait to walk the few feet to the bed. Sweat would pour off him, mixing with hers, as he hovered above her, finding his way deep inside her…making her his.

She squeezed her legs together and nuzzled closer to him still. She could smell sex on him. That extra muskiness underneath it all. She closed her eyes, inhaling his scent and their youth. This was all too good. It was too easy to slip back into six years ago, before she was even pregnant with Johnny.

He brought his arm back from across the bar and wrapped it around her, pulling her closer. He positioned her to face him, and their bodies were touching, face to face, chest to chest, hips to hips. He moved, pressing against her. Damn. He wanted her as much as she wanted him. She opened her eyes.

"Are you sure it's a good idea to hold me?" She balanced on her tiptoes as she spoke into his ear.

"Feels like the best idea ever." His words were mellow in her ear, and he pressed against her once more.

"Mmmm…" She exhaled audibly as she fought to focus. "But everyone has a phone. They're going to snap pictures of us."

"Yeah? So?" He pulled back but kept his hands wrapped around her waist. "I don't have a wife who's going to get mad. Any reason you can think of you don't want to be in the paper with me?"

"No." She wanted to be anywhere and everywhere with him.

"Okay, then." He nuzzled her ear as he spoke.

She placed a hand to her forehead, calming herself. "I'm lightheaded, and I haven't even had a sip of my drink yet."

He smirked. "Well, let's rectify that." He took his arms from around her waist and grabbed the drinks off the bar. "C'mon. There's a table in the far corner in the back. Bartender told me. We can have some privacy." Reale released a deep, sexy growl. "He warned it might be loud, though, because of the proximity to the band." He raised his eyebrows, grinning.

She nodded. "I think we can handle it. You?"

"Something tells me we'll be fine."

"Yeah." She smiled and followed him across the room and to the tiny table hidden in the back of the bar.

****

"Okay, in sixteen seconds, name sixteen animals that start with the letter P."

"Sixteen?" Sitting across the table from Mandy, Reale leaned forward, smiling. This was the dumbest game he had ever tried to play, but she was loving it. And to see that smile—damn, he would have played hopscotch on the bar. The bar was quiet now that the band had finished their final set, and the bartender had only a few stragglers, but at—he glanced at the time on his phone—three forty, most everyone had moved on for the night. Probably gone home to hook up or sleep it off. Unfortunately, the latter was the only choice for him tonight.

"C'mon. No cheating. I saw you glance at your

phone. No searching answers."

He smiled. She was so relaxed right now; he hadn't seen her that way since those few, freaking amazing nights on Fire Island. Damn, it was incredible to be here with her again. She tossed her head, her eyes glassy from the alcohol, her defenses down.

"Hey, rock star, that's the game. Sixteen animals. And just so you know, your son can get to the letter X." She shrugged. "I think it's impossible to get beyond, but we'll see." She raised her eyebrows as she held his designer watch in her fingers. She pressed the stopwatch.

"No, wait." He held up his hand, laughing, and took another sip of his drink.

"There's no waiting." She giggled. "Three seconds are gone. This is the championship round. You're going to looooossssseeee...." She giggled as she sipped her margarita.

"Okay. Okay. Panda. Possum...puh..." His mind was blank when he stared at her.

"That's all you've got? Two animals?"

"No, no. Uh...Peter! Paul. Petunia."

She put up her free hand. "Those are names. Not animals."

"Oh, no." He shook his head. "People are animals. And I know a Peter and a Paul."

"You know a Petunia?" She tilted her head.

"Okay, no. I don't know a Petunia. But I know a Pat. And a Philip."

"All right. All right. I guess I'll let you have those because of your compelling argument, and besides"—she shook his watch in her hand—"you're out of time."

"Damn. Does that mean I lose?"

"Yup." She leaned forward closer to him. Her breasts were resting against the table. Damn, they looked good. "And if you stopped staring at my breasts for a moment, you'd realize that you losing means I win."

"Oh, really." He leaned closer still, until he could feel her warm breath on him. She was barely an inch away. It would be so easy to kiss her… "And what do you win?"

"How about another margarita?" She held up her nearly empty glass.

He took it from her hand and placed it onto the table. "Sorry, champ. You've been nursing that thing for hours. One's your limit. I'm already going to be carrying you out of here."

"Nonsense." She waved him off and stood to show. "See? I'm—" As if on cue, she wavered, and he jumped from his seat to steady her.

He eased her back down into her chair. "As I was saying. I'll be carrying you home."

"Home." Her word was wistful.

"You want to go home?"

She shook her head. "No. Not at all. I never want to go." She reached out and grabbed his arm. "I want to stay. With you. In Manhattan. Forever."

He stroked her hair lovingly. "I want that too, Mandy. Tonight was amazing, but we have responsibilities elsewhere."

"Yes." She sighed.

"And I know you're burnt out, and you need way more than one night of fun, but we need to get home to John."

"Yes." She swallowed hard, and her eyes filled

with tears.

"Mandy? What's up?"

"Am I the worst for wanting to be away from him for a night? Truth be told, I never even checked in with Jess."

"Because you knew he'd be fine."

"Yes, but he's sleeping at her place, and what if he needs…?"

"Mandy. I've been texting her. John is fine. Fell asleep at eight thirty because they were watching a movie, and she carried him to bed. He's fine. And happy. See?" He held up his phone for her to read the texts that had gone back and forth during the night.

She studied the phone. "You did that? While I was partying?"

He chuckled. "You were hardly partying. You've had three-quarters of one margarita. But yes. I checked in on our son. And he is our son. As much my responsibility as yours—"

Before he could finish his words, she stood, and leaning across the table, she kissed him full on the mouth.

Chapter Seventeen

Oh. No. Amanda stood in the doorway between her living room and kitchen, watching Reale Lynxx crack eggs and move about like he was their live-in chef. Which could be fine. Fun even…if it didn't mean seeing him here this morning meant he absolutely, positively spent the night. And considering the mood she was in last night… Oh. No.

"Mornin', sunshine." He grinned as he carried a pan full of scrambled eggs with a wooden spoon sticking out the top toward the kitchen table. He waved with his free hand.

She hovered in the doorway, her terror momentarily forgotten as she lifted her nose into the air, sniffing, following the scent of good coffee with as much finesse as a bloodhound on a cold fall morning hunting quail. Mmm. She approached the kitchen—and Reale—warily.

"Um, Reale…you're here."

"'Course I'm here. Making breakfast. Had some groceries delivered. We only got home a few hours ago."

Home. Was he living here now?

"Uh-huh." She scratched an itchy spot on her scalp. Johnny was at the table, good. "Thanks for picking up Johnny for me."

Reale whistled and winked at her. Damn, he was

too happy.

Johnny never looked up, completely locked into his tablet. Huh. She had a strict, no-tablet-at-the-table rule, but right now, she'd make an exception just to find out if she had broken her own strict, do-not-sleep-with-your-rock-and-roll-ex-boyfriend-no-matter-how-sexy-he-is rule.

"And um, where did we—or more specifically, did you—sleep last night?" Her heart pounded in her chest.

"Don't you remember?" He waltzed past her and placed his scrambled egg pan onto the stove before stuffing two slices of whole grain bread into the toaster.

She turned to him, mortified. "No. Uh, I'm sorry. But uh…"

He smiled, grabbing his pan again and crossing to the table, expertly sliding eggs onto Johnny's plate. "Seconds." He nodded toward Johnny proudly.

"But, you slept where exactly?"

"Babe. You were drunk. I carried you in the house, changed you into your PJs, and slid you into bed. I slept on the couch. Scout's honor." He held up his peace fingers, making a V.

"That's the wrong sign, dumbo." She smirked. "So nothing happened?"

He came closer, whispering so Johnny couldn't hear. "As tempting as it was, what with your ruddy glow and contagious laugh, I figured after you had sung every song on my last CD to me, twice, you were perhaps a bit too intoxicated to partake in any additional activities that evening. Or morning."

She slapped her hand to her forehead. "I am so embarrassed."

"No." He shook his head, twirling the wooden

spoon in the eggs. "Don't be, babe. You were having fun. You were beautiful, and your voice sounded pretty darned good."

"Oh, sure." Her gaze followed him around the kitchen, and she shielded her eyes from the glare of the one tiny window. "Could someone please close that?" She nodded to the curtains at the window.

"Migraine?" His happy demeanor darkened.

She shook her head. "No." She placed the side of her hand to her mouth, whispering so Johnny couldn't hear. "Hangover."

"Ah." Reale chuckled as he closed the curtains with one hand. "Luckily for you, I happen to be a leading authority on such conditions."

"Oh, I'll bet." She rolled her aching eyes.

He stood tall, squaring his shoulders. "Let's leave the snide remarks at the door, shall we, and see what Dr. Reale prescribes?" He held up the pan, nodding toward the eggs. "Like a greasy breakfast."

"Fine." She shuffled into the kitchen and toward her chair.

Before she could sit, he snuck up behind her, patting her bottom. "I would check that nasty attitude if I were you."

Shaking off her fog, she whipped around to face him. He was grinning, the big, sexy louse. Darn him. His white teeth were gleaming, his eyes sparkling.

He raised his eyebrows in a dare. "Wanna push that attitude?"

He picked up the wooden spoon he'd used to scoop the eggs, and God help her, she giggled in response. A warmth rose from her belly, flushing her cheeks, as a definite dull ache radiated its way downward. Her nipples hardened in response and poked through her flimsy T-shirt. His eyes flashed to her nipples and back up to her eyes again. He was too much. She needed to sit to release some of the mounting pressure. Darn that Reale Lynxx, and darn her body for reacting toward him in this way.

"Wanna push that attitude?"

She bit the corner of her lip, smirking. Heck yeah, she wanted to. "I guess it's best if I don't."

She smoothed her oversized pajama bottoms beneath her and sat in her chair as he eased it to the table for her.

He nodded. "That's better." He pointed to her glass. "Drink your juice."

She lifted the short juice glass, spotting pulp. "Is this fresh squeezed?" She glanced at him. "You made this?"

"You bet." He nodded. "Found a juicer packed away in the back of the cabinet with all the pots and pans. I'm surprised you don't use it. I mean, you're a health freak, so why not?"

"I'm hardly a health freak." She took a sip and placed her glass back onto the table. "And yeah, well. Time. You know?" Time, and fresh fruits and veggies were way too expensive to waste them on a juicer.

"Okay." He nodded, giving a small smile. He understood. "Eggs are coming and"—he leaned over, dropping toast onto her plate—"toast. The bulk of the food and the grease from the margarine, although it's some healthy, low-fat crap, will begin making you feel better. Drink more. The orange juice will help hydrate you. Force down as much water as you can stomach today."

"Thanks."

"You're welcome." He stood beside her, shoveling a few more scrambled eggs onto her plate. He leaned down over her, so close. He smelled so darned good... Was he going to kiss her? She glimpsed Johnny still locked into a game. He'd never know. She turned toward Reale, raising her mouth, her breathing racing faster and faster...

"One margarita." He chuckled. "What a lightweight." He smiled and kissed her on the tip of her nose, laughing under his breath.

"Ha, ha." She turned to face her son and grabbed her glass of orange juice. Sure, she was edgy and tense, but she'd have to cool it for a bit. They were here—the three of them together—and this was an incredibly nice Sunday morning. It was almost like they were a real family. "Um, any coffee? It smells delicious."

"Finishing brewing."

She nodded, glancing at the cabinet where he'd found the juicer. Was it possible he'd found her mug— the one he'd given her—hidden back there too? She stole a peek at him. If he did, he wasn't talking. She turned to her son who still had not acknowledged her. "Morning, Johnny. Did you have fun with Aunt Jess last night?"

"Um-hm." Johnny swooshed his finger across his tablet, all but ignoring her.

"Nope. No way." She reached across and placed her hand on the tablet, flattening it to the table. "You're not ignoring my question over a game."

"But I was almost past that level," Johnny whined as his gaze found hers.

"Well, I don't care if—"

Reale stepped up. "May I?" he questioned Amanda as he placed her coffee—in her mug—before her, like he did every morning, all those years ago. He'd found the mug, but why not mention it? Had he forgotten?

"Uh, yeah. Yes. Sure." Glancing at her cup, she eyed the cartooned cityscape of Manhattan with the little red heart painted above their building. That heart was as bright as ever, even after countless hand-washings. She shifted in her seat. Yes, it would be better if he didn't remember, but damn, how she wanted him to. The aroma of her coffee snapped her from her melancholy. She peeked into the cup. The coffee smelled so good. It couldn't be her canned coffee she'd bought on sale at the drugstore.

Reale spoke calmly to Johnny. "John. Your mom has a rule, and we had a deal. No tablet at the table unless its homework at homework time. Isn't that right, Mom?" He turned to her.

"Uh, yes. That's right." She held her cup tightly, feebly covering the design, desperate for cream, but her head was booming, and the refrigerator was so far away.

Reale shrugged, still speaking to Johnny. "Sorry, little man. Tablet off the table. Besides, I want to hear some applause and rave reviews for my extra-super-deluxe scrambled eggs." He popped over to the toaster and pulled out two more pieces of well-browned bread. He plopped them onto a nearby plate and spread margarine across the top, and then reached back and grabbed the tiny container of half and half from the fridge.

She took a sip of juice while she waited.

"Hey, buddy." Reale smiled at his son. "It's not

231

just my eggs that rock. No one, I mean no one, can make toast like me. And my fresh squeezed juice, fuhgeddaboudit."

Johnny giggled as Reale slid across the room, delivering toast to Johnny with the container of cream tight in his other hand. Reale didn't just walk—when he was "on" like he was this morning, the man could glide across a room, and she couldn't help but get caught up in it. *Darn your sexiness, Reale Lynxx*. She sighed as he poured cream into her cup, and then lifted and twirled the cup, stirring the cream into the coffee without the need of a spoon.

She glanced up at him, taking in his gorgeous but tired face in the low morning light. "Thank you."

"You're welcome."

She held her mug in her hands. Morning coffee. From Reale. In her mug. Just as he had once promised he would always bring her. She lifted the cup to her lips, inhaling the aroma so good it was nearly orgasmic, and took a long gulp. Dear God. This was the best coffee she had ever tasted. It was mellow and rich but light, like the flavor hovered above her tongue instead of coating it. Her eyes widened as she looked up at Reale.

"This is the best thing I've ever had to drink. Ever." She stared into her cup, mesmerized. "What is it?"

He shrugged. "Coffee."

She shook her head. "No way, mister. I've had coffee. I've served a million cups of coffee. What the heck is this?"

"If you want to know, it's Jamaican Blue Mountain."

"Jamaican Blue Mountain." She repeated the name, committing it to memory. "Well, now I'll never be able to go back to my usual swill, thank you very much. I've got to pick some up next time I'm at the store."

"Nah." He waved his hand away as he poured coffee into his plain, white porcelain mug that came from the diner. Those plain mugs were gifts from Nick, along with most of her dishes. Placing the coffee pot on a trivet on the table, Reale sat down in the chair opposite her. He raised his mug. "I'll keep you in coffee."

"Well that's very nice of you, but our arrangement specifically states you only support Johnny. And since he doesn't drink coffee…" She patted Johnny's hand as he shoveled in another bite of Reale's eggs. "I'll be buying this for myself. A special treat."

"The coffee runs about five hundred dollars a pound. There are cheaper brands and much more expensive ones. But this is my favorite."

She placed both hands on her cup, holding it still, terrified to spill a drop. "Five hundred dollars a pound? How much would this cup of coffee I'm drinking cost?"

"I don't know. What's a pound of coffee make, thirty cups? So whatever five hundred—"

"Over sixteen dollars a cup."

"Yeah?"

She nodded. "Five hundred divided by thirty is roughly sixteen dollars and fifty cents a cup."

"I'm amazed you can do that in your head."

"I'm amazed I'm drinking sixteen dollars' worth of coffee in one cup." She shook her head. "Wow. My pound of coffee costs four bucks."

He tilted his head. "Can you really call that

coffee?"

She laughed. "Hey, remember the fabulous coffee you used to get us from the street cart on Bleecker?"

"Remember?" He smiled, sitting back. "I'm still trying to reproduce that coffee. I used to grab as many cups as I could carry and pour it into your mug." He pointed to her coffee. "That one. You remember?"

She nodded. She would never forget. Never. And apparently, neither would he.

"Damn. That guy used to charge us twenty-five cents a cup. What a deal." He shook his head at the memory. "That was because of you, you know." He nodded to her.

"What?"

"We got cheap coffee because the guy had a crush on you."

She scrunched up her face. "No way. Not a chance."

"How could you doubt it? You are still the most gorgeous woman I have ever known."

She ran a hand through her matted hair as heat rushed her cheeks. "Oh? Is it my oversized plaid pajamas? Or my tangled hair and teeth that feel like they are wearing a fur coat?"

"Yes." He grinned. "All of it. You're stunning, Mandy."

She shook her head, sighing. "Thank you, Reale." Her ears heated as embarrassment flooded over her. She leaned back, grasping her mug in her hands, sipping her coffee. "Mmmmm. Heaven." She glanced at him. "He only charged us a quarter a cup because of you."

"He had a crush on me? No way. He used to stare at you constantly."

"No, he didn't have a crush. But he knew you were a struggling musician, and he wanted to help us out."

He narrowed his eyes, thinking. "Really? Then why'd he charge us full price after we comped him tickets to that show on Bleecker?"

She put a hand to her mouth, giggling. She glanced at him and leaned forward, her shoulders bouncing up and down in time with her chuckling.

"What?" He tilted his head.

She doubled over in her seat, peals of laughter falling from her. The laughter came faster and faster and harder and harder, her sides aching and her chest burning. Her pounding head throbbed, but she couldn't care. She was laughing too hard. She gasped for air, barely able to breathe. She slapped her leg and then sat back as she gripped the table for support.

"What? Mandy?" He was laughing along with her. "What's so funny?"

"He stopped—" She chortled. "I'm sorry." Laughter overtook her again.

"C'mon, Mand. What's the story? I knew you knew it."

"The coffee guy. He stopped giving us cheap coffee after he heard you play because he thought you were so—"

"What?" He chuckled, caught up in her laugh. "He thought I was so great I wouldn't need it?"

She shook her head, almost falling off her chair. She glanced at Johnny who was grinning as he bit into another piece of toast. She turned to Reale. "No. He thought you were so *awful* he didn't want to encourage you!" She fell to the floor, laughing, her sides aching.

Reale's booming laugh echoed through the kitchen.

"He did?"

She nodded, sucking in huge gulps of air between laughs.

"Oh, Mandy. I never knew. That explains why he didn't come to another show even when I offered."

Still on the floor, she sat up and gripped the chair, leaning against it.

"Mommy's on the floor!" Johnny clapped, thrilled.

Reale gazed at her sitting there. "How come you never told me?" He put out his hand to help her up, and she accepted. Little zaps of electricity shot up her arms as he guided her to her chair.

She climbed up onto her seat and wiped away her tears from laughter. "Because he was wrong. And I would never let anyone discourage you. Or hurt you."

He winced at her words.

"Oh, I—" Damn. She looked away, settling into the chair.

He reached out and took her hand, stroking it with his strong, talented fingers. "Hey. It's okay. I've made peace with…everything. This time I had John to myself, I realized how hard being a single parent is. And I spent some time trying to see the decision you made from your point of view, and honestly, although I'm not happy with it, I understand now what you did was incredibly selfless and brave."

"It was?" Her eyes widened as her breath raced again.

"Yes." He lifted her fingers to his lips and kissed. Warmth radiated through her body. "I can't say I'm happy with how it all happened, or that it took this long for me to find out."

She nodded. "I know. I'm sorry."

He shook his head. "I don't need you to be sorry. As hard as it was for me to understand, I know you did it for me." He ran his free hand through his spiky hair. "And damn, that's a huge weight for both of us to carry."

"Yes."

He leaned forward and wrapped both hands around hers. "So we shouldn't anymore. We have to let go of the past if we're going to go forward."

"What?"

"I'm talking about moving forward, Mandy. As a family."

"Uh…" Slipping her hand from his powerful grasp, she turned to Johnny. "Did you have enough to eat?"

He nodded.

"I would think so. Why don't you head into your bedroom for a few minutes to play a game while Reale and I have a grown-up conversation?"

"Okay." Johnny stood and picked up his empty plate.

She put her hand on his. "I've got it, don't worry."

Johnny smiled as he grabbed his tablet from the counter and took off for his room. She watched him go and then turned back to face Reale. His intense eyes were locked on hers.

"A grown-up conversation, huh? Sounds heavy." He sat back, twirling his fork.

She placed her elbows on the table and her head in her hands, rubbing her temples. "Reale. Moving forward. As a family. What are you saying?" She lifted her head, searching his eyes for the answer.

"I think it's kind of self-explanatory, Mand."

"But how do you propose we do that? How?" She

shook her head. "How do we move forward?"

"We decide to forgive each other."

"But Reale. I thank you for your effort in trying to see my side over the decision I made all those years ago, but…"

"But?" He raised his eyebrows hopefully.

"But all I see is anger when I think of what you did to Johnny and me. *Your* anger. I don't see your decision stemming from any place of care or concern. Even if it was skewed."

He nodded. "I know." He locked his gaze on hers. "Are you ever going to be able to get past this?"

She leaned forward and stroked his arm. "I don't want to hold a grudge. I like being with you, and I love that Johnny has his dad. But I've told you before, you and I…" She shook her head. "We can never be."

"But what about last night? It was like old times." He nodded to her coffee mug. "The two of us, in Manhattan."

"Yes. And we were both playing a role. Darn, Reale, I was even wearing the same clothes I used to wear when we were together. Literally the same clothes."

"But we were happy last night. We could have that again. On tour. We could travel the world and—"

"Wait, wait, wait." She put up her hand, stopping him. "On tour? Reale. Did you learn nothing over these past few months of being Johnny's father? We can't start him in school and then yank him out. And I'm finishing school myself. We can't up and go to…*wherever* with you."

"I'm not being foolish. I've given it some thought. I would get him tutors. And lots of guys bring their families on tour. They're on the road together." He shook his head. "Mandy, last night, there was something there."

"Yes, but how can I trust that you won't rip Johnny away from me again the next time you don't like what I do?"

"It's not that simple."

"No, it's not. But we've spoken about this over and over. You have unlimited means and resources. Anytime you want to, you can yank Johnny away from me. And I have no recourse. I'm unable to fight you. I have no money and no power. How can I know it won't happen again?"

"You have to trust me."

She squeezed his hand. "I want to, Reale. God knows I want to. This is not about getting even. I'm not holding a grudge. But you put me through hell. And Johnny too. On purpose. With no ulterior motive except to hurt me and get even. How can I ever get past that? When will I ever be able to let down my guard and know we're safe?" She glanced at the table and back to him. "I imagine this must be what it's like to be an abused woman. To believe in your soul you're with the right man...until that first time he hits you. Then all trust is broken. No matter what he says, how can you ever believe that right hook isn't going to be aimed at your head again? And Reale, could you ever respect me if I put Johnny in the way of that punch?" She shook her head as she let go of his hand. "God knows I would never respect myself for going back."

"So that's it?" His eyes were alive with fire and pain.

"I can't see any other way." Her throat ached as

she choked out the words.

He nodded, swallowing hard. "Well." He stood.

"You're going?" She glanced up at him.

"Yeah." He scoffed. "I think it's best."

"Okay." Her stomach clenched and her voice faltered. She was right in what she said. And he should go. But why did it ache in her soul? She stood. "Uh, thank you, Reale. For last night and this morning. For all of it."

"Sure." He nodded toward Johnny's room. "I just want to say goodbye."

"Of course. Go ahead."

"Nah. I'll say goodbye here if you don't mind getting him for me."

"Oh, uh…" She turned and walked to Johnny's room, feeling Reale's gaze on her. She took a deep breath and pushed open the door to Johnny's room. "Johnny? Come say goodbye to Reale. He has to go."

"What? No." Johnny tossed his tablet onto the bed and crossed his arms. He sat tight on his bed.

She sighed. "Johnny, please. Please. Come." She had no patience right now.

Reluctantly he hopped off his bed and made his way to the kitchen. She followed.

"You're leaving?" Johnny's face fell as he stared up at Reale. "I don't want you to go." Johnny clamped his arms around Reale's waist.

"I know. I gotta get some stuff done, buddy. I need to get some work done today."

"Can I help?" Johnny looked up at his father with such expectancy Amanda's eyes filled with tears.

"Sorry, little man. I need to record. I'll pick you up Tuesday morning when Mommy starts her shift, okay?"

He ruffled Johnny's hair and unattached his son.

Her ovaries ached as she watched them together. Reale walked to the kitchen door, and she followed. He pulled open the door, and she held it for him.

"Well, uh. Bye, Mandy."

Her throat tightened as she fought back the tears in her eyes. "Bye, Reale."

"Mommy?" Johnny tugged on her pajama pants. "If Reale is leaving, what are we going to do today? I want to do something fun!"

She sighed, fighting back tears as Reale walked out the door, and all the joy she had felt went out the door with him. Lumbering back to the table, she fell heavily into her chair. She spun her mug with her fingertips. They had been so happy last night. So happy together. How could it hurt this much just a few hours later? Of course. It's like Jess had told her. The higher you fly, the farther you fall.

That was the risk of happiness.

Chapter Eighteen

"It's nice of you to be here for Johnny. And…with me," Mandy whispered to Reale as they stood together inside the door of John's kindergarten classroom. They were apart from the small group of parents, and they were all watching as each child approached the teacher, Mrs. Flagstaff, to tell his or her name and get a nametag. It was the parents' job to wait patiently.

"Of course."

She went on like she always did when she was nervous. "It's nice that he has both parents here. I mean, he's one of the only kids who has two parents present."

"Yes." No way he was going to miss John's first day of kindergarten, and no way Mandy could handle it herself. Jess had texted him a week ago to tell him Mandy was a hot mess about the whole thing, bawling her eyes out through her shift at work. He would never make her go through this alone. "Look." He pointed to the Lynxx backpack tucked neatly into John's cubby. "Nice fit, right?"

She nodded. "Maybe I should have snuck Peanut into his backpack. Just in case."

"No, Mandy. Peanut's waiting at home where he belongs."

John glanced at them and waved. They waved back.

"Oh, my goodness." She placed a shaking hand to her chest.

Even though they weren't touching, he could feel her body tensing next to him. "Mandy, you just need to hold it together a few more minutes."

"I know." She sniffed. "I promised myself I wouldn't cry until I was out the door, but he looks so grown-up sitting there in his uniform, doesn't he?" She shook her head and smoothed her hand down her beautifully simple, navy-blue dress with a loose-knit, navy cardigan thrown over. She slid her heel out and back into one of her beige pumps repeatedly. "Oh, it's his turn." She pointed to John.

Reale grabbed her hand, and she inhaled as he held her protectively. Tears formed in her eyes as John walked to the teacher and proudly called himself "John."

She turned to Reale, her eyes wide. "John?"

She mouthed the word, and Reale smiled.

"Okay." She collected herself, her gaze following John as he walked back to the thick, robin's-egg-blue carpet. She exhaled when he sat. She looked around the room and leaned toward Reale. "I knew full-day kindergarten was too much. For heaven's sake, it looks like a college classroom in here."

He nodded. "Yes, posters of furry monsters like the ones on the walls here are hanging in lecture halls of major universities across the country." He prodded her with his elbow.

"Oh, ha, ha." She turned to him. "You don't think it's too grown-up?"

"I think it's perfect." It was. The problem was, he wasn't perfect. He was far from it. And because of that, the other more "proper" Long Island families avoided him, and he and Mandy were isolated from the rest of the group. That was fine for him—gave them a chance to speak without bothering anyone—but would his fame and rep forever ostracize his family? He glanced at Mandy. Yes, she and John, they were his family, whether they lived together or not. She began nervously picking at her nails. The poor thing.

He leaned over to whisper in her ear. "The classroom is amazing, bright colors, a friendly teacher. And the school is state-of-the-art, I mean, did you see the music room? They have a full-sized baby grand." He stood tall.

"I did see that, yes."

"Wow." He shook his head. "School was nothing like this when I went." He turned to her. "Thank you, Mandy. For putting in all the time and research to find this school. And thank you for writing the letters to get him in."

"Well, we never would have gotten in at this late date without your celebrity name and money."

"Then I'd say we make a good team, how 'bout you?"

She glanced up at him. "Yes. I suppose we do."

"Okay, mommies and daddies!" Mrs. Flagstaff clapped her hands. "We are getting ready to start our morning game, so we'll need for you to head to the cafeteria." She picked up a guitar and started strumming.

"Oh, my gosh," Reale whispered. "The woman plays guitar too!"

Mandy giggled. "You want me to give you some alone time with Mrs. Flagstaff? She couldn't be a day over seventy-five."

"Cute, Mandy. Really cute."

"Okay boys and girls, let's sing the 'Goodbye Song.' You'll learn it soon, but for right now, follow along. The words are over the whiteboard."

"The words?" Mandy grabbed Reale's arm, wrapping her hand around the sleeve of the dark gray sport jacket she had asked him to wear. "He can't read well. What if he's the only one?"

"Mandy." He bent down to whisper into her ear. "That one kid over there is chewing her hair." He pointed discreetly to another. "That one is picking his nose, and yup, you got it, eating it."

"Oh, gross." She wrinkled her nose, turning away.

"And that one over there." He nodded with his chin. "The one with the short cut hair, he has been staring at the same ceiling tile since the moment he sat down. May not be on the same planet as the rest of us."

She giggled, and the sound was more beautiful than any melody he had ever written.

"I think John's got this. Let's give him some credit. He's freaking amazing."

"Yes, he is."

"Come on." He took her by the hand, and it felt so damned right. Having their son in this school and walking out of class together filled him with a sense of completeness he had never before felt. "As great as she is as a teacher, I can't listen to her sing anymore. Mrs. Flagstaff is going to develop a node if she sings that way any longer." He scowled. "Somebody's got to teach her to stop straining her voice."

"Well, it's the last verse." Mandy pointed to the words over the whiteboard.

"Oh, whew." He gripped her hand tighter. "Come on. Let's head to the cafeteria for the Boo-Hoo breakfast."

"The what?"

"Wait." He pulled back, staring at her. "Are you telling me there was an email I read that you didn't?"

"I may have been in denial these past couple of weeks." She shrugged. "But don't worry, all immunization records and papers from the doctor and such have been turned in."

"I have no doubt." He smiled. "But that doesn't change the fact that you don't know about the Boo-Hoo breakfast." He tugged on her arm, pulling her gently. "Come on. I'm taking you. All the pastries you can eat and all the tissues you need to blow your nose."

She hesitated and turned to look at John. "I need to say goodbye."

He held her firmly. "Nope. Un-unh. The rules say we leave without a fuss. No more hugs or kisses. The poor kid's been slobbered on enough."

She turned to Reale. "I don't think I can do this."

He nodded. "Yes, you can. Because it will give him the confidence to know he can do it."

She nodded, swallowing hard.

"Mandy, I will be there with you. Every step of the way."

"Promise?" She gazed up at him with her giant jade-colored eyes that were filled with so much vulnerability his heart lurched.

"I promise." He squeezed her hand as he led her out of John's classroom and down the hall.

****

"Here." Reale handed Mandy what must have been

the fortieth tissue.

"Thank you." She dabbed beneath her beautiful eyes and blew her adorable nose. He reached out his hand again, and again she placed her used tissue into it. "You don't have to—"

"Mandy." He cocked his head.

"Thank you."

He jogged to the nearest garbage and tossed in the tissues before hurrying back to her side. "I've got to say it again. This is the best smelling school cafeteria I've ever encountered. Smells like a restaurant, doesn't have that horrid smell of warm plastic trays and brown slop I remember from grade school. The menu says they're having whole grain pizza and organic steamed carrots for lunch. With organic low-fat milk and a low-sugar chocolate chip cookie made with coconut oil." He smiled at her. "Mandy, this is your dream menu for John."

"I suppose." She glanced wistfully about. "And I did pack him a lunch just in case."

"Yes." He nodded. "The boy will not be hungry. For sure."

She glanced up at him, her eyes widening. "Do you think he understands it's okay to eat what he wants? I mean, either one? He doesn't have to worry about wasting today?"

"Mandy. Please. Please stop worrying. You explained everything, and he's a smart kid. And he'll be home in a few hours."

She nodded.

"Hey." He held up the remains of his cinnamon roll. "These pastries are fabulous. You ready for a muffin?"

"No, thanks." She rubbed at her belly again. "I can't eat right now." She glanced away and back. "I guess I'm attracting attention with all my crying. There's a couple who has been staring at us nonstop. Or more likely, you have a fan alert."

"Oh, I doubt that. My demographic seems to be angry young men and the occasional pissed off teen girl."

"Well, Mr. and Mrs. Preppy over there"—she nodded discreetly—"haven't taken their eyes off you."

He glanced their way and back. "Really, Mandy? You think matching plaid jackets and duck boots over there are listening to me rant and rave onstage about the state of society?"

"You don't rant and rave. You make incredible, cutting-edge music. You are a genius."

He chuckled. Damn, she was some support system. "Well, genius may be pushing it a tad, but thank you." He took a deep breath as happiness washed over him. This must be what it's supposed to feel like to be a father: contented. His son was happy in a great school, and he was here to pick up the pieces for his loving and emotional other half. To support her anyway she needed. Damn, yeah. He hadn't felt this sense of accomplishment, maybe…ever.

He smiled at Mandy as Mr. and Mrs. Preppy began walking toward them.

"Oh, crap." Mandy patted the tears under her eyes. She turned, glancing up at Reale. "Am I a mess? They're coming our way. I don't want to talk to them if I have makeup running all over my face."

"You look beautiful." She did. Absolutely stunning.

She smiled, sighing as the couple approached. She was the first to offer a greeting. "Hello!" She spoke brightly. "I'm Amanda."

She put out her hand, and the woman took Mandy's hand, shaking it. The woman's hand was like a limp fish.

"I'm Marjorie. With a J," the woman said, letting go and turning to her husband. "And this is Arnold."

"Also with a J?" Reale chuckled as he reached out his hand to shake with Arnold. Arnold's hand was soft and hot, and his shoulders stooped forward when he shook hands. Definitely a pencil pusher of some kind.

"Uh, no." The woman raised her eyebrows, stepping back from Reale as if he smelled like he hadn't showered in a month.

"Um. Anyway. Nice to meet you. I'm Reale." He put out his hand for the woman, but she dismissed him with a prim smile.

"Yes. We know who you are."

"Okayyyy…" All the happiness he had felt a moment before drained from his head down his body and out his toes. His body tingled with adrenaline. He felt alive, but in a different way—a primal way—as if something were about to attack, and it was his job to defend.

Mandy wedged herself in front of Reale, addressing Marjorie with a J. "Do you have a son or daughter in Mrs. Flagstaff's class?"

"A son. Arnold Livingston Scottsdale the third."

"Wow." Reale nodded. "Great name."

"Thank you." Marjorie with a J looked him up and down, from his thousand-dollar shoes up to his fitted, white shirt with the top two buttons undone. He'd offered to wear a tie, but Mandy said no. She never wanted to change him—she only ever wanted to play by the rules. Marjorie with a J gave a thin-lipped smile. "It's a family name. Obviously."

"Obviously." Why was he letting her get to him like this? What did he care if she was a snotty bitch?

"Well." Mandy cleared her throat. "It looks like our son Johnny is in class with your son. Do you call him by his full name? Arnold?"

"Yes."

Well of course they do, Mandy. Of course. But God love her for trying. Marjorie with a J pursed her blood-red-stained lips.

Mandy flashed a radiant smile, wasting it on these two stooges. "Well I only call Johnny 'Jonathan' when he's in trouble. You know how that is."

"Not really, no." Marjorie with a J crossed her arms before her.

Arnold with no J spoke up. "Is John…Johna…" He was struggling with the name.

Were these people for real?

Marjorie with a J turned to him. "With an NY dear. A *nee* sound. Like you're saying the word knee." She lifted her wool-clad leg in her sensible pants and tapped her knee. "John-knee."

"You know this, Arnold." Ire rose in Reale's belly. "Almost like you're saying Prep-peee."

Mandy smirked.

"Yes, of course." Arnold continued. "Is John-*knee*…"

"Very good, dear." Marjorie with a J patted Arnold's quilted arm.

"Often a discipline problem?" The two preps held

their breath as they waited for an answer.

"What?" Mandy stepped back, the look on her face morphing from amusement to horror.

"Excuse me?" Reale stepped forward as he forced his racing breath to slow. How dare they ask such a question?

"Why would you ask that?" The look on Mandy's face changed again from vulnerable and hurt to strong and powerful. "He's a five-year-old boy."

Marjorie with a J turned her shoulders so she could speak to Mandy, obviously trying to block out Reale. "But that haircut of his. All pointy and standing up." She mimed along with her words. "And considering the male influence in his life…"

"I beg your pardon?" Mandy took a step back from Marjorie with a J. "You're worried about a haircut? And you have no business passing judgment on anyone, especially someone you don't even know."

"We know plenty." Marjorie with a J tossed her pointy nose into the air.

"Really?" Mandy released her arms to her sides. "What do you think you know?"

"We know he almost killed a train filled with children."

Mandy dropped her chin, speaking slowly. "That's an exaggeration and you know it."

"Mandy." Reale touched her arm, desperately wanting to disengage.

"No, it wasn't. And isn't." Marjorie with a J shook her coiffed head, and not a single dark brown hair moved. How much hairspray did someone use to make that happen?

"You have no idea what you're talking about."

"No, you, Amanda. You're the one who has no idea. If you did, you and your son would have stayed away from him forever." Marjorie with a J shook her head, nearly *tsking* Mandy. "He was *drunk*, driving a train filled with children." She glanced at Reale, narrowing her eyes, daggers shooting from them.

"Yes, I was." Reale stepped forward and stood tall. "And I apologized over and over again. Although nothing can make up for it, I have made amends with the families. And thank God, no one was hurt."

"Thank God?" Marjorie with a J turned to Reale, her face reddening. "God wouldn't waste his time on...on *you*." She practically spit her word. "And I know the truth, Mr. Lynxx, or whatever your real name is. I know that train filled with children toppled, and there were more injuries than anyone admitted to, and I know your legal team did everything in their power to cover it up. Nearly killing a large group of kids isn't great for record sales, huh?" She raised her eyebrows and licked her lips. "I know this because my best friend, Patty Beaufort, her daughter was on that train." Marjorie with a J stepped closer to Reale, crowding his space. She reeked of foul-smelling perfume. "Does the name Ansley Beaufort ring a bell?"

"Can't say it does, no."

"Figures." Marjorie with a J stepped back. "I'm sure you've forgotten all about it." She shook her head in the most condescending way possible and yanked her jacket at the waist primly.

"No, I most certainly have not. But there were a lot of names involved."

"Of course. Arnold?" She turned to her husband. "It's time we go."

"Yes, yes." Arnold exhaled, visibly releasing some of the tension he was holding in his sloped shoulders.

Marjorie with a J glanced back and forth between Mandy and Reale one last time. "And don't even think about our sons becoming friends. I would never agree to a play date, even with both nannies on close watch."

"Don't worry." Mandy shook her head. "John-*knee* doesn't have a nanny, so it won't be a problem."

"Huh!" Marjorie with a J gasped. "Come on, Arnold." She grasped her husband's quilted arm and dragged him away and toward the small, remaining group on the other side of the cafeteria. As the Scottsdales approached, the group huddled around them. They glanced toward Reale and Mandy, collectively shaking their heads. Crap.

Reale inhaled deeply, afraid to even look at Mandy. Damn it. Why did this have to happen to her? His breath raced faster and his throat ached. Why? Why did his stupid, out-of-control, juvenile behavior have to hurt the two people he cared about the most? Would John be ostracized because of him? Would Mandy be shut out from the school? Would they miss out on everything because of him? How could he fix this?

Mandy's warm hand slipped into his. She interlaced their fingers, squeezing tight. She leaned toward him. "Well, what can we expect from people who name their son after a horrible disease?"

"What?" He turned toward her. "What disease?"

"The kid's name is Arnold Livingston Scottsdale. ALS. Same acronym as Amyotrophic Lateral Sclerosis. Lou Gehrig's disease." She shook her head. "Poor kid. Hope he survives them okay." She turned to him, gazing up at him, and his heart swelled. "Thank you,

Reale."

"What the heck are you thanking me for? Didn't you hear what those people said?"

Mandy shrugged. "The Scottsdales? Oh, who cares what they say. They're entitled to think whatever they want, and unfortunately, say it too. As long as nothing affects John-*knee* negatively." She giggled. "Anyway. Thanks for supporting me through this morning. I never could have gotten through it without you."

"Yes, you could have. You're the strongest person I know. But I'm glad you didn't have to. I'm glad we were together."

"Me too." She stood on her tiptoes and wheeled toward him, kissing him on the cheek. "Come on. You have plans?"

"No." All he wanted was to be with her. Always. That's all he had ever wanted. His cheek warmed where she had planted the kiss.

"Then why don't you come with me to pick up Johnny's first day of school cake and grab some decorations."

"First day of school party?"

"Yup." She plopped both hands on her hips, smiling. Her eyes were still glassy from the tears. "How 'bout it?"

"Sounds perfect."

"Good." She nudged him with her elbow. "And that way you can keep me from peeking into his classroom window and getting us kicked out."

He sighed. Unfortunately, he was the one at risk of getting them kicked out.

"C'mon." She nodded to the door. "We'd better get out before they come in for lunch at ten thirty, and we get found out."

He squeezed her hand. She pulled ahead to leave the cafeteria, but he held her tightly. She turned back.

"Reale?"

"Thank you, Mandy."

She smiled, and hand in hand, they left the cafeteria together.

Chapter Nineteen

Amanda and Johnny stepped through her front door that led directly into the kitchen.

"Surprise!"

"Guys!" She placed a hand to her heart, overcome that so many people—she scanned the crowd—yup, everyone from the diner who wasn't working, Jess and both her parents, Amanda's boss, Nick, and Reale were all crammed into Amanda's tiny kitchen, blowing noise makers and wearing hats. A few of the guys from the diner kitchen were eyeing Reale curiously, but everyone was acting ultra cool. No one appeared the least bit star struck or surprised that a mega rock star was standing in her kitchen on the South Shore of Long Island.

"Happy First Day of Kindergarten, John!"

They all yelled in unison, and Johnny beamed. His head swiveled from side to side as he glanced around the room, taking in first-day-of-school banners and superhero posters. He spotted Reale and ran to him, jumping into his arms. Amanda's heart swelled.

Jess slipped to her side, carrying two short plastic cups filled with red wine. "That's one dopey grin on your face."

"Well it's a big day." Amanda hung her "good" bag on a hook by the door, the brown leather bag with a simple flap front she reserved for special occasions.

"First day of kindergar—"

Jess waved her off. "That smile isn't because of school."

"I beg your pardon?" Amanda turned to Jess. "For me?" She pointed to one of the red wines Jess was holding.

Jess nodded.

Amanda took a sip of her wine, tossing her ponytail. "Mmm. Delicious. Thanks for bringing it."

"I didn't." Jess raised her eyebrows, biting the corner of her plastic cup.

Amanda glanced at Reale, and butterflies fluttered through her belly.

"He brought the right organic, sulfite-free one and everything."

"Yes, he's always been considerate about those sorts of things." She squared her shoulders and turned back to Jess, trying to mask the excitement she was feeling around Reale. "What is it from, then? The, 'big, dopey grin' on my face?"

"Really?" Jess plopped her free hand on her hip and cocked her head.

"Who wants cake?" Jess's mom, Lynda, wielded a giant knife, holding it over the way-too-big cake decorated with seven superheroes made out of icing, and a plastic superhero crawling over the side. She flashed a giant, subtly glossed smile as she held back the sleeves of her maxi-length, soft, blue kaftan dress. Her dark hair with a few gray streaks fell around her shoulders in an effortless manner. She glimpsed Amanda and winked. She was stunning but a bit scary with that knife.

"Good grief." Amanda nodded to Jess. "Your mom

has a weapon. She's not mad at you right now, is she?"

"Un-unh."

"Reale? You'll help me, please?" Lynda batted her perfectly made-up eyelashes at Reale as he sprinted to her side.

Amanda stifled a giggle and turned to Jess. "They're a thing? Reale and your mother?"

Jess nodded exaggeratedly. "Ohhhhh, yesssss." She took a sip of her wine. "He has been her assistant setting up. Hanging the streamers where she wants them, reaching the high spots…" She shook her head. "He and Nick have been running full speed getting everything done for her. Reale even sent his driver to pick up extra ice because she didn't think there was enough. She thinks Reale's awesome."

Amanda nodded. Awesome. He was pretty awesome…when he wanted to be. She rubbed at the tiniest little stabbing pain in her gut.

"Just like Johnny's her surrogate grandson, she's taking on Reale as her stand-in son-in-law. Or as she likes to say, '*Soon*-in-Law.' "

Amanda giggled, putting her hand to her mouth. "I'm sorry, Jess."

"Don't be." Jess waved her free hand. "I'm used to the constant pressure of her wanting grandkids. My dad's been on his cell since he got here, so Reale will keep her distracted for a while. C'mon."

"Just a sec." Amanda stepped forward and grabbed Johnny's hand. "Want to make your announcement?"

He nodded. "I get to do the first show-and-tell!" He beamed as everyone clapped.

"What are you bringing, Johnny?" Nick held his hands out wide as he grinned at Johnny.

"I don't know yet." Johnny's face scrunched into a scowl.

"How about my famous spinach pie? I'll make a special one for you to bring in and share with your class." Nick beamed at Johnny.

Amanda smiled. "It's not for six weeks yet, but thanks, Nick. We'll keep that in contention."

"Why so far away?" Jess refilled her glass as she spoke.

Amanda shrugged. "Who knows? But Mrs. Flagstaff chose him to go first because of his excellent behavior." She raised Johnny's hand and kissed it.

"Well the first piece of cake is for you, Johnny." Lynda pinched his cheeks.

Jess grabbed Amanda's free hand and pulled her into the quieter living room as Johnny bounced up and down next to Lynda, waiting for the first piece of cake. "Let them eat cake. We need to talk."

Careful not to spill her wine, Amanda collapsed onto the couch, kicking off her too-tight heels. She could feel Reale's gaze following her. Jess sat next to her.

Amanda reached around and grabbed a tired foot, rubbing. "Damn. I work on my feet all day and they don't hurt, but put them into heels for a couple of hours. The ache is right at the ball, you know? These things can't be good for your body." She shook her head, her attention settling back on Jess. "I'm glad you and your mom are good. I hate it when you two are at war."

"I know you do." Jess paused, slipping off her silver sparkle ballet flats and tucking her feet beneath her. She smoothed her short, flowered dress across her lap and adjusted the shoulder straps. She held her wine with both hands, facing Amanda. "Do you miss your mom?"

She shrugged, raising her eyebrows. "She never took the time to know me. All she ever did was push me to live the life she thought I should live."

"Without Reale."

"Yup." She sighed. "You and Lynda may be at each other's throats, but it's because you love each other. My mother and I, we never talked. There's nothing to miss."

"Thank goodness that won't happen to Johnny." Jess smiled. "Thank goodness he has both of his parents, and they're not going to try to force him to be something he's not."

"Amen to that." Amanda raised her cup in a toast.

"Anyway, seems my mom has made peace with the fact that I'm an actor." Jess took a long drink of her wine and rolled her eyes. "Well, going to be an actor anyway."

Amanda put her hand on Jess's arm. "You are an actor, Jess. You just need that right break to come along."

"I guess." Jess smiled. "But we're not talking about me. What's going on with you and Reale?"

"Nothing." Crap. She had no interest in talking about this tonight or anytime. "Is that what you wanted to talk about? Sorry to disappoint you. But there's nothing to discuss. We're both being civil for Johnny's sake. That's it. I want cake. You? It's red velvet." She stood, hoping to get a reprieve from talking about Reale. Her bare feet were chilly against the cool floor.

Jess stood next to her. "How does your kid even know about red velvet? That's such a southern thing for a little New Yorker to like."

She shrugged. "I've got no idea, some superhero's color I guess. Whatever, I want some."

She stepped toward the kitchen, but Jess grabbed her by the sweater and pulled her back. She nodded toward Reale.

"Amanda. The man stares at you constantly. He forgave you for keeping the biggest secret of his life *from him*. Can't you forgive him for suing for custody?"

"He didn't just sue for custody." She forced a smile, trying to keep this conversation and the party lighthearted for all of their sakes. Her empty belly ached. "He won and he took Johnny away."

"For less than a month, and obviously he learned the error of his ways."

"But would I have Johnny back if that accident hadn't happened?" She searched her friend's eyes for the answer.

Jess slumped her weight onto one leg, standing closer to Amanda. "I'm not the one you need to ask. And it's not him either. That one you have to ask yourself. And while you're at it, you need to figure out if the accident on Fire Island hadn't happened, and Reale hadn't been there, would you ever have told him he has a son? These are questions only you can answer."

Jess was right. These were the questions Amanda struggled with nightly.

"Amanda, he stayed in contact the whole time he had Johnny. You video chatted with Johnny almost every night. And Reale didn't up and leave the country with Johnny like you were terrified he may do. Reale screwed up, yes, but so did you."

Amanda started.

Jess sighed. "Yes, Amanda, you screwed up too. But who cares? The blame game has to stop. Enough checking off who hurt whom worse, or whose sin was greater. You don't want to live like that. You both screwed up, and you know what? You'll do it again and again. Everyone does. It's just in your case the screw-up makes the papers because he's Reale Lynxx. The most important thing is that you don't screw up Johnny."

Jess nodded toward Johnny who was sitting on Reale's lap, shoveling in a giant bite of cake. Amanda smiled, and Reale turned to her. He smiled back.

Jess shook her head. "Amanda, you love him. With every ounce of your soul. They—those two blondies over there—they're your life. Don't let fear rule you. You're smarter than that."

"I'm trying not to repeat my mistake."

"Then don't. The only mistake you made is keeping a secret from that man. Don't do it again. Everything's out in the open now. All cards are on the table."

Swallowing hard, she glanced at her friend. "But my job is to protect Johnny."

"Yes. And to give him everything he needs, including his father."

"But what if his father hurts him?"

"Like abuse?" Jess furrowed her brow.

"God no. But what if he tries to take Johnny again, and we get into another mess?"

"And what happens if you hurt Johnny?"

"Me?" She scoffed. "How could I hurt Johnny?"

"By keeping him from his dad. By refusing to give him the family he could have—the three of you, every day of the week." Jess reached out and took Amanda's hand, squeezing it. "By being so damned stubborn you all lose. Amanda. Go get more out of life, for both of you. Get out of the diner. Get your nursing degree. Go get the life you deserve—the life you and Reale planned all those years ago. So you were sidetracked. Who isn't? I'm supposed to be in Greece right now, but I'm here, still trying to save up to pay for the damned trip."

"Jess…" Amanda smiled at her friend. "You know, if you ever decide to diversify, you should think about becoming a therapist or a spiritual guide or something. You've really got your stuff together."

Jess laughed, tossing her long black hair. "I don't have my shit together, Amanda. No one does. We're all just getting by, day by day. You're no more messed up than the rest of us. I promise. And this…" She pointed toward Reale. "This isn't beyond fixing if you would allow it."

Adrenaline coursed through her as she glanced at her son, sitting in his father's lap, giggling. Reale caught her eye and nodded to her, and goosebumps covered her arms. God, what she would give to make it all work.

****

"That was a great party." Reale sat on the front step next to Amanda, so close their bodies were touching—shoulder to shoulder—and it felt too good to move. She wiggled her bare toes against the cold concrete.

"Yeah. Thanks for everything you did, Reale." She sighed.

"What did I do?" He took a long drag of his beer.

Sexy. Everything that man did was sexy. And damn, he was so handsome. Her body warmed, and a definite ache settled deep within her. If only this had all gone a different way. If only he were handling her now instead of a beer. She turned and took a sip of her own beer, trying to cool down. *Okay, focus.*

"Let's see…" She held up her hand and counted on her fingers. "You were with me at school, running around all over town after party decorations because they didn't have Back-to-School party supplies at the first two stores, to the bakery to get the cake, back to the diner to get the platters of food, setting everything up with Lynda while I went to get Johnny…"

"That's nothing. I was happy to do it."

She turned to him, taking in his angular features and the lines around his eyes. "Reale. You had to have a security detail tag along. You spent your day doing the most boringly average jobs. You could have picked up a phone and had Madison Square Garden decorated for John, and I know it. But you didn't. You stood, in all your rock star greatness, in my tiny kitchen and charmed everyone from the diner."

"Wait. Rock star greatness?" He chuckled, grabbing the back of his neck with his hand.

Her eyes followed and landed on his scruffy beard. "I love that beard."

He ran his hand up and down, scrubbing his face. "Yeah?"

"Oh, yeah." Damn, wasn't it hot for a September evening on Long Island?

Keeping his head turned to her, he pressed tighter to her shoulder, until the weight of his body nearly knocked her over, and it took effort for her to stay upright. *Bring it on, Reale*. Maybe if he pushed a little harder she would be lying on her back on the front stoop, with him hovering above her... She breathed deeply, inhaling his sexy, dangerous scent, her eyes closing. The weight against her shoulder stopped as he draped his arm around her and pulled her close. She leaned against him, inhaling the gorgeous night air, safe and protected up against Reale Lynxx. Exactly as it was meant to be.

"Mand?" His voice purred in her ear. "Doesn't this feel like being on the fire escape of our apartment on the West Side?"

"Mmmm..." She didn't dare open her eyes. As long as they stayed closed, she was twenty-one years old and the girlfriend of Reale Lynxx.

"Jesus." He chuckled. "Some nights we were so cold. We used to light tons of those little...what were they? Tea lights?"

She nodded.

"By the time I'd light the last one, the first one was burnt out." He chuckled. "They never did a damned thing. I used to wrap you up in blankets and hold you close. It felt so good."

"Yes." She pushed closer to him.

"I think we used to be out there more than we were inside."

"No." She turned to him, her head resting under his chin, her cheek pressed against the opening at the neckline of his shirt. "We were in bed more than anywhere." She glanced up at him, her lids heavy, her limp body growing more and more achy...desperate for his touch.

He ran his hand up and down her spine before letting it settle on her lower back. She tilted her chin upward. They were so close, her lips were parted, and his breath rushed into her...filling her. Her chest heaved with her quickening breath.

"Reale..."

"Baby..." He leaned over, and his mouth found hers. He kissed her once so gently.

She opened her eyes and stretched upward. She needed more of him...now. He locked his lips to hers with more force. His kiss was warm and strong and hungry. His free hand cupped her cheek as he kissed her over and over, pulling her closer. His mouth opened hers, and his tongue found its way in.

"Mmm..." She moaned into his mouth.

He pulled her closer and turned her toward his body, tight against him. "You are so sexy." He grunted his words as he kissed her over and over, pulling them to their feet. They stood on her porch, as her arms snaked around his neck, and his strong hands clamped on her waist.

"Oh, God..." She pushed closer and wrapped one leg around his hip.

He reached around, grasping her leg, hoisting her up easily.

She straddled him, wrapping both legs around his waist. "Inside." Her word was a breathy whisper. "Reale. Take me inside."

His body stiffened.

"Reale?" She pulled back, gazing down at him as he looked up into her eyes. "What? Why are we stopping?"

His eyes were glassy and filled with lust, but all he

did was shake his head.

"Reale?" She tapped on his shoulder so he would loosen his grip. She slid down his body and stood before him.

"I can't, Mandy."

"Can't what?" She shook her head.

"Take you to bed."

Her eyes widened, and an ache formed in her throat. "Why not?" Everything raced through her head at once. Was he still too angry? Was it an image thing? Did he need to be dating someone high profile? Was he not attracted to her after all? "Reale?" Her eyes danced back and forth across his.

"I don't want to be with you if it can't be like it was."

"When we were kids? Reale, how can it be like that? We're parents. You're a superstar."

"I mean, when these damned imaginary walls weren't between us. I've forgiven you, Mandy. I think maybe I'm even beginning to see your side. But you're still angry about what I did. I can feel it in you. In the way you're holding back the tiniest bit."

"Reale. We're on my front porch. I have neighbors. I'm not holding back."

"Really? There's no part of you that's still angry?"

She glanced away and down at the chipped cement beneath their feet. She curled her toes and released them.

"That's what I thought."

"It just happened, Reale. I'm scared." She glanced up at him with wide eyes.

He stepped as close to her as they were moments before, their bodies tight to one another. His hands lay heavy at his sides. She stared up at him.

"If I took you inside and made love to you, Mandy, I would do it because I knew in my heart that if you got pregnant again, you would tell me. And we would raise this baby together. I trust what you did, and I believe your reasons. I'm willing to let go. Are you? Can you trust me like I trust you?"

"I need some time."

"Time." He nodded, stepping back. "There's no way I'm going to taint the memory of us with anger."

"But this…" She waved a finger between them. "It's just for tonight."

"That's the problem." He gave a small, sad smile and reached out to brush a hair back from her face. His fingers cascaded around, rubbing her swollen lips.

"Reale?"

"Get some sleep, Mandy. I'll be by to see John tomorrow if it's okay."

"Of course it's okay. He doesn't have school because of the staggered kindergarten entry."

"I remember." He let his hand drop, and she shuddered. He pulled out his phone and texted something. He held up the phone, waving it. "The car is waiting for me down the block. Just texted my driver. Do me a favor?"

"Anything." And damn if that wasn't true.

"Would you go in and lock up? So I know you're inside safely."

"Oh, yeah, okay." She stepped back from him, and every cell in her body ached. This was wrong. So wrong.

"See ya', Mand." He put up his hand, giving a wave.

She turned and stepped inside and then closed the door between them. She rested her forehead against the doorframe as he slid into the backseat of his black, ultra-expensive sedan. In a flash, he was gone. She lifted her head and stared at the dark night as she bolted the lock on the door, once again shutting Reale Lynxx out of her life.

Chapter Twenty

Amanda sighed, clenching a pot of fresh brewed coffee in one hand while rubbing the dull ache on her forehead with the back of the other hand. She stared out the diner window. It was a gorgeous, warm, late-fall day, right around sixty-five degrees. It was the Friday before Thanksgiving week, the week they had to decide what they were doing about Thanksgiving. Damn. This was the first holiday season with the three of them together. But were they together? She'd ordered a turkey and had already picked up cranberry sauce. The rest she'd get as they got closer. But the problem wasn't the food, it was who was—or wasn't—coming to dinner. She hadn't seen much of Reale since that night of Johnny's first day of school, but he really should be with Johnny on a holiday…which meant he'd also be with her.

A few leaves scuttled across the parking lot, blowing in the gentle breeze. What a day. And man, it would be an exceptional day to be in Manhattan. A day to walk through Central Park and sip cappuccinos in the Village, a day to pop in and out of galleries and breathe in life and excitement. Heck, it would have been a gorgeous day to pack up Johnny and go apple picking somewhere on the Island, tossing on a warm sweater when the evening grew chilly, and catching a high school football game…the three of them, snuggling under a stadium blanket, hoping they were cheering for the right team. She sighed again. It was Reale's day to pick up Johnny; Johnny was sleeping over at his dad's. Lucky kid. Whoever said the days were getting shorter wasn't living Amanda's life—her days were unbearably long. And damn, they were lonely.

They had fallen into a nice enough routine, dropping off Johnny together on many days and picking him up on a schedule, but that was as far as it went. Always. It was rote. And boring.

"Miss?"

She turned. Oh, man, she had forgotten Old Man Howard the Grump was her only patron right now. Oh, great. Maybe tonight would be the night she could retire on the fourteen-cent tip he left. She glanced over her shoulder into the kitchen at Carlos the cook, silently chopping his veggies for the evening special of frittatas; the same special they ran every…single…Friday night. She never needed to check the specials; they never changed. Month after month, week after week, year after year. She yawned. Behind Carlos was Nick, who was in his tiny diner office doing the books, same as he did every Friday before the dinner crowd.

"Coffee?" Old Man Howard waved his cup in her direction.

"Oh, yes, sure. Sorry." She snapped to and smoothed the front of her constrictive uniform. The uniform was always a nuisance, but tonight it was so tight and binding it was oppressive. Pushing her discomfort aside, she walked to Howard's table to refill his coffee cup, as she had done so many times before. And would do so many times again. So, so many times.

"Miss? You're overflowing the coffee!" Howard

stood and stepped back from the table.

She righted the pot and jumped back herself. She placed the pot of coffee on another table and sprinted to the kitchen to grab a towel. Carlos looked up from his chopping as she grabbed towels and a cup of ice in case she had burned Howard. Thankfully the diner was mostly empty, and she could tend to the elderly man she may have scalded with hot coffee.

"I'm so sorry. Are you burned?"

"No." Howard shook his head.

"Oh, good."

"I could have been."

"Yes." She dabbed at the table as she removed the drenched placemat and silverware. "There's, uh, no charge for your lunch today." Great, another nine bucks she didn't have blown on soup and coffee. Nick wouldn't want her to pay, but what could she do? She'd spilled the coffee.

"I would think not." Howard sat at another seat, cleaning his glasses and otherwise collecting himself. Thankfully he wasn't burned and no coffee had spilled on him. "That's the problem with your generation," he muttered. "No responsibility. It was your job to pour coffee, but your mind was off daydreaming about something else." He shook his head, scowling.

No responsibility? Her chest heaved and her throat constricted. Her heart raced faster and faster, and she clenched the damp, dirty towels in her hands. *Let it be, Amanda.* But deep inside a tiny worm of anger was burrowing in her gut, needing a release. "Excuse me, sir, but you have no idea what you're talking about."

"I know what I saw." He humphed and turned away.

Walk away Amanda. Just walk away... But damn, she was sick of it all. "And what did you see? That I'm human? That I made a mistake? That in all the countless times you've eaten here, I accidently overfilled your coffee cup and offered to pay for your lunch?"

"In my day we took our jobs seriously."

She stepped forward, closer to him. "I would appreciate it, sir, if you wouldn't presume you know anything about me. I am raising a son—on my own—working to pay for everything he needs while I send myself to school. You eat here every day, and you leave fourteen cents for a tip. We survive on tips. And you require a heck of a lot of service with the perfect crackers and soup temperature, and what do we get? Fourteen cents. If we're lucky. So why not get off your high horse and stop telling people what's wrong with them? I made a mistake. That's it."

A mistake. Not the first and certainly not the most significant. She wasn't infallible. She had never even entertained the thought, but maybe she *did* make a mistake. And maybe those people in her life that mattered most were willing to forgive her for it. She glanced at her watch. Two oh three. Reale was probably at school, waiting to get Johnny. Her heart raced with desire to get to them.

"I will be speaking to your boss, Mr. Nick, you can be sure of that."

"Go right ahead; he's in the backroom." She pointed to the kitchen area with her thumb.

Howard straightened up and adjusted the belt on his corduroy pants. "I eat here every day. You'll lose your job. Then what will happen to your son? You and

273

your butterfingers had better learn to be more careful."

"I'll tell you what happens to my son." Her chest heaved with her hurried breath. "He gets the best education this damned island has to offer thanks to his rock star father. And I'm leaving to go pick him up. My son. Don't you dare bring him up or intimate that I don't take care of him. And as far as careful, that's the last thing I need. To be more careful."

She untied her apron and stormed away. She stood behind the diner bar. Her chest heaved and her hands shook as she texted Jess. *Had it out with O.M.H.T.G. Fuck it all.* She tore open the top buttons of her uniform.

She turned to see Carlos in the kitchen with his mouth open, framed by his dark black beard. He lifted his white chef hat and used his forearm to wipe away the sweat on his forehead as he stared without blinking. Nick stood next to Carlos with a look of surprise on his face. He ran a hand over his perfectly combed gray hair. *Beep*! She glanced at her text.

WTF? Awesome! Go to him. Now.

She turned to Nick. "Nick, I love you, but I—"

Nick put up his hand, silencing her. "Amanda. You're a good girl. Maybe too much of a good girl. Don't worry about us. I'll get you covered. And don't quit. Not yet. Go to Johnny and that rock and roll boy. Have a night off. Be young."

Beep! She glanced down again. *I'll babysit!*

She grinned. God love Jess. "Nick, I would kiss you if I had the time." She rushed toward the door and grabbed her old, brown work sweater—the one with holes and always smelled of matzo ball soup and antiseptic—and caught her reflection in the dessert case behind the bar. She was a mess in her rumpled uniform and half-up hair, but she didn't have the time to care. She yanked open the diner door.

"I'll collect next week!" Nick yelled after her.

She stepped out of the diner and sucked in a deep breath of the glorious air. Hell, yes. It was high time she did *something*.

****

"Mandy?" Reale's face brightened as she walked into the cafeteria where all parents assembled to pick up their children. Reale was early, hanging off in a corner by himself, while the Long Island preppy mothers congregated on the other side of the room. She glanced their way but didn't recognize any of them. Panic overtook her. Where was everyone? Had she forgotten a field trip? The preppies looked her up and down as she scooted toward Reale. They whispered as she walked by.

She ran a hand through her hair, adjusting the tendrils that hung down. Did she look that awful? Oh, the hell with it. Who cared? That was their issue, not hers. "Hey, Reale. Where are all the parents in Johnny's class? We didn't miss a trip or anything?"

"No way. I don't know where they are. But nice to see you."

She smiled and her tight shoulders relaxed. "I'm sorry, I know tonight is your night, but I got antsy at the diner. I was hoping, maybe the three of us could go…I don't know, be bad."

"Bad?" He raised his eyebrows, smirking. "What are you and John doing that constitutes being 'bad'?"

She shrugged. "I don't know." Her spirits dropped.

"I think it's a great idea." He took her hand and

squeezed.

She exhaled. Good. This would be good. And later she'd talk to him, and Jess said she would babysit, so—

"Mr. Lynxx?" The principal with short, cropped, blonde hair, wearing a yellow suit in almost the same color as Amanda's uniform and a name tag that read *Ms. Ronebarth—Principal*, walked forward. She turned to Amanda and raised one arched eyebrow. "Hello, Ms. Simmons."

"Ms. Ronebarth." Amanda shook her hand and smiled at the coincidence of colors. "We've only spoken on the phone."

"Yes." Ms. Ronebarth nodded. "I'm glad you're here as well. I understand this is Mr. Lynxx's afternoon to pick up Jonathan."

"Yes." She nodded as an "off" feeling developed in the pit of her stomach.

"Good. I have been wanting to speak to you." Her gaze jumped from Reale to Amanda and back again. "Both of you. Would you two come with me to my office?"

Amanda hesitated.

"We have plenty of time. Jonathan won't be out of class for another twenty minutes."

"Fine." Reale held out his hand for both women to walk before him.

Just walking past Reale and his chivalrous act made Amanda ache for him in that certain way. *Oh, Reale.*

The three of them walked down a bright, sun-filled hallway covered in positive affirmation posters and student artwork.

"It's amazing how much work they've done

already," Amanda chirped, but neither Reale nor Ms. Ronebarth responded. She glanced at Reale who kept his gaze on the floor before them.

They stopped before Ms. Ronebarth's office door, and Ms. Ronebarth pushed it open, allowing Amanda and Reale to enter before her. Amanda sat in one of the two chrome and black leather chairs facing a mahogany desk, and Reale joined her in the other. She glanced at a full-sized bookcase holding books about child development, all in alphabetical order. On her desk Mrs. Ronebarth had a simple, all-in-one computer and three pencil cups, one for black pens, one for red pens, and one for pencils.

Behind Amanda the door clicked shut, and Mrs. Ronebarth walked past. She sat at her desk and steepled her fingers, leaning forward. Before her on the desk was a manila envelope. She sat back and opened the folder. "Jonathan has been a wonderful student."

"Has been?" Amanda cocked her head.

"His test scores are excellent. He's very bright."

"Thank you." Amanda squirmed in her chair, feeling small.

"Test scores?" Reale turned to Amanda and then Mrs. Ronebarth. "How much testing is there in the first few months of kindergarten?"

Mrs. Ronebarth smiled. "He doesn't know he's being tested, I assure you. But he reads. And most children do not when they begin kindergarten. And he understands many advanced concepts."

"This is all good." He sat back. "You had me worried there."

She glanced at the papers in the folder again. "As a matter of fact, Mrs. Falstaff recommended he be placed in an advanced group, and I would have approved it."

"Would have?" Amanda's voice was weak.

Mrs. Ronebarth cleared her throat and closed the folder. She sighed, spinning in her chair before settling in dead center of Amanda and Reale. "There have been complaints."

"About Johnny?" Amanda sat forward, her muscles tensing. "Johnny is the sweetest, nicest child. You can ask anyone—"

Reale took Amanda's hand and squeezed. "Let's let Mrs. Ronebarth explain." He blinked slowly as if they spoke a secret language.

She nodded, trying to calm her breathing.

"The complaint wasn't about Jonathan. It was about his show and tell."

"What did he bring in?" Reale looked at Amanda.

She shrugged. "The bow to his archery set. I made him leave the arrows home."

Mrs. Ronebarth nodded. "Yes. And many of the students loved it, and they wanted to touch it and try it, but Mrs. Flagstaff told them they couldn't load anything into it—likes pencils or whatever kindergarten children think of—because it was a dangerous weapon. So…"

Reale nodded. "The kids went home and told their parents that John, the son of a rock and roll bad boy, brought a dangerous weapon to school."

Mrs. Ronebarth nodded solemnly. "And many, well, most students in his class didn't come to school today."

Amanda sat forward. "He was alone?" Her heart raced.

"No, no." Mrs. Ronebarth shook her head. "Two

other children came in. The three of them had a wonderful day." She sighed. "Mr. Lynxx, Ms. Simmons. I don't pass judgment on what people do in their lives. You two have been nothing but lovely, respectful, and articulate in your correspondence. Your son is wonderful, bright and well-mannered. I don't read much of what the media says about people, nor do I believe it or care. My school has been on the receiving end of some horrible press through the years—parents who were angry at the school or me in one way or another. I am not one to play into drama or stupidity. However, I am a businesswoman first and foremost." She nodded to her bookcase. "All these books on education? That's not my job; it's my teachers' jobs. My job is to keep a school running. And when a classroom of eighteen students suddenly has the potential for a drop rate of fourteen or fifteen..." She placed her hands together and squeezed. "These parents network. Even my waitlist won't sustain us for long. You see, I find myself in a difficult situation."

"Why would they leave your school?" Amanda searched Mrs. Ronebarth's eyes. "I mean, I've done the research. You have no competition."

Mrs. Ronebarth sighed. "Thank you, Ms. Simmons. But the problem is, if enough of my parents leave to go to my competitor—who is not as good as we are, I agree—but if they all go, my competitor's school will quickly become the better school."

Reale leaned forward. "So just by us being here, I'm risking my son's education?"

"In a way, yes."

He stood and paced in a tiny circle. "This is like that Groucho Marx joke. 'I refuse to join any club that would have me as a member.' " He shook his head. "This is ludicrous."

Amanda's stomach flipped. "There must be some way to fix this."

Mrs. Ronebarth sat forward, speaking directly to Amanda. "Please understand. I am in no way insisting you leave. That would be against the law. I am simply telling you as soon as one year from now, if Jonathan stays, his education and the school will change drastically."

"Maybe a little change is a good thing." Reale ran a hand through his hair before letting it drop. "The preppy faction has enough pull to change the course of this school?"

"If they all leave, I'm afraid so, yes. If I no longer have a budget to keep my top teachers employed and to maintain all the specials we offer…" She tilted her head. "I find myself in an impossible situation, Mr. Lynxx."

He dropped down into his chair, defeated. "So even if I funded your school until John was through high school—gave you the what, millions…?" He raised his eyebrows in question and Mrs. Ronebarth nodded. He continued, "There would be no kids left for him to go to school with. There would be no need for most teachers, so your school would minimize in size, and all those activities that make it special would disappear." He shook his head.

"I'm afraid so." She nodded.

"What can we do?" Amanda sat forward, wringing her hands.

"Take the week. Talk it over while Johnny's home on Thanksgiving break. Your financial means will make it possible for you to educate Jonathan in any way you'd like—private tutors, home schooling…"

"No." Amanda shook her head. "No. He needs socialization. I kept him from his father for too long, and he's only ever had me. I refuse to have him locked away, being educated in a house somewhere. I don't care how large."

"Have you considered relocating?" Three lines formed vertically on Mrs. Ronebarth's forehead as she narrowed her eyes. "There are excellent schools all over the country. Many places are far more accepting and welcoming to parents who are in the arts. This particular group of parents I have is tough. None of them have ever ventured past the country club on Saturday nights. Yes, my education is excellent, but are you sure you want your son surrounded by that?"

Amanda started, sitting back. In all her research, she had never considered the parents of the kids Johnny would go to school with. All she ever thought about was his education.

"There are excellent schools in Manhattan you may want to consider. I know not everyone wants to raise a child in the city—"

"We love the city." Amanda and Reale spoke in unison and turned to one another.

Ms. Ronebarth nodded. "Then for goodness' sake, consider it. I will give you the name of a couple of places, and I'll happily pull some strings. There's one in particular. It specializes in flexible learning schedules for families in the arts."

"But moving Johnny… He has friends."

Ms. Ronebarth nodded. "Yes. Like I said, it's your decision." She glanced at the clock. "It's almost three. I have to prepare for dismissal."

"Of course." Reale nodded, standing.

"I've been given an ultimatum by the parents. I'll need to know your decision as soon as Thanksgiving break is over."

Ms. Ronebarth held out her hand to Reale who shook it and then to Amanda. Amanda shook her hand as well, although her gut ached in response.

"Well, thank you." Ms. Ronebarth held up her hand, and Amanda and Reale walked out of the office together.

****

Her eyes were brimmed with tears. He could see them, and damn, he was the cause. Once again he was hurting them—the two people he loved most in the world. How could this happen? Maybe they would have been better off without him after all. He glanced out the window as the drab landscape of the Long Island Expressway whisked by. John was pushed up against him, wedged between Reale and Mandy. She'd asked to go home so she could change out of her uniform, but then what? They were going to have a family afternoon, but Ms. Ronebarth put a damper on that.

And what about those other families? Could they be so narrow-minded they would make a child pay for his father's sins? And what were those sins? He never stole. Never cheated. Never hurt anyone on purpose. So he drank. Lots and lots of people did, including those damned preppy fathers who cracked open their first beers on Sunday morning after church and continued drinking all day. What, that was okay because they had a set of barbecue tongs in their other hand? Or because they were drinking on freshly laid pavers on a landscaped backyard in the heart of suburbia? Why was that better than drinking through the night and making music that people enjoyed and loved? Music that affected people. Why was he the bad guy? Was it because he had short, spiky hair? Because he cursed once in a while? What man didn't? Come on, those preppy dads cursed a blue streak when they were alone on a golf course and messed up their backswings. And yes, the accident was horrific and could have been so much worse, but it could have happened to anyone. Anyone. It was just that when he did it, it made all social media platforms in a matter of minutes.

But no. No. He wasn't the victim. He had toppled that train. And children had been scared. And some had been hurt. And God—he sighed—it could have been so much worse. He was to blame. And he took full responsibility for it. People have always loved to demonize rock and roll, but Reale Lynxx gave them fuel for their fires. He made his fortune by giving people what they wanted—a bad boy they could love to hate. And now his family had to pay the price.

He turned to Mandy, catching the graceful angle of her face. She reached up and tucked a stray hair behind her ear. Whether he was right or wrong didn't matter. They were in a messy situation, and it was because of him.

The driver turned the car off the exit, but still no one but John had spoken a word. When John first climbed into the car, he was so excited to have both Mommy and Daddy pick him up. He was filled with stories about his awesome day with only three kids in the class, and he chatted non-stop all the way from the North Shore to the South. But it was Friday, and even

John eventually grew tired, so he dug into his healthy snack of organic cheese sticks and homemade granola, and his conversation died off as they sat in early traffic going east on the LIE. But the worst part of the trip was Mandy hadn't said a word. Not one. She nodded and smiled and hand sanitized John while producing his snack, she hugged John and clapped after he sang his ABCs in French, but she didn't utter a peep. And it was freaking killing Reale.

The car pulled into her short driveway, and she turned to them, not making eye contact. "I need to change quickly, and Johnny, you should run in and pee." Finally, her gaze found Reale's. "Will you wait? Please? While I change and get Johnny set? I mean in the house."

He started. If he hadn't been there, if he hadn't known what had happened in Ms. Ronebarth's office… It didn't make sense. Mandy's body language—the way she was sheepishly speaking—it sounded like she was blaming herself. But how?

"Yes." Carrying John's heavy Lynxx backpack, Reale climbed out of the car after Mandy and John. He held the house door for them after she unlocked it. He glanced at the key in her hand. How divisive keys were. He hated that she had a key to one place and he to another. He used to love using their keys to let her into their apartment. Loved it.

"I'll just be a minute." She scooted through the door and slid John out of his blue blazer before taking the backpack from Reale. Methodically, she hung them on the hook in the kitchen and then peeled off her old sweater and oversized patchwork bag. She hung them next to John's Lynxx backpack and blue school blazer.

John ran for the bathroom. "Gotta peeee!!!!!" He bolted down the short hallway leading to the bathroom, and Reale chuckled.

Mandy turned back to Reale, dropping her chin and then squaring her shoulders, staring straight at him. "You okay for a minute while I grab a shower? I want to get rid of the smell of diner. I'll be quick."

"Take your time." His feet were as heavy as if he were wearing lead boots. Damn, how he wanted to go to her.

She smiled. It was all cordial but so polite and contrived. He shook off a chill. He didn't want this with Mandy. He wanted their real, honest, gritty life back.

"There's wine in the fridge. And hummus too if you're hungry," she called over her shoulder as she walked away. "You know where the chips are—over the stove."

He nodded as she disappeared into her bedroom. He liked knowing his way around. He stood alone in Mandy and John's kitchen, taking it all in—the hominess, the organization—but underneath it all, something was missing. Behind the stove were broken pieces of white subway tile. The simple, basic faucet in the sink had a constant drip, drip, drip. He went to the wall and switched on the overhead lights. Sure enough, one of the light bulbs was out in a high hat that required a ladder to reach. It was like the front stoop with the chipped cement. Little things needed attention. He stood tall and breathed deeply. What was missing from this picture was a man. Someone who could handle all of the handyman jobs for her while she concentrated on the more important issues.

He opened the fridge and glanced in. He wasn't

hungry, not after the meeting with John's principal, but curiosity and a desire to mark this territory as his own overtook him. He abandoned the fridge to scour the cabinets. He knew what was in them. Plasticware in the lower cabinets, cleaning supplies in the locked cabinet under the sink, and dried pantry goods in the higher shelves: black beans, taco shells, veggie puffs, healthy fruit gummies. He stepped back from the opened cabinet as a feeling of possessiveness practically strangled him. He didn't choose the food, didn't shop for it, and didn't pay for it. He wasn't in this picture. Here he was, in the only house his family lived in, and he wasn't a presence at all.

"Dad?" John materialized, dressed in sweatpants and a superhero T-shirt. "Where are we going?"

"I, uh…" His gaze fell on his son—his short blond hair, his bright blue eyes, his lopsided smile—and he exhaled. He was wrong; his presence would always be here, as long as John was. So shouldn't he make this house as good for them as he could? Starting tomorrow, if Mandy let him, he'd take care of the handyman jobs around the house. Yes, of course he could hire a fleet of people to do the jobs, but that wasn't him. Or Mandy. And that would have been like inviting another man to come piss along the border of the property, marking it as his own. Like hell he was going to allow that.

"Dad?" John cocked his head, smiling at Reale.

"Oh, uh, I'm not sure."

"Sorry to keep you waiting." Mandy walked into the kitchen, and he forgot what he was going to say. His gaze ran up and down her in her faded skinny jeans and an oversized, light-gray sweater that hung over her hips and covered her hands. Her thumbs stuck out of thumbholes, and her hair, freshly washed, hung in waves over her shoulders. Her lips shone with the lightest pink gloss, like they were slick from kissing, and her giant green eyes were highlighted with eyeliner and mascara. She didn't need any makeup, she was most beautiful without, but damn, she looked gorgeous standing before him. Over one arm hung a quilted black vest. She stood near the coat hooks at the door, transferring the contents from her old quilted bag into her newer, brown leather one.

"I, uh…" She walked to Reale as he fought to calm his racing breath. "I know it's your night with Johnny. You're sure you don't mind if I tag along?"

"N-no." He shook his head. Were they going to pretend the afternoon had never happened? "I would love it."

She placed a warm hand on his, and bolts of electricity shot up and down his arm. "I know we need to talk, Reale. Could we maybe go have some fun with John and then talk later after we drop him off at Jess's?"

"Yes." Hell, yes. Yes, in every way.

"Thank you." She hesitated. "Did you have any particular plans?"

"I was thinking outdoor go-carts. Since it's warm tonight."

She nodded, her eyes sparkling as she turned to John. "You, mister, you'd better get your warmest superhero jacket. We're going to do some go-cart racing and then…" She turned to Reale with giant, vulnerable eyes. "Burgers and fries okay?"

"Perfect."

"Great." She bounced on her toes. "Okay, you two,

prepare to be schooled by me."

Reale chuckled. "Now I know where our son gets his old man expressions."

She plopped a hand on her hip and smirked.

"You can drive a go-cart?" John turned to his mother, his eyes as wide as hers.

Reale smiled.

"Oh, you'll never be able to catch me. Promise."

Reale squatted down next to John. "Truth is, John, she won't ever leave the starting gate, so every time we pass her, she'll pretend she was a lap ahead. But I'm on to her. I know her."

She smiled, nodding, her face softening. "Yeah, you do."

He stood. "Yeah, I do." They stared at one another for a long moment as color flushed her cheeks. Damn if she wasn't beautiful.

"Mom? Dad?" John turned from one to the other.

Reale clapped his hands together, smiling at John. "Did you grab your jacket?" John walked to the hooks near the door and jumped up, freeing a thick red jacket that hung next to Mandy's old work bag. Reale smiled. "Come on, I've got a race to win."

They crowded by the kitchen door, and Reale held out his hand for his family to walk out the door before him. They stopped on the cement stoop, and Mandy turned to him, sliding the house keys into his hand. He grasped the keys tightly. Damn, he never wanted to let go. Without a word she ran ahead and skipped alongside John, racing to the car.

Finally, despite everything, this was right. He beamed as he watched them, before turning back to lock up.

Chapter Twenty-One

Reale shook his head playfully. "I can't believe you can drive like that. Did you ever put your foot on the brake?"

"There was a brake?" She batted her lashes.

He chuckled and laid his arm across the back of the seat as they sat on opposite sides of the car. It felt so good to be in the back of the car with him, the two of them cruising down the LIE toward Manhattan. As much as she loved their family time, it was special, and nostalgic, when the two of them were alone together.

"It was nice of Jess to watch Johnny again." She sighed. "I just don't want to take advantage. I mean, it was one thing when I was alone, and I know Lynda adores Johnny, but they're my friends, and I don't want to—"

"I'm paying Jess."

"What?" She turned to Reale. "What do you mean paying her?"

"Okay." He put up his hand. "I knew you'd be worried about taking advantage, and she wants to take this trip to Greece, so I figured she's the best possible person we can get for a nanny." He shrugged. "Actors are always starving artists at the beginning, so…"

"Oh." She turned away, trying to process her feelings as the car slowed on the expressway. What was she feeling? Happy? Aggravated? Out of control? She turned back. "And she's okay with that?"

"She resisted at first, but when I explained I'd have to pay someone, she agreed to watch Johnny for free but let me pay for her trip to Greece."

"What?" She sat forward, giggling. "That is so Jess."

He chuckled. "She said it's a win-win for everyone especially her, seeing she has a—let me see if I get this right—'rock star bad boy for a brother-in-law.' " He made air quotes with his fingers.

Her cheeks heated. "She said what?" She shook her head as her temples throbbed. She turned and glanced out the window at the stopped cars around them. The LIE on Friday night was always a traffic nightmare. She turned back toward him; please, please let it be dark enough that he couldn't see her blush. She cleared her throat. "I'm sorry, Reale. She's just…Jess, you know?" She stared down at her feet. "She knows we're not…" She waved a finger back and forth. "You know."

He sat straighter. "No. What?"

"Reale." She cocked her head. "Whatever it would take to make her your sister-in-law. And she's not my sister anyway, so none of it makes any sense." She shook her head, flabbergasted.

"Sometimes nothing makes sense, Mandy. You know that."

She pushed away her awkwardness. "It's a little odd. Her getting paid to watch Johnny."

"I thought it might be. The reason I didn't ask you first was because I thought it could be weird for you. I waited for Jess to be on board and went from there."

"Oh, uh, okay?" What was there to say? It all made perfect sense. "But we can't—" She stopped herself short.

"Can't what?"

She shook her head. "Nope. Nothing." She wasn't going to finish that thought. No way. He wouldn't treat Jess like hired help. He didn't treat anyone that way. It wasn't in his nature. She took a deep breath, inhaling to a count of six. She needed to get the heck out of people's way and stop trying to control everything. She'd learned the hard way that control did not equal happiness.

"Mandy." He took her hand. "If it's too much, we can change. I guess I should have asked first. I'm sorry." The car rolled forward, picking up speed.

"No. No." She shook her head. "It's perfect, Reale. Thank you." She steeled herself, pressing against the buttery warm brown leather seats. "And as far as calling you her brother-in-law, I'm sorry."

"I'm not."

She gazed into his smart eyes, swallowing hard. How many times had she fantasized about being Mrs. Reale Lynxx? And the truth was, until she was pregnant with Johnny, it hadn't been a fantasy. They'd been on track to be married. He'd asked her countless times, and she'd sworn she would. They'd worn those silver bands as if they were wedding bands. The only reason they hadn't gotten married was because she wanted him settled. She hadn't wanted anything, including her, to sidetrack him. And she had hoped her mother would come around and at least get to know him before condemning him. Plus, he hadn't wanted to run to City Hall. He wanted her to have a dream wedding. She'd told him over and over all she needed was him, but he wanted more for her. He'd always wanted more for her.

She shook her head. Damn, how youth always thinks there's endless amounts of time.

"What are you thinking about?"

She looked at him, taking in that face she knew so well. "Just how I always thought there was so much time. For everything."

"And now?" He squeezed her hand.

"And now I have a measurement of time. It feels like yesterday I was pregnant with Johnny."

He smiled. "I would have loved to see you pregnant. I bet you were gorgeous."

She snickered. "If you think a giant marshmallow on two stick legs is sexy then yeah, I was your girl."

"You were my girl." He squeezed her hand again and intertwined their fingers. "And I'll bet you were stunning."

"Reale."

"Mandy." He turned to her. "We need to talk."

She turned so they were facing each other as well as they could, their hands still together between them on the seat. "I know." She nodded forcefully. She didn't want to have this conversation here, in the back of a car, but it seemed some of her most important discussions happened in the backseats of cars. She glanced forward, but the driver was behind a thick plastic partition, unable to hear them.

She turned to Reale. "What do we do about school? I've been over it and over it in my mind, and I don't see the option of the city. I mean, even if you wanted to pay to send him to school in Manhattan and set up a car and driver…between school and his commute, his entire day would be gone. With the traffic, he'd have to leave way before the sun comes up and wouldn't get home until after it goes down. And I'd never let him travel alone, so my schedule would get completely flip-flopped"—she pulled away from his grip, using her hands as she spoke—"and even if you traveled some days or Jess, it would eat up the entire day." She shook her head. "I guess our only option is the number two school."

His eyes hardened.

"It's not a bad school." She kept rambling, sucking in too much air, growing lightheaded. "It's fine. It's more than fine. It's an excellent school. People all over the world would love to have their child attend a school like this. It's excellent." She nodded. "Yes, yes excellent. I mean where I was going to send him, our public elementary, that's borderline fine, but private school, even the number two private school—" Her words were falling out of her like they were cascading over a waterfall.

"Mandy." He cut her off with a sharp tone. "Breathe. Please. Baby. I'm so—"

"I'm sorry." She blurted the words, looking up at him, her eyes aching with tears.

"Why are you sorry?" His forehead was creased with worry. "I'm the one who got us into this mess. That damned accident is going to haunt me forever. What an asshole I was to risk those kids." He shook his head. "And now you and John are paying the price. You know as well as I do we'll run into the same situation at the next private school on the island, it'll be no different, and it's all because of me."

She shook her head ferociously. "No. I mean, I'm sorry I kept Johnny—John—from you. He's your son too. I should have told you that night you were performing for the music executive. I should have told you the second I figured it out. We should have raised him together. What I did I did out of love for you, but I understand now I was wrong. I was *wrong*, Reale. I should have had more faith in us and in your abilities to rise to the top no matter what. You wouldn't have given up your dream to work some minimum wage job to support us; we would have made it work. Together. I messed it all up. And I'm sorry." Tears fell faster than she could wipe them away.

"Mandy." He reached down and unbuckled his seatbelt. He slid across the seat, embracing her and holding her, burying her in his chest.

She sobbed harder and blubbered into his T-shirt, "You can't be unbuckled. It's not safe."

"Shhh…" He pushed her back, holding her at arm's length. "What you did was a long time ago. And yes, I struggled with it. And yes, I acted abominably because of it. But I've spent a lot of time thinking it over, and I think I understand why you did it. And deep inside"— he patted his chest with one hand—"I thank you for what you did. For the sacrifice you made."

She sobbed harder, her nose running. "Don't you see? If I hadn't done that, we wouldn't be in this position today."

"Well we'd be married and raising John together, there's no doubt about that."

She moaned in half-ecstasy and half-agony. Shooting pains circulated throughout her body, settling in a low, dull ache. "It's all my fault."

"How can you say that? The fault lies with those judgmental preppies at John's school. Not you."

"If I had been there for you, none of this would

have happened. You would have stayed clean and sober. You would have had someone who loved you on your side always. So much of what you've done these past five years is because of your pain. I know it's presumptuous to say I would have made all the difference in your life, but God knows you would have—and did—make all the difference in mine."

"Mandy." He held her closer as she sobbed against him. He glanced out the window. "Hey. What do you say we stop here and go grab a drink? We can talk."

She sat up, sniffling, wiping her tears against his chest. "Yes. Thank you, Reale."

He pulled her back against him, his strong arms wrapped around her as her body relaxed completely—for the first time in six years.

****

He stared at her as she sat across the table of the red plastic booth, sipping, or rather dragging, at her chocolate milkshake. She lifted it and shook the glass, raising an eyebrow.

"When you said get a drink, I had a margarita on my mind." She pulled at the straw again, her lips making a perfect O. "This thing is so thick it takes actual work to drink it." She swayed her body gracefully to the sound of the doo-wop music coming from an old-fashioned jukebox on the far wall.

He chuckled. "Thickest around. Maybe the thickest I've ever had anywhere. It's not a margarita night. When you need something medicinal, nothing makes you feel better than a chocolate milkshake. It's a proven fact."

"Really?" She took another drag from her ultra-long, red straw before taking the straw between her delicate fingers, stabbing at the shake.

"Uh-huh." He winked as he lifted his shake to his mouth, nearly missing and poking his cheek with the straw, sidetracked as he stared at her. Damn, even with puffy eyes and tear-streaked cheeks she was beautiful.

"How'd you even know about this place?"

"I've been here before. There's someone I visit around here sometimes."

"Will she get mad if she sees you with me?" She raised her eyebrows playfully, but her vulnerability rang through. She didn't want there to be anyone else.

"It's a he."

She scrunched her face, teasing him. "Well, then I know it's a strictly business arrangement. You going to tell me who it is?"

"Nope."

"Huh." She glanced about. "There are a lot of kids on dates. Who knew they'd be so into this retro stuff? One of the girls at a table over there is wearing a poodle skirt." She squirmed in her seat. "And they've all noticed you. You sure you're okay here?"

He looked past Mandy and gave a small wave to a group of girls at the nineteen-fifties styled ice cream bar. "I'm thinking this isn't a tough crowd."

She smiled. "Maybe not. But it's a crowd who has phones, and pictures will be up on social media all night. You sure you want to risk your bad boy image like this?"

"Bad boy." He laughed. "I think it's time to make some changes in my life, don't you?"

She swallowed hard, the color rushing from her cheeks. "If it makes you happy. Sure."

"You make me happy."

"Reale." She sat back, her beautiful face contorting with worry.

"Okay, tell you what. I'll let you in on a secret." He leaned forward like a conspirator and rested his forearms on the table. "I have a surprise for tonight."

"You do?" Her eyes sparkled.

"Yup. The guy who lives around here, he's part of the surprise. I was going to do this over the weekend, but since you're with me tonight it feels right."

"What is it?" She leaned forward, and her soft sweater clung to the outline of her breasts.

"Oh, no, you've got to wait." He signaled for the waitress. A girl in her early twenties nearly tripped over herself getting to him as fast as she could. "Check, please?" He grinned, and the girl's cheeks blushed.

"Oh, there's, uh, no charge, sir. When you picked up your drinks at the counter, they should have told you that." She glared at the ice cream bartender.

"No charge?"

"No, sir." She smiled at him, stalling as she shuffled her feet.

He sat back. He wasn't surprised. He was never charged when he went anywhere. Why was it the people who could afford the most tended to have their lives comped? "Well, that's very nice. Thank you." He reached into the front pocket of his leather jacket lying on the seat next to him and pulled out his wallet, removing a one-hundred-dollar bill and another. "This should cover the desserts for everyone who's in here now and leave a nice tip for you." He read her nametag. "Amalie. Pretty name." He handed her the hundreds, and she took them with a shaking hand. "Thank you, Amalie."

"You're welcome. Thank you." She turned and rushed off. She giggled as she ran to a group of girls huddled at the end of the bar. They whispered as they pointed at Reale, using their phones to snap pictures.

He glanced at Mandy. She was sitting back with her arms crossed and a smug grin on her face. "What?"

She sat forward, smiling. "What? 'What a pretty name, Amalie.' " She rolled her eyes. "No wonder everyone loves you."

He stared into her eyes. "I think we know not everyone loves me."

She shifted in her seat. "It's just an expression. It's fun watching you work your magic. You made her year. And that tip…" She shook her head. "If someone left me that tip… Damn."

Two hundred dollars? After she paid for the other diners, the waitress would clear about a hundred bucks. Mandy was impressed with a hundred dollars? What the hell was happening? He slouched back against the hard, shiny seat, rubbing an ache in his gut. How was it possible the mother of his son, and the only woman he'd ever cared about, was worrying about making tips in a diner? This was wrong. And damn, how he wanted to fix it.

"Mandy."

She shook her head, her eyes level on his. "Reale. No. Please. Not now." She smiled and grabbed her brown leather bag that was lying on the seat next to her. "Come on. Let's go. You've got a surprise to show me."

She smiled radiantly, and he smiled back.

****

"Is this an art gallery or a tattoo parlor?" Amanda

glanced around the small shop, a freestanding building hidden from the street. She hung her bag on a hook near the door next to Reale's jacket as she took in the stark white walls with recessed boxes that held dozens of framed tattoo images. Larger recessed areas were covered in floor-to-ceiling, light wooden planks. Two or three seated cushions sat before a Japanese Shoji wall, small, horizontal wood rectangles framing textured rice paper. "From outside, I thought this place was a garage that belonged to the private home."

"Most people do. It belongs to my friend, Daiki. The house is his, and this is his workshop." He nodded to the Shoji wall. "The place keeps going. There's an art studio back there. Anyway, I met Daiki when Lynxx was on tour in Japan years ago. He wanted to come to the United States to work on his art. He's incredibly talented."

"He does tattoos?"

"That's his medium of choice. You can commission works in all sorts of different mediums if you want, but he prefers flesh."

She shuddered.

"What?"

"Nothing. The word flesh sounds kind of primal."

"I think that's the point."

"Okay…" She walked past Reale, her hand floating across the back of a single, soft, black, leather-and-chrome chair. The room was small and cool but smelled like sweet lemongrass. "Is this where the magic happens?" She nodded to the chair.

"It can be." He pointed to the Shoji wall. "That's a sliding door. There's a table back there. Daiki did my Mandy tattoo in Japan."

"Oh." Her body warmed from her core outward. "You're here to get a tattoo…"

"That says, 'John.' " He smiled.

"Oh, Reale." Her already warm core nearly exploded from happiness. "He'll love that. Where are you putting it?"

"Deltoid. Left side."

"In Kanji? Like the Mandy tattoo?"

"Yeah."

"Reale." A young man entered the building from the outside, wearing a white coat like a doctor's jacket. He walked to Reale and embraced him. The two hugged for several moments.

Reale pulled back and turned to her. "This is my friend, Daiki. And Daiki, this is—"

"Mandy." He stepped forward, taking her hand and pulling her into a tight embrace. He was strong, and he held her for a long time, like they were old friends. Daiki pulled back, smiling at her. "You never had to tell me who she was, Reale. I could feel the energy between you two before I ever entered the studio."

"Oh, I…" Heat rushed to her cheeks again. How was it she'd blushed more in the past couple of months than she had in the six years prior?

"So." Daiki pushed his wire-rimmed glasses up on his nose and brushed back his thick black hair with a single blond streak. "Both of you today?" He glanced from Amanda to Reale and back again.

She shook her head. "Oh, no. I've never. We're just here for him."

"Uh-huh." Daiki nodded. "Don't like tattoos?"

"I like them. On him. It's not my thing. Although…" Although she would love a decoration at her C-section scar.

"Uh-huh."

Daiki leaned back against the chair, cocking his head as he stared at her. His eyes stayed on her face, but they appeared to glaze over, like he was here but not here all at the same time. The way John's eyes did when she wanted him to do his chores. Daiki's brow furrowed, and she swallowed hard, glancing at Reale. Had she done something wrong? Why was he staring?

"Take a look at this." Daiki walked past her and slid open the Shoji screen door, exposing a backroom.

She glimpsed a long, sterile-looking table and similar décor as the front of the shop. He came back holding a bamboo-framed picture of what looked like a curved hook with several infinity symbols off it. She stepped forward. "It's beautiful. What is it?"

"My version of a 'Unalome.' For some people it represents the path to enlightenment. In your case I would imagine this would represent a journey." He smiled sweetly. "And it's not always been an easy journey, has it?"

Her throat ached. "No." Her word was a whisper as she fought back tears.

"I have never placed this particular design on anyone. It's never been created besides this one picture."

"It's beautiful." She choked on her words. "Why wouldn't you?"

He smiled. "My designs are one of a kind. They have an energy of their own. They tell me where they need to go, and this…it needs to go to you."

She drew a deep breath and put a hand to her mouth. She dropped her hand, collecting herself.

"Daiki, it's beautiful. But I've never planned to be tattooed. There's only one spot I would consider, but I'm not ready yet." Sure, she would love something so beautiful over her scar, but what if in the future she had another child?

Daiki nodded, smiling. "Not time yet." He placed the framed art down on a countertop. "Amanda, when you're ready, you'll know where to find me."

She nodded.

"Mandy." Reale stepped up to her and wrapped his arm around her shoulder. She started, caught up in the symbolism, almost forgetting he was there.

Daiki clapped his hands together. "Let's get you started, Reale, yes?"

"Great."

Reale dropped his arm from around her, and she shuddered in his absence. He reached behind him and yanked his white T-shirt over his body in one forceful but fluid movement. She gasped. Her gaze ran up and down his lean, toned chest and abdomen, and she fought to pull it away. His nipples hardened with the chill of the room, and she emitted the slightest gasp in response. He smiled and placed a hand on her cheek. She closed her eyes, nuzzling against him. He nodded, dropping his hand and stepping back. He handed his T-shirt to her, and she held it to her breast, inhaling him.

He pointed to the chair. "There, Daiki?"

Daiki nodded, his arms crossed before him, closed off for the first time since they'd arrived.

As Reale slid onto the chair, she sat on a nearby stool, reluctantly letting go of his shirt, placing it on the stool next to her. "Come on closer." He reached out and grabbed her stool, pulling her toward him. She was tight to Reale's right side, careful not to block Daiki's way.

Daiki left without a word and then returned from the back room carrying a sleek black portfolio case. He sat on a rolling stool on the opposite side of Reale from Amanda. He unzipped the portfolio and flipped through several pictures. "This"—he turned the book toward Reale—"is the name John written in Kanji."

"Nice." Reale nodded in appreciation.

Daiki held up his hand against Reale's deltoid. "You're strong and developed, so the tattoo will take prominence."

Amen to that. She sighed.

"Great." Reale smiled.

"But I want you to consider. Writing the name John here will not leave me room for any other name."

"Well, I have another name. The only other name I plan to have tattooed on me. On my waistband. You know that. You did it."

Daiki nodded. "Yes. That's Amanda's spot, I understand. But I'm not talking about a woman. I'm talking about another child's name."

"What?" Reale sat up in the chair as Amanda leaned forward, steadying herself with outstretched arms to keep from falling off her stool.

Daiki smiled. "I am an artist. I feel people. But it doesn't take a gift to see what's between you two." He flipped the page in his portfolio. "This. This Kanji means 'father.' "

Reale inhaled sharply.

Daiki nodded. "If you tell me here and now, with no hesitation John will be your only son, we'll go forward as planned. But every cell in my body is telling

303

me there will be more children. I'd like to take this Kanji and work my magic. Look at this line and this…" He pointed to the picture. "Do you see how this will sit beautifully inside a mountain? The mountain is strong. It represents constancy and eternity. Mountains change on their exterior, but their core remains firm and still. Loyal. That is you, Reale. You too have been on a journey, and not an easy one. But underneath it all, you know who you are and where you should be."

She glanced at Reale as he wiped a tear from the corner of his eye. He made eye contact, staring at her long and hard. Her body swayed toward him.

Daiki smiled. "It's not an easy thing, Reale, but mountains can move. You're living proof of that."

"I, uh…" Reale glanced down at his lap, and she ached to go to him. To hold him.

"If you need a moment…" Daiki stood.

"No." He shook his head. "No more moments. No more wasting one single second. But the decision isn't mine alone. Mandy?" He raised his eyebrows in expectation, smiling in a way meant only for her.

And here it was. The decision only she could make. After all this time, there was no one else for him and no one else for her. And even if life—and her fear—didn't allow them to be together as a couple, maybe there was another life they were meant to create. A sibling for John. A baby sister or baby brother. Another soul that needed to be on this earth. She and Reale had come together all those years ago to have John. That was certain.

But…it was also to take care of one another. To be together.

And maybe someday, in the deepest part of her

soul where she wanted to be with him so desperately, she could trust him again. And maybe they could move forward. As long as that glimmer of hope flickered somewhere deep inside her, she couldn't shut him out completely.

"I think the mountain will be perfect."

She smiled, and he nodded, a slow, sexy nod filled with promise, as Daiki began his prep work.

Chapter Twenty-Two

"Does it hurt?" Mandy nodded to his dressing. She had both hands tucked under her legs as she leaned forward, concern etched in her beautiful brow. She cared so much about people and their comfort—she would make a fabulous nurse. He'd always known that.

"Nah." He shook his head. "It's tender, but not too bad."

"Maybe we should have gone for the tequila first and not the chocolate milkshake."

He snickered as he sipped freshly squeezed orange juice from a short plastic cup. He held out the cup to her, and she freed her hands, taking it. "You know, Mandy, you never told me how you came up with the name John." He placed his hand on the dressing over his tattoo. "While we wait for Daiki to come back. Can you tell me?"

She sipped the juice and cleared her throat. "I can't wait to see the tattoo not all red and puffy."

"Yeah." He dropped his hand. "So? You're not skirting this. How'd you come up with it? The name John?" He slid over in the chair, making room on his right side for her to sit beside him.

She jumped down off the stool and placed the juice glass on it. She climbed up next to him, sighing. Her small warm body felt so good next to him, so right. The soft material of her sweater caressed his bare chest.

"I thought about it a long time. Nine months really." She chuckled. "It was a hard decision. I wanted a name he would love, but through the entire time I thought of you and hoped and prayed you'd like it."

"I do."

She nodded. "Good."

"Mandy. Where did it come from?"

She turned her giant eyes up toward him, her face soft and relaxed. "I ran through every name I could think of, every derivation of Reale, though there aren't many of those." She giggled. "I thought about Alex after your childhood friend."

"You remember that?"

"Of course." She smiled. "But it seemed wrong, somehow. Over and over the name Johnny stayed with me. It was because…" She chewed the corner of her lip, sitting up and turning toward Reale. "Do you remember our first date?"

"At the bar the night I met you? Of course. Vividly."

She shook her head. "No, I mean the next night when you took me to dinner. Sushi in the Village."

"Of course, you told me you loved eel skin rolls, and when I ordered them for you, you turned green." He chuckled as he leaned down and kissed her on the top of her head. Her hair smelled incredible. He adjusted on the seat, fighting his growing desire for her. How long would he be able to stay this close?

"Well, I've been on vegetable sushi ever since. I don't know what I was thinking. Anyway, it was a gorgeous night, and we sat outside—"

"At a little table that barely had room for one, so we combined our dinners onto one plate."

"And you pulled my chair tight to yours. And halfway through dinner, you wrapped your arm around my shoulder..." She snuggled against him, emitting a sigh that sat right in his groin.

"And I knew you and I had found each other. That we were the lucky ones. The ones who found each other young. That we had found the only other person in our lives who would always matter."

"Yes." She wrapped her arm across his chest and turned to him. "Does this hurt if I lay like this?"

"Are you kidding? No, Mandy, no." Christ no, it didn't hurt. Nothing had ever felt better. Ever.

"Anyway, we sat facing the street, and the sign over the door to the Italian restaurant next door said—"

"Johnny's. Damn. I can't believe I didn't put it together."

"Johnny's. Yes."

"I'm going to start calling him Johnny now that I know."

She shook her head. "No. Please don't. He loves that you call him John. He feels grown-up, and like you said, it's something only you do."

"Mandy." He sat her up and gazed into her soft, giant eyes. "Do you think we'll ever be able to move forward? To have another baby together?"

"I think there's a reason we brought Johnny into this world. And maybe if there's another soul who needs to be—"

"No way." He shook his head. "Don't feed me that crap. I'm not buying it. We brought John into this world out of love. That is the only reason anyone should bring a life to this world. Because of love. It wasn't because he needed to be here. It's because we loved each other, and because of that love—he's here. I'll be damned if I'll think otherwise." His heart pumped and sweat formed on his brow.

She cocked her head. "But that's such a scary thought."

"What is?"

"That it's all up to us, as people. It's much better to think there's a divine force guiding us."

"There is, Mandy. It's called love. That's the force that kept you from nailing me to a wall at the custody hearing, and the force that has you singing to John when he can't sleep. Love is the universe guiding us. If we make another baby, it's because we love each other so much we want to have another baby together. We're not the vessels for a life that wants to come to us. Our love calls that life. We're love—and love is the reason for everything."

"Oh, Reale." She lifted her lips, and he kissed her gently, again and again.

"I'm ready, Mandy. To move forward as a family. Are you?"

"I want to, Reale. With every ounce of my being. But there's so much—I've never even seen where you live."

"Because nothing is home to me. I shuffle from house to house. No place is home. You can see them all, be at them all, have them, Mandy. I'm happy to give them to you."

"I don't want them, Reale." She shook her head, sitting up higher in the chair, and his bare chest grew cold. "I love that you're successful, but not for the money, but because you deserve it. And I love that you can offer Johnny the world. But…" She turned away.

"But what?"

"But money has never been my friend. My mother used it as a weapon, and I'm afraid you did too."

"Mandy, I was impetuous and cruel. I was angry. I'm sorry."

"I know you're sorry, Reale. But what if you get angry again? I can't live like that, being a puppet praying I do everything right so you won't pull it all out from under me again."

"Mandy, that's the last thing I want."

"I know that. But my mother tried to control me with money, and so did you. I don't know how this could ever work. If we were a family, if we lived together…"

He inhaled deeply. God, how he would love to come home to Mandy every day.

"I would always be on the defensive. Worrying the cards were all in your favor. You have the means I can never even imagine. You could grab Johnny at any moment and be gone."

"I wouldn't do that. And I didn't do that. And the truth is, how is that different from now? We don't have to be together for that to happen. I have custody too."

She nodded and her eyes watered. "You're right. But the difference is, now I could bounce back. I could yell and scream and say you're an asshole, but at least I didn't trust you. I would still know I have some control. Somehow force myself to go on and keep fighting you. But if we were a family, if I let my guard down…" She reached out and stroked his cheek gently. He closed his eyes. When he opened them, she was smiling but took her hand away. "Reale, I could never survive that kind of heartbreak again."

He grabbed her hand, and she gasped.

"What's in your bag?"

"My what?" She shook her head, trying to make sense of his seemingly senseless question.

"Your bag. That brown bag on the hook." He nodded toward the door.

"I don't know. My phone."

"What else?"

"Why are you asking? The usual stuff. Mints, my wallet, lip gloss, a mirror."

"How much money is in your wallet?"

She shrugged. "I don't know."

"Enough to call a cab to get home if you needed to?"

"I guess so."

"How about a train pass? For the railroad?"

"Yes."

He nodded. "In case you needed to get to John. I know for a fact, Mandy, you don't bring that bag every day. I've seen you switch bags back and forth. You switch from that older patchwork bag for work to this one when you go out. You consciously made the decision to take money and a train pass with you tonight. Even though you were with me."

She dropped her gaze and then pulled it back up to him slowly. "I didn't do it because of you. I bring those things out of habit."

"At some point, Mandy, you've got to let go of the need for control and trust somebody. And I hope that somebody is me."

He swung his legs off the chair. He stood and grabbed his T-shirt from the stool. "I'll shoot Daiki a text from the car. C'mon. It's time to go home."

She nodded, sliding off the chair, and followed after him silently.

Chapter Twenty-Three

Turkey, turkey, and more turkey. Why did everyone who came into the diner the Tuesday before Thanksgiving order turkey? Weren't they planning to have it on Thursday like the rest of America?

Amanda delivered two white, oversized dinner plates heaping with pressed turkey slices, mashed potatoes, stuffing, and cranberry sauce. Turkey gravy was ladled across the top, dripping down the sides and all over her hands. Ugh. She placed the two plates in her hands onto the table of an elderly couple, smiling at them.

"Anything else for you?"

"No, thank you, dear." The woman smiled, and the corners of her eyes crinkled into crepe-like paper.

Amanda nodded. "Let me know if there's anything you need." She looked into their coffee cups, checking their status, but they were still full. "Okay." She glanced at the elderly man patting his wife's hand before picking up his fork. How nice love was. She sighed.

"Look, dear." The elderly woman held out the corner of her light-yellow cardigan sweater, holding it against Amanda's chick-colored uniform. "As my great-granddaughter would say, we're twinsies!" Her eyes sparkled.

"Oh. Yes." Amanda looked down at her pale-yellow uniform splotched in turkey gravy. "Twinsies." She forced a smile and swallowed hard. "Well, if you need anything else…"

She turned and walked quickly to the large counter. She rushed past and ran into the break room. She sprinted through the small break room crammed with two folding chairs, an unused desk, and a time clock on the wall, pushing open the door leading to the outside. She nearly fell through the door and stumbled out onto the parking lot at the backside of the diner. Through the fading light she glanced at her watch, just about four. Darn, it got dark early on Long Island in November. She shuddered as a chill passed over her. She inhaled a deep gulp of the brisk, late-afternoon air and swallowed a lung-full of cigarette smoke. She turned to Carlos.

"Ugh, Carlos. I thought you were quitting." She crossed to him, coughing and fanning the air as she walked. She glanced at his white chef's jacket covered in as much gravy as she was.

"I thought *you* were quitting." He nodded to her, cocking his head.

She shuffled her feet and stared at her filthy sneakers, kicking a tiny piece of broken asphalt. The aroma from the nearby garbage cans wafted by. She plugged her nose. "I did too. It's not that easy, you know?" She wrapped her arms around herself to stay warm.

"I know." He held up the cigarette before taking another drag.

"But you're gambling with your life, Carlos."

"Aren't you?" He took one more long pull from his cigarette before tossing it to the ground and stomping it out with his foot. "All right, the blue hairs need their turkey week."

"Turkey week? Is that what we celebrate?"

"In diners. You bet. You should know that by now. You've been here forever." He pulled open the door that led back to the break room. "You coming?"

Was she going? Was there any choice? "I'll just be a minute."

"All right. But please don't let your orders get backed up. Not on turkey week."

She nodded. "Promise."

Carlos let the door close behind him as she leaned up against the backside of the diner. Her teeth chattered in the cold, but at least she could be alone with her thoughts for a few moments. No patrons parked back here unless the rest of the parking lot was full, and that wouldn't be for another half hour or so.

Turkey week. Thanksgiving. She turned to her side and rested her shoulder against the cold steel of the building. Thanksgiving was a mere two days away, and they still hadn't set any final plans. Before the weirdness of Friday—when she'd almost quit the diner and nearly got fired, when her son was asked to leave his school a few weeks after starting, and when she and her rock star ex-boyfriend decided there was the potential and possibility of having another child together if it wasn't for her desperate need to control everyone and everything—she was going to ask Reale to have Thanksgiving with her and Johnny. But now? Would he want to come? And when was he going to get tired of playing house without any of the afterhours activities? When would she?

"Hey." Jess poked her head out the door. "You hiding?"

315

"Un-unh." Amanda plopped her back against the wall, letting her head drop with a thud. "Ow."

"Maybe that'll knock some sense into you." Jess joined Amanda, standing next to her and purposely bumping hips with her. "Damn, it's freezing." She shuddered as Amanda stared off into the mostly empty parking lot. "Hey, wake up, sleepy. Bad boy keeping you up late these days?" She raised her eyebrows, grinning.

"No. I haven't seen him. He picked up and dropped off Johnny Saturday, but it was a quick hello. Sunday he didn't stop by at all. We need to decide about school, but we seem to be avoiding it. And each other."

"You ask him to Thanksgiving dinner?"

Amanda shook her head, turning to her friend. She smiled at Jess's loose ponytail and clean makeup. "You're not in character tonight?"

"Nah." Jess leaned up against the wall next to Amanda. She tucked her hands behind her. "I felt like being me for a bit." She shrugged. "Whoever that may be."

"You don't need to know yet. You've got plenty of time. Go see the world. You can figure out the rest of it later. Speaking of, how are the travel plans going?"

"Great." Jess pushed herself off the wall and turned to Amanda. "I'm leaving the first of the year. My showcase will be over, having finished its very limited engagement of four nights." She giggled. "It'll be about the same time Reale leaves for his next tour."

Amanda nodded. His tour. She had completely put it out of her mind. Somehow, if she didn't think about it, she could pretend he wasn't going to be gone for months on end. Johnny would be devastated. She shuddered.

"Amanda? What's going on with you? What are you waiting for? Invite him to dinner already before my mother does." Jess made an O with her lips, blowing out air. "I can see my breath. It's freaking freezing." She shook her head. "So? You inviting him?"

"What if he's tired of all this suburban averageness? He can spend the holidays anywhere and with anyone." Her gut ached as she spoke. What she would give to be with him.

"Ladies!" Carlos stuck his head out the door. "We're filling up in there. Finish your conversation on your own time. I've got orders backing up. You promised."

"Sorry, Carlos." Amanda pulled herself together and grabbed the freezing handle of the opened door from Carlos.

Jess put her hand on Amanda's arm, stopping her. "Amanda, he wouldn't be with you if he didn't want to be. You've given him ample opportunity to get turned off, and he keeps coming back."

She gave her friend a small smile. "Thanks, Jess." She held the door open wider, and Jess walked through as Amanda took one final glimpse at the darkening sky.

****

"Amanda?" Carlos rang the pickup bell, and she turned to the counter. Why was she moving like she was in thick oatmeal? Her brain was foggy, and her arms ached. She picked up another turkey special, and her hands slipped on the gravy.

"Carlos there's too much gravy." She put the plate down.

"Un-unh. Keeps the turkey moist."

"But I've got to be able to deliver it." She wiped her hands in her uniform again. The grease stains had covered her apron and were creeping onto the uniform itself. Great. She looked down at her uniform and back up to Carlos, then held her hands out to her sides. "Carlos, I look like I'm in a Thanksgiving horror movie."

"Aren't you?" He lifted his hand wielding a spatula and pointed to the dining area. "Old Man Howard the Grump. Table Two. Your section."

"What?" She turned to catch Howard pulling out his chair and arranging his placemat at Table Two. Her section. Crap. "Jess?"

"Yeah, I'll help out if you can grab my table in the far corner."

"Fine. Deal. Thank you." Who cared it was the farthest table and the most work? At least she could avoid the whole awkward scene with Howard.

Jess blew by, hustling to grab a pot of coffee. "Howard kinda likes me." She winked at Amanda and with her free hand adjusted her breasts like she was sliding them into a pushup bra.

Amanda chuckled, turning away. "That's disgusting, Jess." She hustled to grab the pot of decaf for one of her elderly tables.

"Disgusting or not, I'm working for a twenty-cent tip. Wish me luck." Jess tossed her beautiful, long, dark ponytail, laughing as she walked to Howard.

Amanda shook her head and retrieved her pot of coffee. She made her way through the diner that was quickly filling up. No doubt they'd have a waiting list in another half hour, all the people needing their turkey dinners two days before Thanksgiving.

Ding, ding! The doorbell rang again as a group came in, this time a family with three kids. Three kids? How can anyone do that? She smiled and pointed to a far booth as she turned to grab regular coffee and three sets of placemats to color on and three boxes of crayons. She knew from experience—for the parents' sakes—it was best not to ask the kids to share crayons.

Warmth radiated through her; dinnertime and kids made her think of Johnny. How was he? Thrilled no doubt, making handprint turkey decorations with Lynda. She'd never guess it by looking at her ultra-glam image, but Lynda was a master with kids. She glanced at her watch: four forty-seven. Darn it. She wanted to sneak out to call Lynda, but she was out of time. Besides, why would she check up on them? That was the control freak in her, the one Reale warned her about. And he was right. She sighed, imagining Johnny baking apple pies with Lynda. Lynda would snap pictures for her, for sure. She chuckled at the image of Lynda, probably dressed in a couture gown with perfect makeup, peeling apples for a pie. She'd do it. Lynda was amazing, just like her daughter. Amanda smiled at Jess who made a screwy face in return.

Ding, ding! What was it with this particular Tuesday night? Oh, yes, vacation week. Everyone would be cooking later this week, so they'd eat out while they had the chance. Two more families entered, one struggling with a stroller, followed closely by a children's sports group of six, seven, eight kids. She counted heads as they walked through the door. Maybe soccer? She pushed two large tables together as she glimpsed their shin guards and long shorts. Yup, soccer for sure. She rushed to get everyone seated and settled with drinks, and the stroller tucked away in the corner near the coat hooks no one but she ever used.

Darn it, why didn't Nick hire a hostess? Most other diners had them, but Nick insisted patrons liked to choose their own tables. Well maybe the patrons did, but it sure was extra work for the wait staff. And although Nick helped out once in a while, he wasn't here all that much.

Ding, ding! She rushed to the office to grab a pad of legal paper for the waiting list. She sprinted back and dropped the pad on the table closest to the door, placing a pen on top. "Please sign in and include the number in your party." She made a general statement, speaking to no one in particular and not bothering to make eye contact any longer. No, it wasn't great for tips, but what could she do?

Ding, ding! Damn. This was ridiculous. She turned to Jess. "Can you text some of the other waitresses? Julia and Becky?"

Jess whisked past, shaking her head. "Both away on vacation."

"How about Vicki?"

"Same thing!" Jess filled soda glasses as she spoke.

"Oh, come on." Amanda cursed under her breath. Holiday weeks were such a tough time to get anyone to work. "Can you text Nick?"

"I already did!" Carlos called out from the kitchen.

She glimpsed Carlos barking orders at his staff as he moved around the kitchen quickly and expertly. There was never a backup in his kitchen. She turned to Jess. "When is Nick going to hire some new people? He has the front end running on the five of us."

"Beats me. All he does is hang a dumb 'help

wanted' sign in the window. It's so old it's fading."

She shook her head as sweat pooled on her lower back and at her hairline. "There must be a hundred applications piled high on his desk. No one's ever right. This is crazy."

Ding, ding! Ding, ding!

"Jesus," Jess muttered as she walked by Amanda. "Didn't anyone stay home tonight?"

Amanda glanced over the expectant, hungry crowd staring at her. She smiled as best she could as she hustled with trays of food and drinks.

"You need more wait staff!" a tall man in a long black trench coat called out.

Like they didn't know. "You're right, sir." She pushed aside her sarcasm and swallowed her agitation. "But that wouldn't help anyway. Our tables are all full. There's…" She glanced at the counter that was also filled to capacity. "There'll be some room soon. Thanks for your patience." The man grumbled something it was better she didn't hear. She nodded in Howard's direction. "Jess, can you push Howard?"

"You push him. I'm not poking that bear with a stick."

She nodded as the din of diners grew louder and louder. *Ding, ding! Ding, ding!* She didn't even bother to look up. Her heart was pumping, and sweat dripped down her temples. A droplet stung her eyes. "Come on, Nick." She kept her head down as she hustled back and forth from kitchen to table and back again. "Get here, get here." As good as it was to be busy, too busy meant less quality service and worse tips, so they'd end up working twice as hard for less money.

Ding, ding! The diner quieted as she set down her

oversized tray and handed out overflowing plates at her table of six. Her six patrons pointed to the door, smiling and talking to each other. Oh, crap. It meant someone they knew had come in. No doubt they'd want her to make another empty table materialize and serve them all at once.

She stood straight and glanced at her next table. Huh. They were doing the same thing, pointing to the door and whispering to one another. Oh, crap. Probably some local celebrity was at the door. Or worse, the mayor or someone who would demand immediate attention. The diner grew eerily quiet, and if it weren't for the smiles on everyone's faces, she would have sworn a masked gunman had entered the building. All right, she couldn't avoid it any longer. Jess was in back, so it was her job to handle this mess—whatever it was.

She turned with a sigh, and her gaze landed on a smiling Reale.

As if on cue, people pulled out phones and began snapping pictures. Reale put up his hand, waving to her, that darned lopsided grin taking over his face. He stood still, as if he were afraid to approach her. Despite the beads of sweat dripping from her temples and all the craziness surrounding them, a smile spread across her face. She nodded and walked toward him.

"You may have picked the wrong night for diner food." She took in all six feet of him, his spiky hair, the short scruff on his face, his buttery-soft, black leather jacket, signature white V-neck, worn jeans, and old black boots. Damn, he looked like a rock star. She sighed, growing dizzy. In his hand he held a large manila envelope.

"I think I picked the perfect night."

A hush fell over the diner as everyone listened to their conversation.

She cleared her throat. "Um, I can't get you a seat right now. But I'd like you to stay."

"I'd like that too." He shuffled the envelope from hand to hand. "How 'bout I help out?"

She craned her neck forward, raising her eyebrows. "Excuse me?"

"I can help. I'm not sure I remember much from when I was waiting tables in high school, but if it'll help…"

"Reale." She shook her head. This was getting weirder and weirder.

"Sure thing." Jess rushed from the kitchen to the dining room. "Hey, Reale. Hang your jacket in the break room and grab some plates from Carlos."

She pointed to the kitchen, and Carlos playfully saluted Reale. Reale waved back.

Jess wiped a bead of sweat with her forearm as she balanced her tray on one hand. "I'll tell you where they go."

"No, no, wait." Grasping her now empty tray with one hand, Amanda let it fall against her legs as she held up her free hand, stopping him. "This is too weird. You don't have to do this, Reale."

"I want to."

"But…" But what? But this wasn't in her control? For once she didn't know how this was going to turn out? Screw it. "Okay. Thank you."

He walked forward, then stopped short just before her. "But before I do, can I steal you away for a moment?"

"Hey, Lynxx." It was the man in the trench coat.

"We're hungry. You take our waitress away, and we'll never get fed. Play on your own time."

Reale nodded, smiling at Amanda. "Okay, then, I'll have to do this quickly." He glanced over his shoulder, smiling at the dozens of people holding phones, recording his every move.

Amanda shook her head. Damn, what a tough way to live, with no privacy, ever. He handed her the envelope.

"What's this?"

"A listing of all my real estate, possessions, and my net worth."

"What?" Her eyes danced across his.

"You said your concern was I had everything financially, so I could disappear with John. This first document." He opened the envelope she was holding and tugged at a legal document, popping the top free from the envelope. "Without pulling it all the way out, it says you own half of everything I have. I spent today doing the legal work. Basically, you're now a multimillionaire and could buy this diner out a thousand times over."

"Excuse me?" She placed a hand to her racing heart.

He smiled. "And this second document"—he slid the first papers back into the envelope and pulled out the top of a second set of papers—"is a pre-nup. It says when we're married, everything is yours, and if you ever decide to leave me, you get everything."

"Wait, wait...*what*?"

He nodded. "All I've ever wanted is you, Mandy. If this is what it takes to give you the security to be with me, if this is what it takes for you to finally become my wife…well then, I'm more than happy to give it all to you." He took a tiny step closer. "All I wanted, all I want, is to be with you and give you everything…and for you to be my wife."

"Your what?"

"My wife."

"Reale." Her heartbeat raced. "What are you saying to me?"

"I guess I'm asking you. Will this make you feel secure? Now can you trust me enough to be with me? The playing field is equal. You can be secure my money can't take John away again, because it's your money now. Everything I have is yours."

"I'll marry you if she won't." It was trench coat man.

She released a nervous chuckle as the collective group of diners laughed and moved closer toward her.

She swallowed hard. Here he was. Offering her everything. But…

"No." She stepped forward and pushed the envelope toward his chest.

"No?" His eyes widened with surprise.

The diner patrons gasped and murmured.

"No." She shook her head. "I mean, I don't need this. I trust *you*, Reale, not the paperwork. I don't want anything for me; I want it for us. I'm sick of trying to control everything. Especially us. Thank you for this incredible gesture, but my answer is no, to that. But…"

He cocked his head. "But what?"

"Ask me again. Without the pre-nup and with no guarantees except one—you love me."

"Amanda Simmons. I have loved you for the past eight years of my life. Would you please do me the honor of marrying me?" He reached into his leather jacket pocket and pulled out a black velvet ring box.

Oh. My. Gosh. "Reale…"

He opened the box, and she gasped. Inside were two silver bands, exactly as they used to wear everyday of their prior lives.

"They're the silver bands we used to wear."

He nodded. "These are platinum, but yeah. Otherwise they're the same." Taking the smaller band from the box, he tilted it toward her. "Look at the inscription."

She took the ring into her shaking hand and turned it so she could see. Her eyes widened as her heart raced. "Is that the *unalome* Daiki created?"

"The one meant only for you, yes." He took her band and slipped it onto her ring finger. "Like you are meant only for me, and I am meant only for you."

"Oh, Reale." She took his ring and slipped it onto his strong, capable finger.

He pulled her to him, and her body molded to his. "I'm covered in turkey gravy. I'm not sure you want to be this close."

"Are you kidding? You think anything, especially a little Thanksgiving gravy, will keep me away from you now?" He pulled her even closer. Her soft breasts pressed against the stiffness of his jacket as she inhaled the sweet smell of vintage leather and Reale.

"I can't promise it will be like it was, but I can promise it will be even better." He smiled, taking her hands and intertwining them with his, holding them to his chest.

"I've got a confession." She glanced at the ground before her and back up to his gorgeous, smart eyes as he waited patiently. "I still have my silver band from all those years ago. It's tucked away in a drawer."

He inhaled deeply. "Me too. Tucked away in a pocket I had specially made for my guitar case. What do you say we wear them on our right hands?"

She nodded. "One hand representing the past…"

"The other, the future. Yeah."

"I love it."

"Good." He smiled. "Here's what I'm thinking. I bought our old building in the Village, and get this, Kevin, the guy whose cable I used to tap? He's still there. With the same yappy pug."

"Oh, Reale, we can't kick him out. We don't need an entire building."

"Of course not. He can stay as long as he wants. And I've got his cable bill covered for as long as he lives there."

She giggled. "I guess we owe him that much."

He nodded, chuckling. "I would say. We'll renovate the empty apartments, knock down some walls, whatever. You can design it any way you'd like. Put all those years of watching home shows to good use. And uh, John…" He stiffened.

She placed her hands on his biceps and rubbed away his tension, as she gazed into his eyes. "What? What about Johnny?"

He nodded and swallowed hard. "I have wanted to ask you this since the moment I found out—I want him to have my name. To be a Lynxx. Jonathan Simmons Lynxx, what do you say?"

She was so overcome her chest heaved as she struggled to breathe. "Why do you think I never gave him a middle name?"

He tilted his head, looking deep into her eyes. "Really? That's the real reason?"

She nodded as her throat tightened. "Deep inside I'd always hoped..."

He reached out and brushed back a piece of her hair, tucking it behind her ear. The gesture was so soft, yet so possessive and powerful. She sighed.

"We'll get him settled into school. Ms. Ronebarth was right. There's a fabulous school in the city on the west side that caters to kids of parents in the arts. Kids come and go based on their parents' shooting schedules or tours. They set up homework plans so they never fall behind." He leaned down, looking into her eyes. "Too much? Or keep going?"

She beamed at him. "Absolutely keep going. Please."

"We'll renovate while we're on tour. And while we're on tour, I'm gonna work on my relationship with the guys in the band. Seems you were right, again. An apology can work magic. And I know you can't just up and leave, but hear me out. Please. I've already shortened the tour. Maybe we could think of it as a sort of honeymoon. With John and the band along." His serious demeanor softened, and his cheeks flushed the slightest bit.

She tilted her head, love overtaking her.

"We'll get back in time for spring semester so you can finish your undergrad, and..." He leaned down, touching his forehead to hers.

"And?" She lifted her eyes expectantly as her body tingled, alive with happiness.

"And you and I will get to work making another baby." He grinned that sexy, lopsided smile. "Damn, how I want to see you pregnant."

"Oh, Reale…" She closed her eyes as he pulled her closer still. Excitement coursed through her body like a vibration. Oh, yes, she wanted to have another baby…his baby. It was the sexiest thing she could possibly imagine. The sexiest thing he could possibly say with that deep, dangerous voice.

"And of course, nursing school, whenever you're ready. As far as the wedding, we can get married any place you want. Europe, the islands—"

"City Hall."

"Yeah?" He raised his eyebrows.

"Yeah."

"Okay, I want this official." He bent down on one knee. "Amanda Simmons, I am asking, on one knee on the sticky diner floor, in front of a whole bunch of cell phones recording every word we say, but no pressure"—he grinned—"will you marry me?"

"Yes, Reale Lynxx. I will absolutely marry you."

The diners applauded and whistled as Nick hollered in appreciation, and Carlos and his crew banged together pots and pans in the kitchen. Reale stood and pulled Amanda close for a kiss. She closed her eyes and breathed him in, his scent, his strength, his love.

He rested his forehead to hers. He pulled his head up and lifted the sleeve of his jacket, glancing at his shiny platinum watch. "Damn it. I don't want to wait anymore. City Hall is closed now, so what do you say we take a quick flight to Vegas? Or else we can marry ourselves tonight, and tomorrow morning we'll be at City Hall first thing? That way John can be with us."

"Sounds perfect. As long as it's first thing in the

morning. I don't want to waste another second of our lives waiting for anything. All I need is you, Reale. That's all I ever needed."

"And God knows I need you, Mandy."

Jess ran up and hugged them both. "Don't forget you need a nearby nanny. In a nice apartment in your building." She stepped back, laughing and wiping her tears.

Amanda chuckled as she wrapped her arms around Reale's neck. "Reale, thank you."

"Thank you, baby. For all of it. For sticking by me through everything. I love you, Mandy. I always have and always will."

"I love you too, Reale."

He held her tightly in his embrace before lifting her off the ground and spinning her around.

Nick fought his way through the crowd, waving his hands. He must have come in the back door sometime during Reale's proposal. "Come on, everyone back to work." He winked at Amanda and shook Reale's hand. He tossed Reale a short, plain, white apron. "Carlos told me you're helping out?"

"You bet." Reale peeled out of his leather jacket and rushed to hang it on the hook near Amanda's sweater. He tied the apron around his waist as Nick handed Reale a giant tray that Reale balanced on his billion-dollar hand.

Nick nodded. "Huh. If you ever get tired of that rock and roll stuff, you've got a job here."

Reale chuckled. "Thanks, Nick. Hopefully waiting tables is like riding a bike. But even so, Mandy and I are only here for today, so you've got to get to work on her replacement."

"And I'm gone come January," Jess shouted from the drink station as she refilled sodas in dingy, saffron-colored, plastic cups. "Heading to Greece! Whoo!"

"But it's hard to find someone right." Nick shook his head, arguing.

"I'll do it." Old Man Howard the Grump pushed his chair back from his table and stood.

Jess spun around to face him as Amanda's jaw dropped open. "Excuse me?" They spoke in unison.

"I'll do it." He gazed around the diner before focusing on Nick. This night was getting more and more surreal. "I lived in Manhattan. I was one of the singing waiters at the deli on Ninth before it closed." He cleared his throat gruffly.

"You're a singer?" Reale stepped closer.

"Damn right." Howard yanked up his pants at the waist. "And a damned good one. And I don't sing that crap you get paid millions to shout at people. I sing opera."

Reale grinned. "That's awesome."

Howard furrowed his brow. "Why…yes. And I was a damned good waiter as well." He recovered his grouchy demeanor. "None of the mistakes this staff makes." He glared at Amanda as he held his head high in the air. "That job was my pride and joy."

She stepped forward. "Then I've got to ask. If you understand being a waiter and working for tips, why the fourteen crackers and fourteen cents?"

"I count crackers because you need to learn precision. The best waiters are the most precise."

"But why fourteen?"

"My wedding anniversary was on July fourteenth. The only things that make me happy are my memories of my late Estelle. Having fourteen crackers makes me feel like she's here with me, and we're having a meal together. I moved out here when she passed. Couldn't imagine being in the city without her. Too many memories."

Tears welled in Amanda's eyes. Yes, she understood perfectly. She glanced at Reale and smiled, before turning back to Howard. "Oh, Howard. I had no idea—"

"And fourteen cents. Well that's because that's all the tip you're worth." He gave the slightest sly grin, his shoulders sloping. "I don't have a lot anymore. Leaving fourteen cents, well…maybe my lucky number will bring you ladies some luck as well." He nodded to Reale. "Seems to me, it already has."

She beamed as Howard put up his hand.

"Don't get all sentimental on me. You were still a terrible waitress."

She giggled and Reale stepped to her. He took her hand in his.

"You sure you can't stay?" Nick begged Amanda and Reale playfully, placing his palms together as if he were praying.

"We're here just for tonight, Nick. Then I've got some serious plans for this one." He raised their intertwined hands, kissing her fingers.

His touch sent tremors through her body. He squeezed her hand before letting go. Oh, how she wished this shift was over.

"It's one night only, huh?" Nick crossed his arms in front of his chest, watching Reale make his way to the kitchen to grab plates.

"Not going to leave you stuck." Reale spoke over

his shoulder as every patron, except Howard, snapped pictures of him.

Nick nodded. "You're a nice guy, Reale."

Reale stiffened, holding his newly loaded tray full of food. He turned to Nick. "Not sure about that one, Nick."

Nick shook his head. "I am. You're not perfect. None of us are. But you're a good man, Reale. You and Amanda come back and eat here for free, anytime you like."

"Thanks, Nick." Reale blushed slightly, smiling from his eyes as Amanda's heart swelled. Gosh how he needed to hear that.

Nick turned to Amanda. "Don't forget me. You bring my sweet Johnny around to see me once in a while, you hear?"

The busboys were so backed up she wiped down a table, prepping it for her waiting customers. She swiped the rag across the table one last time, grabbing any stray crumbs, catching a glimpse of her platinum band on her ring finger. It felt so right. Finishing her table, she turned to Nick. "Of course I'll bring him by, Nick. You've been like a grandpa to him."

Nick waved her off, grumbling, "Customers waiting."

Jess rushed past, carrying her oversized tray filled to capacity. "Hey, Lynxx, you going to stand there staring at your fiancée, or you going to work?"

Amanda glimpsed Reale standing by a far table with a now empty tray, gazing at her. She sauntered to him as sexily as she could while wearing a yellow uniform splattered with gravy and hurrying to deliver mountains of turkey. "Are you taking food orders?" She nodded to the table he was standing beside.

He shook his head. "I've got no clue what I'm doing."

She smiled and placed a hand on his forearm. "Tell you what. How about I take the orders, and you deliver the food. The heavy trays are probably a lot easier for you."

He nodded. "We've always made a good team."

"Yeah." Adrenaline coursed through her as he leaned over for a kiss, his strong lips finding hers. His scruffy beard tickled her in just the right way—in the way it always did and always would. He pulled back, and she sighed contentedly.

"Come on, babe. Orders are backing up. Let's get this food delivered, finish this shift for Nick, and go get married. As soon as possible. What do you say?"

"I say, yes."

"I love you, Mrs. Lynxx."

"I love you too."

He grinned and kissed her again as happiness overtook her. Giddy, she turned on her heels, nearly skipping to take the dinner orders from her new tables, as he rushed to pile his tray with food, and the din of the diner enveloped them.

A word from the author...

I am so excited to bring you *The Risk of Happiness: The Punk Rocker*, Book 3 in The New York Artists Series! I hope you enjoy Reale and Mandy's story, and if you love artists and New York City like I do, be sure to check out the first two books of the series: *Summer of Irreverence: The Rock Star*, and *To Be or Not To Be: The Actors*.

I'm a bestselling author of gritty, slice-of-life romance, and I'm also a yoga instructor who believes yoga can cure just about anything—and what yoga can't cure, coconut can. I adore vintage army jackets, have a secret addiction to the Marvel Comic series on Netflix, and an obsession with Caramel Walnut Brownie Luna Bars... And the absolute loves of my life are my husband and my two young girls.

To find out more about The New York Artists Series as well as my YA/NA series, The Letting, please stop by my website and drop a note! I love to connect with readers.

Happy reading!

~*~

Find Cathrine online at:
http://www.CathrineGoldstein.com

Thank you for purchasing
this publication of The Wild Rose Press, Inc.

For questions or more information
contact us at
info@thewildrosepress.com.

The Wild Rose Press, Inc.
www.thewildrosepress.com

To visit with authors of
The Wild Rose Press, Inc.
join our yahoo loop at
http://groups.yahoo.com/group/thewildrosepress/